Kelly had spent a lot of time over the last three years trying into understand Logan Field. He had seen his bad temper, his intolerance and arrogance; his gift for coping with difficulties. But until now he hadn't appreciated how Logan glittered in adversity. He was like a great actor seizing and subduing an unplayable part. Combined with his ability to assume a role was the cold-blooded nerve of the born gambler.

Imshan was in jeopardy; the greatest coup of Logan's career was menaced by the hostility and greed of the Minister. But Logan was neither worried nor discouraged. What Kelly saw that morning, during the slow, frustrating negotiation which all knew was already doomed to fail, was a man enjoying every moment of the game. It might well be that Khorvan had met his match.

*Also in Arrow by Evelyn Anthony*

# The
# Persian Ransom

## EVELYN ANTHONY

ARROW BOOKS

*To my dear friend*
*Shirley Chantler*
*with love*

Arrow Books Limited
62 – 65 Chandos Place, London WC2N 4NW

An imprint of Century Hutchinson Limited

London Melbourne Sydney Auckland
Johannesburg and agencies throughout
the world

First published in Great Britain by
Hutchinson & Co. (Publishers) Ltd in 1975
Arrow edition 1988
Reprinted 1988

Printed and bound in Great Britain by
Anchor Brendon Limited, Tiptree, Essex

ISBN 0 09 955180 2

# I

When James Kelly told people he worked in Tehran, they were immediately interested. They found the idea of Persia fascinating, especially women. He thought cynically that had he said he was an executive with Imperial Oil in Iran, few would have responded with enthusiasm. The same cynicism, which he preferred to call irony, had chosen the Persian Room at the Tehran Hilton as a setting for a reception in honour of the Shah's Minister of the Economy and his own boss, the chairman of Imperial Oil, Logan Field. He didn't expect that the incongruity would penetrate the chairman's sense of the ridiculous. It was his own joke, to be enjoyed in private.

He didn't hate Logan Field, although a number of people did. He regarded him as a phenomenon, like an electric storm which suddenly blew up, battering at everything in its path. He wasn't just a ruthless tycoon, the caricature of the merciless, power-greedy businessman so dear to the hearts of the left-wing progressives. He was a personable man of superior intelligence and abnormal drive who happened to be at the head of one of the world's fastest growing corporations. Kelly had met him at Mehrabad, the Tehran airport, that morning; waiting in the broiling Iranian sunshine like an ambassador to receive his king, flanked by equerries: the assistant resident director, the field operations manager and his two assistants, with a junior official from the Iranian Ministry of the Economy bearing the Minister's welcome.

Kelly hadn't expected to see Logan Field's wife follow him down the gangway steps. Nobody had warned him. There had been no cable saying she would be on the trip. He had shaken hands with Logan and then come up to Eileen Field. She smiled and the silly shock went racing up and down his nerve endings. Beautiful blue Irish eyes and that soft smile. What in Christ's name had she ever found to love in Logan Field...

He had come to the Hilton early to supervise arrangements for the party. Three years in Tehran had taught him not to rely upon Persian efficiency or punctuality. The big room with its artificially domed ceiling and low lighting from bogus brass lamps was heavily decorated with flowers. Jasmine and lilies overscented the air, but then the Eastern taste in such things was flamboyant. Only in politics, business and sex were the Persians a subtle people. Otherwise their preference was for the vulgar and emphatic. He checked with the head waiter that the champagne was cold and there was a plentiful supply of whisky.

Kelly was a tall man, dark and thin, with hair that had overgrown his collar; he had authority and tact. He had demonstrated both in the last three years. As a result, Logan Field was giving this reception for the most inaccessible and anti-Western of the Shah's Ministers. No doubt that was why Eileen Field had come at the last moment. The Minister liked the company of women; he spoke impeccable English. At five minutes to six the junior executives of the company and their wives began to arrive. James glanced at his watch and, as he did so, Logan and Eileen Field came through the doorway and he hurried to meet them.

On the way to the Hilton Logan had turned to his wife. Kelly ran a Mercedes, but there was a two-tone blue Rolls Royce, with a Mulliner special body, which was reserved for the use of the chairman when he was in the city. Otherwise it stayed in the garage.

Although it was early evening, Tehran shimmered in a dry heat that made the streets dance in a haze; the car was air-conditioned. Eileen Field wore a silk dress and felt quite cold.

'Khorvan won't be there for hours,' Logan said. 'They make a point of keeping everyone waiting. They think it emphasizes their importance.' He lit a cigarette and looked out of the window. His eyes showed irritability. There were deep creases from his brow to his nose and his lower lip was sucked in.

'It doesn't matter,' Eileen Field said. 'Our own people will be there; we can talk to them. I don't mind if he keeps me waiting.'

'That's not the point,' Logan said. 'I mind, because it's an insult to you and it puts me at a disadvantage. We shouldn't have come before a quarter to seven.'

'Then if by some chance the Minister was early, we'd have insulted *him*. It's better this way round.'

He should have appreciated her logic, but he couldn't. He hadn't wanted her to come, and the Minister of the Economy was not part of the reason. He didn't want her to talk about 'our people' and identify herself with him and Imperial; he didn't want her to go in to the party and show what a perfect wife she was for a man like himself. The harshness of his thoughts made him feel guilty. He never wanted to be unkind to Eileen, even in his mind. It wasn't her fault that things were going wrong. He laid his hand on her knee.

'To hell with it,' he said. 'I'm just edgy tonight. Khorvan's been fighting us for eighteen months. It isn't going to be easy to trust him. They're the most difficult bloody people in the world.'

'I know,' she said. 'I know it's going to be a strain on you. That's why I wanted to come.' He took his hand off her knee. That kind of answer, loyal and innocent, only made him feel worse. There were moments when he longed for her to quarrel, or complain, to give him some excuse...

Seated beside him, Eileen shivered in the artificial chill in the car. She wore a huge diamond brooch with a turquoise in the centre. Her earrings and a bracelet matched. The jewellery felt cold and heavy; she had chosen it because the turquoises were Persian, bought as a present by Logan three years ago, after their only child was born. Her reasons for wearing them were not a conscious reminder that he had been kind and loving then; she thought they were a compliment to the Minister. For the last three years she had given that kind of attention to detail, to try and compensate Logan. If she couldn't give him what he wanted in one way, then she could devote herself to the part of his life which she knew to be the most important, the power and progress of Imperial Oil. She had always admired her husband; part of loving him had been her admiration for the qualities in him which were so alien to those possessed by all her family and friends.

His ambition, his energy, his incisive thinking; his dynamic personality which didn't derive its force from inherited privilege or historical exploits performed by others. '*Une force de*

7

*nature.*' She remembered that phrase, culled out of a book, though she had long forgotten the context. A force of nature. That truly described him, and she had loved him for it.

For some months now, she had known that he no longer loved her. As they entered the Persian Room, she slipped her hand through his arm and together they walked towards James Kelly and the other guests.

Habib Ebrahimi moved through the mixed Iranian and European crowd, carrying a tray with champagne, whisky and soft drinks. He avoided the other guests and made his way to the small group standing a little apart. He came to Logan and stopped, offering the tray. The Minister, Mahmoud Khorvan, was standing beside him. Habib had seen photographs of him, and he glanced at him once to provide a first-hand image of his hate. This was the former Iranian patriot who had sold out to the Western capitalist oil company. For a second his black eyes flickered over the Minister's face: light-skinned, black-browed, with receding hair. He was a small man, immaculately dressed in a London-made suit. Heavy gold-and-diamond cuff-links gleamed as he waved his hands. He was talking to a European woman wearing fine turquoises, and he was looking as if he were enjoying himself. Habib Ebrahimi looked at her too, for a moment. He had seen her come in with Field. She was the wife of the chairman of the oil company which was trying to link itself like an octopus round the throat of his country. Habib was a humble man, but he knew his enemies. He served them with their alcoholic drinks, observing that the Minister upheld his Moslem principles, at least in public, by drinking orange juice, and did what he had been told to do. He had been working at the Hilton for the last six months; when the reception was arranged, Habib suddenly became important. His friends had explained to him how he, the one who sat and listened at the feet of others, was to be of service to the common cause.

He gave a little bow to the Minister and withdrew a few paces. He passed a tall Iranian in army officer's uniform, and stopped at a word from him. He didn't look up. A hand, thin at the wrist, with long fingers and thick knuckles, lifted a glass of whisky from his tray. Habib went on, his head down, not looking up. He knew Colonel Ardalan. He was a brave man, and dedicated, but Habib prayed with what superstition remained in his soul, that he would never see the Colonel any closer.

'It's going well,' Logan spoke aside to James. 'Do you think he's enjoying himself?'

'The hell of it is,' James answered, 'you only know when they're not. It's like trying to do something to please them. If you do it they're not grateful; if you don't they never forgive you. At a guess I'd say Khorvan was in a good mood. Largely thanks to your wife; she's marvellous with people.'

'Yes,' Logan said. Eileen was laughing at something the Minister had said. Khorvan was grinning, his head slightly tilted back. Iranians didn't laugh loudly like Westerners. He touched her on the elbow. 'He's enjoying himself,' James said. 'When he starts pawing it's a good sign.'

'You've done a great job,' Logan said quietly. 'You've justified my judgement a hundred times over, and I'm always pleased about that! How does it feel to have rescued the economy of Europe?'

James shrugged. Logan in an expansive mood embarrassed him; he didn't need a layman's assurance that he had brought off a crucial political coup under the guise of a business negotiation. He had seen the opportunity present itself and his years of public service in the Foreign Office had enabled him to take advantage of it. He had to remind himself constantly not to be a snob. In his heart he despised industry and had little in common with Imperial Oil. He had met Logan Field at a city lunch; he had no idea that he had registered with the oil man as anything more than a Foreign Office under-secretary, holding forth on the Middle East over the table. The offer of the job as resident director of Imperial Oil in Iran had come when he was disillusioned and rebellious. His path to a Grade I Ambassadorship had been blocked, unfairly as it seemed, and a posting to Finland appeared to be a retrograde step. The prospect of Finland had daunted him for weeks. He had little private money and diplomats were notoriously underpaid. The massive salary offered by Logan Field, with stock options, had made up his mind. He went to see Logan and accepted the offer after an excellent lunch at the Savoy.

There had been resentment among the senior executives of the company at the chairman giving such an important job to an outsider. That was why Field referred to his judgement being vindicated. He had chosen a man who could deal with the Iranian Government, and this in effect meant dealing with the Shah.

'It's bloody marvellous,' Field went on, speaking low. 'The biggest oil-field in fifty years – and the breakthrough on oil prices for Western Europe. Christ, James, we'll go down in history!'

'I'm not trying to be pessimistic, but I won't believe it till I see the Minister actually sign the heads of agreement.'

'With the Shah supporting it, he's no alternative,' Field said. 'But I want him on our side, James. I want things to go ahead as smoothly as possible. And as fast. I know this party doesn't mean a damn, and tomorrow morning he'll start trying to squeeze our balls over the terms, but all the same, I'm feeling bloody confident.'

James didn't answer. He sipped his whisky and watched Eileen Field. She was taking a great deal of trouble with the Minister. He wondered if Logan realized how much she contributed. He was too fair-minded to criticize Logan Field because he happened to be in love with his wife. He insisted that he admired Logan's dynamic qualities and it couldn't be denied that, when he wanted to, Logan could be charming. But he was a man motivated by things rather than people; he had a famous collection of Greek antiquities and when James admired it, he had told him frankly that it was better than money in the bank. It was typical of an attitude that irritated James intensely. Everything had to have a purpose; if it wasn't power then it had to be profit. He thought that Eileen Field looked very pale.

'I'd like to give a private party for Khorvan,' Logan was saying. 'Something very special. At your house; it's more intimate than an hotel.'

'He's unlikely to come,' James answered. 'Ministers very rarely accept private invitations, but we can try.'

'Let's join them.' Logan moved towards Khorvan. 'You ask him.' James was surprised when the Minister accepted.

'I shall be delighted,' he said. 'I must have another opportunity of talking to this charming lady. She has been telling me all about you, Mr Field.' For a moment there was a hostile gleam in his eyes. Logan saw it and responded with a friendly smile.

'We shall certainly have a party, Minister. On condition that you are the guest of honour. I'll suggest a suitable date at our meeting in the morning.'

The waiter was back with the tray. Logan took another whisky. Habib waited, submissive and silent, while Khorvan ignored him.

'How long do you expect to stay in Tehran?' the Minister asked Logan.

'For as long as it takes to conclude our business.'

'And your charming wife?'

'She may go back ahead of me. We have a little daughter at home. She doesn't like to leave her for too long.'

'Ah,' said the Minister, not understanding. Daughters were not important and he couldn't see what difference it made if they were left behind. He had little sympathy with Western sentimentality over children; but then he had little sympathy with the West. The chairman of Imperial Oil, trying so hard to ingratiate himself, had no idea what it had cost Khorvan to agree with the Shah that the British company should be admitted to partnership with the National Iranian Oil Company to develop Imshan. Nobody knew how he had writhed and twisted in his efforts to block their negotiations. He had used cogent arguments to defeat American interests; there were enough American troops and bases in Iran without permitting them another hold in what was expected to be the biggest oilfield in the Middle East. The Minister hated the United States and resented its influence in his country; he was able to say truthfully that the Soviet Union would be entitled to take offence if the Americans were admitted as partners. There were other contenders: a consortium of French and Germans, and the Russians had also sent a team. Until James Kelly obtained a private audience with the Shah, Khorvan had been gently steering Imshan in the direction of the Soviet delegation. He glanced at Kelly. His appointment to Tehran by Imperial was a very clever move. The Shah had been impressed by his diplomatic record; he considered himself as more than the equal of any businessman, and in general he despised them. But with Kelly he could discuss the wider implications of the oil-field.

The first audience had been followed by private meetings during the next six months. Europe was facing bankruptcy because of the rise in oil prices. Khorvan viewed this prospect with indifference. His own political leanings were to the Left and he bitterly resented decades of exploitation by the West. The Shah's decision to start lowering the oil price without appearing to do so had been communicated to Khorvan after his last audience with James Kelly.

To Khorvan, the implications were disastrous. When he heard the decision, he had to pretend to agree with it. Disagreement with the Shah's policy was followed by dismissal. Only by seeming to acquiesce could he hope to sabotage the plan. He had agreed with the choice of Imperial Oil as the company which would develop the field. His unquestioning acceptance of the Shah's views left him in charge of the final negotiations.

He gave Eileen Field a charming smile. The waiter was at his elbow again and he took another orange juice. Whatever the executives of Imperial Oil thought, visibly congratulating themselves and imagining that the attentions of a pretty woman made any difference to him, Logan Field had not won yet.

'I shall be delighted to come to your house, Mr Kelly,' he said. 'Now if you will excuse me, I must mix with some of your other guests.' He walked away into the crowd.

'I'd better do the same,' Logan said. 'Look after Eileen, will you?' He had moved away before James could answer. He turned to Eileen with eagerness.

'You're looking marvellous, as usual. And you certainly made a hit with the Minister.'

'He likes women,' Eileen said. 'So do most Iranian men. I don't think it means anything. He was very easy to talk to and he has quite a sense of humour.'

She had met James soon after he joined Imperial. He had been invited to dine at their house in Eaton Square, a privilege Logan reserved for the top executives in the company. It was an evening he had never forgotten. He thought Logan's wife looked extremely frail; he learned afterwards that she had been desperately ill after the birth of their only child and had not long been out of hospital. There was an immediate rapport between them. They had many interests in common, and she seemed grateful for the effort James made at entertaining the other guests. She seemed to him the last woman in the world to have married a man like Logan Field. They met several times after that; Logan valued his qualities as a guest. Before he left for Tehran he was invited to a lunch given for one of the Arab sheiks, and to a large company cocktail party, where he spent most of the time talking to Eileen in a corner.

He watched her at that moment and wondered just how much she liked him. He had no idea what made him ask the question, but he did.

'I'm surprised Janet isn't with you. I thought Logan was sure to bring her.'

Janet Armstrong was not Logan's secretary in the conventional sense; she had been a brilliant student at the London School of Economics and was his personal assistant. She had worked for Field for the last two years. She was the most efficient and intelligent woman that James had ever met, even in the exalted climate of the Foreign Office where clever women floated by like leaves in autumn. Janet Armstrong had the mind of an exceptional man, with no visible feminine weaknesses like sentiment or emotion. He wouldn't admit that she was smart and attractive because he disliked the type so much.

'No. Logan left her behind this time,' Eileen answered him.

He had a thin, intellectual face with eyes that were alert and yet warm. She had liked him almost too much when she first met him. It was as if they had known each other for years. Suddenly she put her hand through the crook of his arm. There was no mistake about the way he closed it against himself.

'Let's sit down for a minute,' she said.

'There's a table over there.' James steered a way through the crowd towards a little gilt table with empty chairs along one wall. He sat her down.

'I'll go and get us both a drink,' he said. 'Don't let anyone come and drag you away.'

'I won't,' Eileen promised. She felt very tired and her head was aching slightly. She had tried very hard to amuse the Iranian Minister, hoping to please Logan. Perhaps it was her imagination, but the more she tried to contribute to his business and fill out her role as the chairman's wife, the more irritated he became.

James came back, carrying two glasses of champagne.

'Thank you, James. You're a darling.' She took the glass and let their fingers touch.

'I wish you'd tell me what's the matter,' he said quietly. 'I know there's something. There's nothing wrong with Lucy, is there?'

Eileen shook her head.

'Oh, good Lord no. She's fine. Growing sweeter and prettier every day. Logan absolutely worships her.'

'I'm afraid I can't imagine him as the doting father, but I'll take your word for it. All right, if it's not Lucy, then what is it? You can tell me. You know that.'

'I know I can,' she said gently. 'I feel I could go to you with anything, James, and you'd help if you could.'

'That makes me very happy,' he said. For a moment he covered her hand with his. Communication was passing between them. It was very disturbing. He looked at her, and she knew that if they'd been alone he would have kissed her.

'I can't talk about it. Not yet anyway. But I promise you, if I talk to anyone it will be you. I think I see Logan making signs at us. We'd better go.'

She got up and James pulled back her chair. He bent down to her a little way.

'Damn Logan,' he said.


There were three people in the upstairs room in the apartment block on Torshab Road. The three-roomed flat had been rented two months previously by an American who described himself as a student of archaeology and explained that he wanted a base in Tehran during his visits to the dig near Persepolis.

He was twenty-eight, tall and squarely built, with blonde hair that was cut unfashionably short, and a Nordic face with blue eyes. The name on his passport was Peters. The last two names under which he had operated in Europe were Rauch and Glover, and in Guatemala he was known as King. The name which really belonged to him was well known and respected in Cleveland, Ohio, but he had ceased to think of himself in connection with it. He hadn't been back to the United States in five years. There was an FBI warrant for his arrest waiting if he returned.

14

Of his two companions, one was a girl, the other a slight, wiry Syrian. The girl was sitting beside Peters and she had one hand laid in a proprietary way on his knee. She had green eyes and her dark hair had been hennaed; her mother was German and her father Lebanese. She was twenty-five years old and she carried a French passport in the name of Madeleine Labouchère with an address in Paris. She had met Peters in Dublin, where they had been attending a secret conference with some of the extreme left wing of the Provisional IRA. As a result she and the American had joined up. To Madeleine, that was the most important thing that had ever happened to her since her political conversion. She had lived with many men, as any liberated woman should do, but never before had she been in love. She was sitting close to him now, waiting for the telephone to ring. It was past one o'clock in the morning; the room was grey with cigarette smoke, and there were empty coffee cups piled on the brass table. The Syrian, who was working in the Embassy as a commercial attaché, yawned and stretched his skinny arms above his head.

'He should have rung through an hour ago.'

Peters shrugged. 'Maybe the party went on past midnight. They've got plenty to celebrate.'

The girl leaned against his shoulder. She lit a cigarette.

'They won't be celebrating for long,' she said.

'It's a masterly plan,' the Syrian said. 'But assassination would have been simpler.'

'Murdering Khorvan won't stop them,' Peters answered. 'It would just have brought Ardalan's butchers swarming all over Tehran. It was a stupid idea, my friend, and rightly vetoed by the Committee.'

The Syrian shrugged; he didn't seem to mind the correction.

'I'm not complaining about the plan,' he said. 'It's very well worked out.'

'I majored in history,' Peters said. 'All the patterns are predictable because events repeat themselves. And this way, we'll come out of it without shedding blood.'

'You're becoming squeamish,' the girl said.

'Would you kill in this particular case?' He looked down at her.

She didn't hesitate. 'If there was no other way – yes.'

'Well it won't arise,' he spoke to the Syrian. 'I'm in charge of this. I said there'll be no killing and no need to kill.'

'You can't have a revolution without blood,' Madeleine said. She didn't want to make him angry, but she had to disagree.

'I don't dispute that,' Peters answered. 'I've done my share. But this is going to be different. We'll come out with a moral victory.'

'If the story gets out, you don't think public opinion will congratulate you for kidnapping...' Madeleine began, and then the telephone rang. It was the Syrian who answered. He only said, 'Yes,' and then listened.

Habib was in the kitchens of the Hilton hotel. Most of the staff had gone home and the clearing up after the oil company's reception and dinner was finished. He was using the telephone in the chef's office.

'I'm sorry to be late. I hadn't finished work. They were all here tonight and the wife is with him. He expects to stay for some time. She also, but will return before him. There are no immediate plans to go back.' As he spoke he glanced behind him, afraid that somebody might have heard a noise from the outside of the office and would then come to investigate.

'Good,' the Syrian said. 'You've done well.'

The voice at the other end sank lower.

'The Colonel was here.'

'Don't worry, he would be. Why should he notice you? Be brave, my brother. Forget the Colonel.' He hung up.

'Well?' Peters was on his feet.

'He got close enough to hear that Field has no immediate plans to return to England for the moment. Also he's brought his wife with him. That's good. It'll make it easier still. But she's going back earlier, so we can't waste time. And he was very frightened because Ardalan was there.'

'I'm not surprised,' Peters said. 'Anyone with sense is frightened of Ardalan. I heard you reassuring him. I don't suppose he did anything to draw attention to himself?' He asked the question calmly.

The Syrian looked at him for a moment before he answered.

'If he did,' he said, 'the one thing he knows as a connection with us is this telephone number.'

16

'Get him out of Tehran tomorrow. It's safer. Ardalan can smell fear at fifty yards.'

'I shall see to it,' the Syrian said. 'So the date is set.'

'We go the day after tomorrow,' Madeleine answered. She got up and began collecting the dirty coffee cups. 'Paris and then London. We split up in Paris and arrive in England separately.'

'From there we will make the final preparations,' Peters said. 'Resnais will join Madeleine in Paris and they'll come in together.'

'Good luck then,' the Syrian said. He came and shook hands with Peters and the girl. He gave them a little bow as he stopped by the door. Then he quietly raised his fist in the clenched salute and went out.

Madeleine took the cups out to the kitchen; she was not a domesticated girl. At home in Beirut there were a dozen servants in her parents' house. She had reacted violently from a luxury she considered sinful and degenerate. At first she had worn shabby clothes and prided herself on being unkempt; even before she broke with her family at twenty, she had delighted in flouting her German mother's insistence upon neatness. But now that she had fallen in love with Peters, she indulged in pretty clothes and paid attention to her looks. She wanted to please Peters with all the passion of her quasi-Oriental upbringing, but above all she wanted him to say he loved her. She was too realistic to expect him to mean it. She left the dirty cups in the kitchen and followed him into the bedroom. He was stripped to his trousers and the sight of the muscled body aroused her. She came and stood close, pressing herself sensually against him, her arms twisted round his waist, stroking him with her hands.

She started murmuring to him in French; she found English a coarse, unromantic language, as bad as German. He put his arms around her. Later she said to him over and over before she drifted into a satisfied sleep that he was wonderful and she adored him.

Peters didn't answer. She was a ferocious woman and he admired her dedication. But he didn't love her and he wished she wouldn't indulge in sentimentality. There was no room for emotional entanglements or for any other commitment outside their common cause. This didn't exclude sex, or even living

17

with a woman, but it was more important to him that they worked together than that they went to bed. He moved away from her and immediately he had forgotten she was there. His mind was alert and concentrating on the details of the plan ahead.

This had been formulated at the conference held in Munich in May. It was easy for the members of the Central Committee to meet in Germany rather than attract attention by asking its European members to travel to Damascus, where Israeli intelligence would have been alerted. There was a large work force of Arabs in the Federal Republic and it was simple for the Palestinian members to travel in as casual labour, while people like Peters arrived as tourists. The meeting had been held in the house of a German dental surgeon in a working-class district. Non-European patients came and went without causing comment. They had held their conference during his surgery hours. Peters had been a member of the commando group of the Palestine Liberation Forces for the last two years. He had travelled to Egypt from Central America under the auspices of the Marxist cell with whom he had been operating in that area. He had been invited to Munich as a special observer. He had left the city with the Committee's mandate to carry out the most vital mission against the forces of Western capitalism since Nasser closed the Suez Canal.

James Kelly lived in a beautiful nineteenth-century house in Shemiran, a select suburb on the lower slopes of the Elburz mountains which lie behind Tehran. It was built of pink stone, domed and turreted, with exquisite stonework tracery, and set in a large, secluded garden. He had rented it when he first came to Tehran, appalled at the prospect of living in one of the hideous modern houses which the newly rich Iranians were putting up in the city. The house was ramshackle and in poor repair, but there was no limit on the company's funds and he had transformed it into its former beauty.

The car had brought Eileen and Logan back ahead of James. She got out and stood for a moment in the moonlight. It was a warm still night and the scent of the jasmine from the garden was very strong. In the sky above, an enormous moon hung like a great pearl. The twentieth-century city, with its ugly buildings, its Arab-traffic-logged avenues, and its modern hotels, might have been a thousand miles away; the house and its fragrant garden, with the delicate sound of the fountains which James had put in order, made sense of the magic that Westerners found in Persia. Now the ancient name was changed, the ancient rulers vanished. The son of an army sergeant sat upon the Peacock Throne, and the Persian aristocracy, weakened and effete, were overridden by the brash and ambitious middle class, gorged with wealth from the great mineral resources they controlled. It was an ugly contrast in the country whose poetry and marvellous decorative arts were among the wonders of the world.

'I'm going in,' Logan said. He had waited for his wife, as she paused, and had seen her look upwards and around her. It was a magnificent night and he too was aware of the jasmine and the interplay of shadows in the garden. Not so long ago he would have taken her arm and suggested they walked for a while before going to bed. But not now.

'I'm dead tired,' he said. And then he added quickly, 'You must be too. It's been one hell of a long day.'

She followed him inside the house without saying anything. Eileen had stayed there twice before; the room was simply furnished but in excellent taste. James had hung some fine Gelim rugs on the walls and displayed a collection of rare Luristan bronzes and Nishapur pots in a wide niche above the bed. It was comfortable and in some ways spectacular, but she thought how masculine it was. She wondered why he had never married and, because she was tired and on edge with Logan, she suddenly said so.

'I wonder why James is still a bachelor?'

Logan was undressing in the bathroom with the door open.

'I've no idea. There's nothing wrong with him – we checked all that.'

'How do you mean – checked?'

She couldn't undo her dress without his help; she unfastened the brooch and took off the earrings, holding them in her hand.

'Checked in what way?'

'We had him checked out,' Logan sounded irritated. 'It's always done. Cuts out trouble later. You know I won't have homosexuals in positions of responsibility.'

19

'My God,' Eileen said. She turned away and dropped the jewellery on the dressing table. 'I think that's disgusting! I wonder what he'd say if he knew?'

'I doubt if he'd be surprised. They've had enough trouble with pansies in the Foreign Office. You've got no right to criticize.' He slammed the bathroom door.

For months she had held herself in control; ignoring his bad moods, excusing outbursts when he was rude. He had changed towards her and she had begun to suspect why. She had tried hard not to be hurt, deluding herself that it was the result of overwork and strain. Seven years of marriage; the first four had been dogged by miscarriages and the birth of Lucy, which had changed everything.

She went and pulled the door open.

'Don't you slam the door on me!' she said. He was already in his pyjamas. He looked first surprised and then he grew red.

'Don't bloody well shout at me!' he said. He came out, pushing past her.

'I'm not shouting,' Eileen said. 'I just won't put up with your bad manners! I think it's disgusting to pry into people's private lives and I said so!'

He turned and looked at her. The last months had been a strain upon him too. His voice was lower, calmer, but it was more wounding than his rage.

'I'll run my business as I think best,' he said. 'What you think doesn't interest me. If all I had to do was live in a bloody broken down house in the Irish bogs and think about how to get money out of my son-in-law instead of doing a day's work, I might have time for your high principles. Unfortunately I haven't. So you can stuff them!'

'I'll give you the three hundred pounds! I'll pay you back the damned money you gave him! Then you won't have to throw it in my face.'

She sat on the bed and began to cry. He had given her father three hundred pounds towards a repair bill for fencing round their land at Meath House. She had written her father an angry letter, reproaching him for sponging on Logan yet again, and been fobbed off by a telephone call full of apologies and charm. Her father despised Logan Field. He thought he was common and trumped up and that the life he lived was a waste of time.

Logan did none of the things of which John Fitzgerald approved. He disliked horses and was bored by racing; he shot reasonably well but without much enjoyment. He was always travelling and chasing himself, and her family thought it was just as well he was so rich because everything else about him was ridiculous. They were not aware of the dynamic personality which had first attracted her. They merely considered him exhausting.

After a moment she felt him sit beside her.

'I'm sorry, darling,' he said. His arm came round her shoulder and pulled her against him. 'I'd no right to say that. I was a rude shit. I'm sorry.'

She couldn't answer immediately. Her emotions were confused; hurt and anger struggled against a feeling of deep despair. When she raised her head he was staring at the ground, his free hand clenching on his knee.

'I'm sorry,' he said again, and she knew that he meant it.

It was not the moment for discussion, but she felt a lemming urge to hasten the process of disintegration.

'What's the matter, Logan? What's happening to us?'

'Nothing,' he said. His arm slipped away from her. 'We're just over the top. We need a good night's sleep. You probably need a holiday.'

'I've never had a holiday without you,' she said slowly. 'I don't want one now.'

His head turned towards her and then away.

'It might be a good idea. Give us both a chance to think things out.'

Eileen got up and searched for a cigarette in her bag. She found his lighter thrown on the bed.

'I've known we were drifting away from each other for some time. I thought it was just a phase – but it isn't, is it? Please. Look at me. Tell me the truth. Is there someone else?'

He glanced up; his expression was unhappy. She knew by the set of his mouth that it would soon be resentful.

'Leave it alone, for Christ's sake, Eileen. Don't start all this tonight.'

She started to cry again.

'I can't. I can't live with the uncertainty. You didn't want me on this trip; you did everything to stop me coming. We haven't slept together for months. You're always too tired or you brush me aside. I know there's somebody else. There has to be!'

'All right.' He got up and stood facing her. 'All right, you want to force the issue. There *is* someone. I can't go on pretending either. Oh Christ!' He picked up the lighter and threw it across the room.

She didn't say anything. She had asked for the truth and he had told it. He was in love with another woman. Suspecting it was not the same as knowing it. The certainty was not a relief. It was like a wound. The extremity of pain was yet to come. At that moment, seeing her face, Logan Field didn't know who he hated most, himself or her. As long as he didn't have to hurt her, he could retain affection for her and even try to avoid a crisis. Nothing was decided, certainly in his own mind, so long as she didn't take the initiative. But she had made him admit that he didn't love her, and from that moment it became a fact.

'Who is it?'

She had stopped crying; she sounded calm. He had never seen her look so bloodless, the dreadful colour accentuated by the blue dress. There was no going back now, and his distress was changing into anger. He was a man who welcomed decisions and hated any kind of vacuum, but this particular decision had been forced upon him. It was her fault and he was already blaming her so he could excuse himself. So long as she asked questions, she would get the answers.

'Janet,' he said. 'I want to marry her.'

Eileen said quietly, 'I see. To have more children?'

'Not necessarily.' Now he was retreating. This was a truth he couldn't face; the gnawing disappointment that after Lucy's birth, his wife could never have another child. One girl, one beautiful precious little girl, to inherit all that he had created...
He couldn't admit that he wanted to remarry because he wanted a son to follow on. It sounded grandiose and ridiculous. But for three years he had been frustrated and guilty because it happened to be true. He saw Eileen put up a hand to the back of her dress.

'Here,' he said, 'I'll undo that for you.'

She stepped away from him.

'No. No thank you.'

She put both hands to the neck and ripped the back apart.

The dress slid down and she stepped out of it. She had a beautiful figure, narrow hipped – too narrow – with small breasts and the very pale skin that went with her colouring. He had desired her and loved her, and for the first four years, in spite of losing her pregnancies and being ill, they had known intense happiness. He had been so proud of her; proud of her charm and her good breeding, showing her off like a treasure. He had been tender, according to his moods; he had known that she loved him. And she had given him the child that he loved more than anything in the world . . . Sexual desire did not awaken, seeing her; conscience made him step towards her.

'Eileen –'

'How could you?' Her voice was quiet but full of contempt. 'That awful woman. I'll go home tomorrow. It'll be less embarrassing for everyone. There's a sofa in the next room; I'd be glad if you'd sleep on it tonight.'

She went into the bathroom and locked the door.

## 2

Janet Armstrong was asleep when the call came through from Tehran. She lived in a small flat in Chelsea, part of a conversion of a Georgian house in an elegant and expensive square. She had rented it for a year and six months ago Logan Field had bought her the lease. It was beautifully decorated in the best contemporary Italian style, and it was a faithful reproduction of her own personality. Crisp, clear, brilliant and positive. The bed was circular; Logan had thought it funny and refused to sleep in it when she first brought him there. He had soon admitted that it was more comfortable than the bed in the Dallas hotel room where they had first made love. It happened by accident; neither had anticipated that a late night conference would end in his hotel suite with him taking off her clothes at three in the morning. It began with a casual touch and ended in a sexual storm that left them both astonished.

As she woke and reached for the telephone, she registered the hour, five-thirty, and the time change in Iran, and she knew it was Logan. She pulled the telephone onto the bed; her blonde hair was cut short and streaked with silver lights; he had asked her to let it grow because he liked playing with long hair when he made love, but Janet had refused. Long hair was untidy and a nuisance. Also it didn't suit her. She had employed no feminine tricks to catch him; nobody could have accused her of behaving like the secretary in every cliché-ridden situation, angling to marry the boss. She had never thought of a closer relationship than working for him, until they exploded together in Dallas. Then, added to the intense interest they shared in the company and the natural fluency with which they worked together, had come the dimension of perfectly matched sex.

'Logan?' she said.

His voice was clear; for once the line worked without atmospherics.

'Janet – it's me. How are you?'

'I'm fine. You woke me up. How's everything going?'

It was typical that she mentioned the business first.

'So far, everything's fine,' he said. 'I have a meeting with the Minister this morning. Then I hope to see the Shah. I don't know how long I'll have to wait for an audience, but if it's weeks, I'll come back home and go out again. It looks all set though. We had a big party for Khorvan and he was perfectly friendly. Kelly said not to be surprised if he didn't turn up and that would have been a bad sign. But it went off very well. How's everything your end?'

'Going smoothly. There's a bit of a panic about the rig drilling on Block 211/6; apparently they keep losing bits down the hole and they're worried about next month's long range weather forecast. Jenner's dealing with it. He's flying up to Lerwick today and out to the rig tomorrow. There were items in all the financial columns about you and Imshan. The same old photograph – you'll have to get a new one taken, darling. I'll fix that up when you get back. The reaction on the market has been very optimistic. There was a big article on the Shah in *The Sunday Times* apropos of the oil-field. Oh, and I hear the Saudi Ambassador asked for an appointment; nothing's been fixed till you get home. Is that all right?'

'They're getting the wind up their asses,' Logan sounded gratified. 'Once we get Imshan into full production they won't be holding the cards any more. We can tell them to go stuff themselves.'

He had always used what he thought of as 'men's language' to Janet, without any fear of offending her. He was only coarse in front of Eileen when they quarrelled.

'Listen, Eileen's coming home.'

'Oh? Why? Nothing wrong with Lucy, I hope?'

She sat upright, tensing slightly at the mention of his wife. She always asked after the child; it was her only concession in the game, because she knew how much Logan loved her. She had seen her several times when she came to the house in Eaton Square and thought her a lonely, over-protected little girl, in dire need of brothers and sisters. She had said so to Logan.

25

'No, Lucy's not the reason. I'm afraid things have come to a head.'

'Oh God,' Janet said. 'Jesus. Has she found out?'

'I told her,' he said.

There was a sharp crackle down the line, and she guessed that he was having to shout.

'I can't talk about it now. I want you to come out here. I'll need someone to act as hostess. Can you come out by the end of the week?'

'I don't know –' she was shouting back at him now; the connection had deteriorated. 'I'll see what's on this morning and I'll ring you tonight. At James's – about seven – your time.'

'All right. Seven o'clock. Take care of yourself.'

'You too,' Janet said. 'I love you.'

She hung up. She got out of bed; she wore a silk pyjama jacket, and her legs were beautifully shaped. She went into the bathroom, all white carpet and glass, drank some water and looked at herself in the mirror. A face that was pale without make-up, grey eyes that needed mascara, and a mass of curling silvered hair. She was thirty-one, with an early marriage which had ended in divorce after three years behind her and the prospect of marrying Logan Field suddenly ahead. She was healthy and she was still young. She could give him children, and she would. She would never be a wife like Eileen Fitzgerald, but then he hadn't been content with a graceful ornament. Logan wanted a partner and he wanted a big family. Looking in the mirror, Janet made up her mind that she was going to give him both.

She smiled, unaware that she did so. Happiness and excitement made her beautiful. She didn't think about Eileen Field. Janet was not without scruples, but she had never seen any reason to feel guilty about the other woman. Eileen Field had married him and had the chance to make him happy. If she had failed, that wasn't anybody else's fault.

She showered, made up and dressed quickly. She loved going to the giant Imperial building off Cheapside She loved her smart office outside Logan's and the sense of excitement it gave her to get down to work. Power had always fascinated her. And Logan personified power. Her own secretary, a middle-aged spinster of superb efficiency who had been with Imperial for fifteen years, was surprised to hear the crisp, aloof Mrs Armstrong humming under her breath as she read through her mail.

Eileen slept late. James's houseboy knocked on the bedroom door with coffee and orange juice, but since nobody answered he took the tray down to the kitchen. At seven o'clock, Logan had come into the bedroom to dress. He had glanced at her lying asleep, one arm above her head, and felt a pang of real regret. Last night had been an ugly incident which made him feel uneasy and ashamed in the chill of daylight. But there was no going back, even had he wanted to. Rejected as she was, she had suddenly been able to despise him, and he hated the feeling. He had been able to despise her family while loving her; in his opinion they were useless parasites, contributing nothing but funny stories and racing anecdotes to any conversation, completely disinterested in world affairs, in industry or politics. Her mother had died after their marriage; she was a tall horsy woman with a soft voice and her daughter's blue eyes. Logan had tolerated her, but John Fitzgerald he actively disliked. A sponger, a snob – he had been sending money to the old humbug for years, knowing that he was never grateful. Now that was over too; there would be no more milking of the English son-in-law. He had picked up his clothes and slipped out of the room. Downstairs he lit a cigarette, sent the houseboy who appeared from the kitchen to get him coffee, and put through the telephone call to Janet. He left the house before James Kelly came down to breakfast.

In the Syrian Embassy, the commercial attaché who had spent the evening in the flat on Torshab Road was writing a report.

The commando unit was ready to go on its mission; Peters and Madeleine Labouchère were booked out on a flight through to Paris and then on to London the next day. Resnais would join them independently. It should take about a week to perfect the final details of the operation and they expected to complete it within ten days at the latest.

Peters had told the Syrian to get the little waiter Habib out of Tehran. There was no reason in the world to suppose that

Colonel Ardalan had noticed him among the crowd, or that he could ever be connected with what was to come. But Peters never took chances. Which was why he was just a series of aliases to Interpol, a faceless shadow with a deadly record of terrorism. The Syrian had to find Habib Ebrahimi and make sure that the million to one chance didn't happen.

Mahmoud Khorvan received Logan Field, James Kelly and the assistant resident director, Ian Phillipson, in his office at the Ministry. It was a large modern building, square and ugly like all the new buildings in the city. It was garishly furnished, with thick crimson carpets and gilt chandeliers; a huge Harrods reproduction desk and fake Chippendale chairs completed the effect of incongruity. A large colour photograph of the Shah with the Empress and the little Crown Prince hung on the wall behind Khorvan in a carved gilded frame. A signed photograph stood by his right elbow. Coffee and orange juice had been brought in for his visitors. His secretary, a slim, beautiful girl, poured and passed the cups. The smell of Turkish cigarettes was strong; the Minister smoked sixty a day. Although he never drank at public receptions, especially where foreigners were present, part of his bookcase contained a cocktail cabinet with every kind of alcoholic drink except wine, which he disliked. His favourite was malt whisky. He greeted Logan courteously, Kelly with amiability, and the subordinate hardly received an acknowledgement. Kelly had long since realized that they were not a gracious people. Khorvan offered cigarettes; all but Logan declined.

'Now Mr Field,' he began. He spoke very good English and understood even better than he spoke. He had spent three years in London studying economics and it was during that period he had developed left-wing sympathies. 'I have given very careful consideration to your offer. Very careful. I have reached an unfortunate conclusion.' He made an arch with his fingers and looked at Logan. Logan didn't move; no change of expression, not a muscle twitch. The Minister admired him for this; he might hate the man and try to wreck the negotiations, but at least he was going to enjoy himself. James leaned a little forward, instinctively prepared to be the diplomat.

'Not too unfortunate, I hope, Minister.'

'It depends on how serious you were when you submitted this offer,' was the answer, directed at Logan.

'We have never entered any negotiation except on a serious level, Minister,' Logan spoke curtly. 'Please explain why you find the offer unfortunate. I had been told it was acceptable.'

'Acceptable to me, yes,' Khorvan said pleasantly. 'But to a higher authority – not.'

'What's wrong with it?' Logan put out his cigarette in the visitors' ashtray. He wasn't in the least worried by Khorvan. Nobody with any experience of the Eastern methods of conducting business would have expected anything but a last minute haggle over terms. He had come prepared to give something away.

'Let us consider the proposition as a whole,' Khorvan said. 'There were many contenders for the right to develop Imshan. Because of the size of the oil-field, every one of them was prepared to offer as much or more than you, Mr Field. But His Imperial Majesty decided in favour of a British company. Thanks to the persuasive powers of Mr Kelly.'

'It was more of a political decision than an economic one,' James interposed. 'His Imperial Majesty is a very great man. He thinks in global terms.'

'His decision to allow your company to export your share of the oil produced at Imshan at a discount on the OPEC price will not only have world-wide repercussions, but it will inevitably undermine the solidarity of the oil-producing countries. It will also, if I am not mistaken, enormously enhance Imperial's position as a major oil company. You could become as important as Exxon.' Khorvan looked at them in turn. 'Yet in exchange for this, you propose to give no more than any of your competitors.'

Logan leaned forward.

'As I see it, Minister, our contribution to the joint venture with the National Iranian Oil Company is to develop the field at Imshan. The cost of this development alone will be in the region of three hundred million dollars to produce up to six hundred thousand barrels a day. There will also be a township, hospital, schools, full modern amenities in an area which is deserted at the moment and a pipeline to the refinery at Abadan. Finally there is the commitment to expand production up to a million barrels a day. If there's anything more the Shah wants us to do, I can't think what it is, but I'm naturally anxious to hear.'

'His Imperial Majesty has made a gesture which will save the West from bankruptcy and revolution,' Khorvan said coldly. 'The price of oil is causing such massive inflation that a total breakdown is inevitable. Everyone knows that. The United States would like to declare war on the Arab States but she cannot because they are under Soviet protection. Governments are plotting and negotiating to try and save themselves; they cannot use the Israelis as a pawn because the Arab forces are equally well equipped, as the last conflict proved. So His Imperial Majesty decides to save you. Once it is realized that Iran is letting some of its oil go at lower prices than is agreed between the OPEC countries, the others will have to reduce their prices in turn.'

'Without any disrespect,' Logan said, 'This is not just a philanthropic gesture. The situation you describe is only too true, Minister. We are on the edge of disaster in the West. But if Europe suffers a complete economic breakdown the result will be chaos followed by a Communist revolution. Iran could not hope to survive it unscathed. The Shah knows this. He is certainly saving us by breaking the price formula, but he's also protecting himself.'

There was silence after he had spoken. Khorvan sipped his coffee. He didn't hide his resentment and James tried to warn Logan not to say any more. But Logan ignored him. He leaned back in his chair and he seemed perfectly relaxed.

'I take it you feel our investment is insufficient,' he said. 'What else do you suggest?'

'You talk of building a pipeline to Abadan,' Khorvan said. 'The distance from Imshan to the refinery is too great. For the quantity of oil that Imshan will produce, we want a separate refinery. Built by you in exchange for the discount on your oil price.'

Logan looked at James. He turned back to Khorvan.

'No mention of a separate refinery was made to Mr Kelly.'

'No,' the Minister agreed, 'but it was to me. His Imperial Majesty is determined that a refinery should be built at Bandar Muqam, near Imshan on the coast. And that whoever goes into partnership with the National Oil Company should finance it. He considers that is a fair contribution.'

The suggestion had come from Khorvan himself. He knew the Shah's determination to squeeze the last dollar out of Western investors in Iran. The refinery investment would be a major step in the long-term industrialization of the country. If Imperial Oil wanted to develop Imshan and to break the oil price to save the West, then it was up to them to find the money. Logan lit a cigarette.

'The cost of a refinery big enough to cope with even half of Imshan's eventual production would be in the region of another three hundred million,' he said. 'An investment of three hundred million, or possibly more because of inflation, would wipe out our profit margins for the next ten years.'

Khorvan said nothing. He made an arch with his fingers and looked at the tips of them.

'I'm afraid it's not possible,' Logan said. 'No company in the world would agree to such a deal. My board wouldn't sanction it even if I recommended it. Surely you can appreciate that.'

'I do,' Khorvan said. 'But unfortunately it is not my problem, Mr Field. I am not negotiating for our oil; you are. If you really cannot see your way to building the refinery, then the deal must be offered to someone else.'

'That's perfectly fair,' Logan said. 'But exactly who is in a position to undertake this? Don't tell me Exxon, because I know as well as you do that Iran doesn't want America having an interest in such a vital asset. You've got enough American soldiers and bases here already. You couldn't let them within a mile of Imshan without having Russia breathing down your neck.'

Khorvan looked at him with dislike. He had turned rather a sallow colour, a sure sign that he was close to losing his temper. He wasn't accustomed to the tone used by Logan.

'There is a Franco-German consortium,' he said.

'I know there is,' Logan shrugged. 'But they won't be able to make an investment on this scale for no profit either.'

James spoke to Logan. He could feel the tension in the atmosphere.

'Perhaps we should go away and look at the figures.'

'I know the figures,' Logan answered. 'So does the Minister.

If we build this refinery, we have no profit for ourselves. It's as simple as that.' He offered his gold cigarette case to Khorvan.

'No,' the Minister said, forgetting his manners. 'I only smoke Turkish.'

'I used to like them,' Logan said. 'Now I use these things.' He held up a mentholated filter tip cigarette. 'They're supposed to be safer. I don't suppose it makes any difference. *"La illah, illalah wa huwa qadir all kulli shayy."* '

James nearly fell off his chair. 'There is no God but Allah and he is powerful over everything.' He had no idea that Logan knew a word of Arabic or Farsi. Even Khorvan showed that he was impressed. Field looked at him and the hard lines of his face creased into the smile which held such charm.

'And if Allah wills that we build you a refinery, Minister, then who knows? I'll take Mr Kelly's advice. We'll go away and think about it. It would help if we could have another appointment with you before the end of the week.'

Khorvan stood up.

'Unfortunately I am going out of Tehran.'

Logan didn't move.

'Then when will you be back?'

'In ten days' time.'

'I think we should have a meeting before then.' Logan stood up. 'I have an audience with the Shah and I can't go to the Palace with this question unresolved.'

Khorvan hesitated. He had no knowledge of a date being fixed and he was unprepared. The last thing he wanted was for Field to bring the question up before the Shah until he had undermined the whole negotiation.

'How long will it take you to consider your figures, Mr Field?'

'When do you leave Tehran?'

'On Thursday. I don't like to travel on a Friday.' As a devout Moslem, he avoided working or moving about on the equivalent of the Christian Sabbath.

'Then it'll take us until Wednesday morning,' Logan said. 'Mr Kelly will fix the time with your secretary.' He held out his hand and gripped the Minister's hand until it hurt. 'Good morning, Minister.'

Khorvan sat down as they filed out. He had no intention of leaving Tehran, and as soon as Field had gone, he put through a call to the Palace and asked to speak to the Minister of the Court. He learned that, although the British Ambassador had made a formal application for Logan Field to see the Shah, no date had been given. Logan had scored a point off him that morning, but it was insignificant beside the battle Khorvan had just initiated with that impossible demand. They couldn't hope to comply and he was confident that he could make their refusal seem like intractable greed to the Shah. Once it became a matter of government policy, Iran had no choice but to force the terms upon the Western company or suffer a loss of face. Either way, Imshan would not fall into the hands of Imperial Oil and Logan Field; and the Russian technologists, with all due modesty, could re-present themselves.

Peters had finished packing up; all that remained of his possessions were a toothbrush, shaving kit and pyjamas. Enough to see him through one night. He had been brought up with what he described as 'things'. His mother collected ornaments; the house in Cleveland was like an obstacle course, strewn with her expensive, maddening knick-knacks. His father had cars, a workroom full of gadgets; for his eighteenth birthday they had given him an elaborate hi-fi system which he had never used. They were 'thing' people, obsessed with what they owned or wanted to buy. They couldn't understand his contempt for material possessions. There were three children, an older sister and another boy, described by his mother as an afterthought. Peters thought this the most humiliating thing he had ever heard; the fact that it was always said with an arch smile and a pat on the boy's head only made it seem worse. He had resented it, but his brother didn't seem to mind.

He was the odd one out, the silent introverted child, the withdrawn hostile adolescent; a sharp stone in the family sand-pit. His sister had gone through college and business school, married a keen young advertising man and moved to San Francisco. Peters hadn't seen or heard of her since he left America. His younger brother was going through school when he took off; he seemed cast in the same plastic mould as his parents and his sister.

Peters had never explained to them why he diverged; he had found it impossible to communicate because their words didn't mean the same thing as his. When they talked of freedom, he saw it as conservative repression; his freedom was nothing but anarchy to them. Morals meant sexual behaviour to them; to him they were an ethical approach to humanity which didn't include copulation. Success was a word that they used like a weapon. He had to succeed. At school, at college, with the neighbours' daughters. He had to compete and be better. The effort not only repelled him but with all his soul he rejected the prize. He didn't want to better his friends in order to win the approval of a generation which he despised and whose standards he refused to accept. He had worked at school and taken his degree at college, but not for any of the reasons put forward by his parents. He wanted to study life and history, to understand the riddle of the world he lived in without accepting ready answers. He never discussed anything with them or confided in them. They complained, sometimes to his face, that he was a stranger. Peters had long recognized this and adjusted to it. Birth was an accident; he had been left at the wrong doorstep.

He was not aware of being lonely until he went to Kent State University. He didn't mix readily with the other students, although he found the atmosphere the most congenial he had experienced so far. There was a revolutionary spirit on the campus, a liberality of thought and a lack of convention which stimulated him. He made a few friends, discontented intellectuals from similar backgrounds to himself, and formed the first deep relationship of his life. Andrew Barnes was his thesis adviser in political science; he was twenty-six years old, and Peters just eighteen. Barnes was slight and limped after an attack of polio as a boy; he was quiet and serious, with a sense of humour that was usually at his own expense. By contrast, his favourite student was powerful, with a talent for athletics which would have brought a different character into the top ranks of college football; Peters was reserved and silent, Andrew Barnes loved talking. He initiated Peters into the pleasures of debate; he taught him to think and to express his thoughts. He overcame the younger boy's inclination to hold back from things and people that he disapproved of, and he preached the gospel of change through attack. Attack through education, debate, ideas. And as a last resort, through confrontation. Barnes was a Marxist; he would have rejected in horror the accusation that he lived a life of Christian unselfishness, wholly devoted to the welfare of others, a fearless champion of the less fortunate, determined to withstand injustice and to work for the improvement of society. To Barnes the word connoted people; he lacked the cold intellectualism that sees humanity in terms of economics. To him, political science was about human beings and his concern for them gave his own political beliefs a shining sincerity. He was the most attractive person Peters had ever met. His personality gathered a devoted group of student disciples around him, but for Peters the first term at Kent under Barnes's auspices was the step on the road to Damascus.

All his life he had felt rootless, condemned to a life of rejecting without an alternative choice. Listening to Barnes, he discovered a new meaning to existence; a light shone at the end of the tunnel which had seemed so dark and lacking in direction. All the resources of love that were in him found a double outlet. The frail, impassioned teacher took the place left vacant by his parents, and because he was light miles away from the limited, conventional father with whom Peters had no point of contact, he never mentioned Barnes or let his parents meet him.

Barnes's teaching gave life a purpose for Peters; he adopted the political beliefs with the fervour of a personality starving for something to fight for. He would have followed Andrew Barnes to hell and out again, and on the 18th of June in 1968 on the campus of Kent State that was exactly what he did. It began as a protest against the Vietnam war; a number of students had been called up for military service, a rally was organized and its leader was Andrew Barnes. There had been other demonstrations; Peters had taken part and recognized the pattern. Speeches, slogans, an outbreak of stone-throwing against the police. The ugly baton charges, violence, injury, retreat and regrouping. When the National Guard were called out, he and Andrew Barnes were in the front ranks. He remembered afterwards, seeing the troops with their levelled weapons and trying to get in front of Barnes. There was a second baton charge, more violent than the first; some of the student ranks gave way, there was a horrible confusion when people seemed to be running in all directions and there were shrill screams from frightened girls. Peters heard Barnes shouting, telling them to hold on. And then the shots cracked out. Until the first students fell, everyone thought the troops were firing over the heads of the crowd. There was a lull of a few seconds when there was no sound at all but the echo of the rifle shots. Then the first screams of horror unloosed the panic and Andrew Barnes fell with a bullet in his chest.

For years afterwards, Peters woke from the nightmare where he was kneeling in the dirt, surrounded by fleeing, shrieking people, holding the dying man in his arms. His memories were confused. He had heard the groans of pain as Andrew Barnes bled from the mouth and seen the head fall back suddenly as if he were holding a puppet and the string had broken. He was weeping when the police arrested him; it took four of them to drag him away and wrench the dead man out of his arms. He had been punched and kicked, fighting like a madman on his way to the police wagon. Inside, with his hands handcuffed behind him, he was punched in the kidneys and in the groin and beaten up again in the station. His parents had come to bail him out and there was a moment when they saw their bruised and beaten son when they reached out to him without conditions. But it was too late. Although they joined the outcry against police brutality and the murder of the students on the campus, Peters didn't identify with them in any way. Their concern, their indignation meant nothing to him. The best human being he had ever met had been killed by the society which they and their generation represented. Barnes and the seven dead students were acclaimed as martyrs. There was a national scandal and world condemnation of the massacre at Kent State. Peters said nothing. He spent ten days in hospital and then returned to the campus. It was not the same and never would be. The limping figure, his head thrust a little forward as he tried to match the quicker walk of his students, was no longer part of Peters's life.

There would be no more evenings spent debating, no suppers eaten in Barnes's house where the talk went on into the night. When the press talked of martyrdom it was a cliché which Peters dismissed with contempt. They hadn't known Barnes or loved him. Only Peters and the group which had been close to Andrew Barnes knew the extent of the crime that capitalism had committed. For most of the students at Kent that day in June would leave a scar, mental or physical. But most would go out into the world and be absorbed into the society they hadn't been able to change.

This was not for Peters. If Andrew Barnes had shown him the meaning of warmth and disinterested love for his fellows, the National Guardsman who took aim at him and fired had taught Peters what it meant to hate. And to hate with a single-minded, pitiless intensity that gravitated naturally to the ultimate extreme of which the gentle Barnes would never have approved. Only violence could hope to overcome the organized violence of modern society. Absolute ruthlessness and total dedication to the cause were the requisites of revolutionaries if they were to be effective in the struggle.

By the time Peters graduated he was a leading member of the extremist Marxist cell that existed within the student organization. He was a marked agitator. Without saying good-bye to his parents, he took a plane down to Mexico. After that he shut his mind to them completely. He never felt an exile. He lived and moved among people like himself; dedicated, efficient, perfecting themselves for the work in hand. He learned to kill, to use explosives, to travel long distances under rough conditions. He was sent to Chile where he did valuable work, organizing sabotage and leading a brief guerilla expedition against an army camp. He stayed long enough to see Allende triumph and he was in Germany when he heard that the brief Marxist reign was over and the oppressors had gained power. In Bonn he and Madeleine Labouchère hi-jacked a Lufthansa 707, killing a steward and injuring three of the passengers. As a result of negotiations, four Palestinian terrorists were released from jail and he and the girl were given a safe conduct to Syria.

He stood by the apartment window for a moment; the sun was setting fire to the roofs of Tehran. There was no view but the streets and the blocks of buildings. An ugly city, built on a barren plain.

He had grown to love the real Iran, with its infinite variety; the lush northern slopes of the Elburz mountains leading down to the Caspian shore; the incredible carpet of spring flowers round Kerman, which had inspired the carpet weavers for a thousand years; the aridity of the Zagros mountains, broken

37

by little green valleys and clear streams, which contrast had fired the poetic soul of ancient Persia and produced immortal verse; the brutal heat of the yellow deserts and the almost spiritual uplift occasioned by the beauty of the mosques at Isphahan; the marvels at Persepolis the city of the great Darius where he had helped with excavations. This was the land that drew pilgrims from the Western world, eager to sample the fruits of the ancient culture and exquisite visual arts of the great Aryan race that had been both conqueror and civilizing influence in the Eastern world. As a people they were proud, treacherous, cunning and deeply hospitable; the inequality of life between the rich and the poor was as harsh as anything he had witnessed even in Central America. He had thought himself immune to misery and disease after seeing the plight of the Indians; it was the gross display of wealth in Iran that brought his rage to the surface. He hated the rich, wherever they clustered like sores on the body of the working masses.

Over-fed, artificial, swollen with profits, they lived in luxury and idleness while others slaved and hungered. Age had not mellowed Peters. He knew nothing but the reasoning of fanatics like himself. He made love to a woman who two years before had knelt in the passenger lounge of an Israeli airport and sprayed women and children with machine-gun fire. There was no weakening of his resolve, no change in his opinions. But this time he didn't want to kill. He would have to be careful of Madeleine. In one way she was a bad choice. She had a light trigger finger and she wasn't influenced by age or sex. But a woman was essential and he felt he could control her. Now that the time was so near, he wanted to start off. He wanted to be on the plane and come down at Orly.

Madeleine was in the dingy little kitchen and he heard her singing. She never suffered from nerves; danger excited her, like sex. She was a remarkable specimen of the modern Arab woman, in spite of her German blood. Tough, determined, unscrupulous, and fierce; her nearest equivalent was her blood enemy, the female Israeli. She might set light to the bedsheets but it was impossible to love her in the conventional sense. For this reason alone, she was the perfect complement to him.

They drank a bottle of wine, ate an excellent kebab which she prepared, and made love till they were both exhausted. By nine the next morning she had left the flat and he was driving in a taxi down Eisenhower Road towards Mehrabad airport.

'I hear you're going back tomorrow.'

Logan found her reading in James's shady sitting room; the windows onto the garden were open and the evening promised to be cooler.

'Yes,' she said. 'James managed to get me a seat for tomorrow morning.'

Now was the moment for him to retract, to make some move towards her, however slight. In spite of the hurt which was so real it was like a physical pain, she still hoped. Whether it was because some love for him was left or out of cowardice, she didn't know. He seemed cool, even impatient, as if having to talk to her was an irritant.

'I've asked Janet to come out. We've run into trouble with that bastard Khorvan. I'll have my hands full out here for some time. Why don't you go to Ireland?'

It had never occurred to her to go home. Her father wouldn't be sympathetic. He'd thought she was a fool to marry Logan anyway and he'd say she was an even bigger fool to walk out on the money now.

'I could take Lucy,' she said.

Immediately he frowned.

'No,' he said. 'I don't like her being dragged around. She's all right where she is, in her own home.' He lit a cigarette. 'We'll sort things out when I get home,' he said. 'I'm sorry it's turned out like this. I'm sure you know that. But I can't give any time to it at the moment. I've got to get Imshan settled first.'

She got up and went to the garden door.

'You certainly know your priorities,' she said quietly. 'And as far as my child is concerned, if I want to take her home with me, I will.' She walked out into the garden without saying goodbye.

James Kelly drove her to the airport. He had given her the address of his solicitors.

'They're a bit old-fashioned; they're not the kind to deal with a bastard like Logan, but they'll know who to recommend. Promise you'll go and see them.'

They were waiting by the departure lounge; the flight had been called and she was just about to go through passport control. Two Iranian police were checking the passengers and their hand luggage with a detector. They were running the detector over the canvas grip carried by a man immediately in front of her. He was tall and blonde and looked like an American junior professor.

'I will, I promise you,' Eileen said. 'I don't know what I would have done without you, James.'

He smiled; his dark hair flopped over his forehead as he bent down to her. 'You'd have been all right,' he said. 'You've got the guts of the Irish. Goodbye, Eileen. I'll ring you in a couple of days. Take care, and don't worry. And if you want me, just cable and I'll come home.'

She reached up and kissed him; she felt his hand grip her shoulder. Then she turned, as the flight was called for the last time. She passed through the detector screen and was given back her handbag. She followed the blonde man into the departure lounge and across to gate 7.

An Iranian woman, wearing the chador, her face covered to the eyes, paddled a few steps between them. She carried a little boy with wistful black eyes, greedily eating his fist. There was no resemblance, but Eileen thought of Lucy at that moment. From the moment she came back from the fashionable nursing home, the child had been in the care of a nanny. She had been too ill to protest at the annexation of her child. As she boarded the plane, she realized that for the first time since she was born, Lucy was going to belong to her. And that she would have to fight Logan every inch of the way to keep her.

She settled into a seat near the Exit door, fastened her seat-belt and opened the book she had tried to read the day before. She was not even aware that the American was beside her. They were each to remember, in very different circumstances, that their lives had joined for the first time when they shared that journey together.

# 3

Jean Resnais passed the time at Orly waiting for Peters and
Madeleine to arrive by watching the girls in the lounge. There
was a pretty blonde who pleased him: a thin, sensual little girl
with long hair and tiny breasts sticking through her shirt. He
could have picked her up easily, and was sorry that he had no
time. He was small and dark, with a sallow, intelligent face; his
clothes were conservative and he carried a briefcase. He looked
a prosperous businessman around thirty. His real age was
nearer thirty-five and he was an expert rifle and revolver shot.
The plane for London was due to leave in an hour; he wandered
over to the Arrivals board and checked. Several women watched
him. The plane from Tehran had landed. Madeleine should
join him in the departure lounge. As far as he knew, Peters was
taking a plane an hour later.

Resnais saw her walking through, carrying one light case;
he went after her, passed through passport control and was
stopped at the security point. Madeleine had gone through. The
London flight was being called. A policeman ran his hands up
and down him, while Resnais stood, with a slight grin on his
face as if it were all a joke, his arms lifted away from his sides.

The detector slid over his hand case and 'pinged' loudly. He
shrugged, opened the case and revealed a metal flask. It was
full of brandy. They waved him on, and he boarded the plane.
He didn't sit near Madeleine or look at the other passengers.
He settled into his seat as soon as the plane levelled off, tilted
it back and went to sleep. He didn't notice Eileen Field because
she was in the front of the plane in the first-class section.

When they arrived in London, he joined the taxi queue outside the No. 1 building. Madeleine was beside him. He grinned
at her, showing his white teeth. They had spent some time in

41

Syria together on a training course and she had never liked him. When he smiled he reminded her of a dog that was preparing to bite.

'Where are you going?' he asked her.

'Victoria,' she said.

'So am I,' Resnais said. 'Why don't we share – these taxis are very expensive.'

'You could have caught the bus,' Madeleine answered.

'I have to get a train.'

'All right then; let's share the next one.'

They got inside and slammed the door. Madeleine gave the driver an address in Pimlico, behind the station. It was a third-class hotel and not too particular about its clients. Couples had been known to take a room for an hour without arousing comment.

'Well,' Resnais said, 'have a good flight?'

'Very smooth. Very boring. I hate flying.'

'You're looking well,' he remarked. He knew, as all the group did, that she was sleeping with the American. He also knew that she disliked him and he was amused by her attitude. He had never accepted women as equals; he had worked with them, but they had one primary function and it wasn't revolutionary. He had never loved anyone in his life, but he had a sentimental attachment for dogs which had almost got him killed. He had adopted a starving mongrel during his stay in the Syrian outpost. When he took part in a dawn raid across into Israel the animal followed. It had run barking towards the kibbutz.

Even so he kept a half-bred Alsatian in his two-roomed flat in Paris. A friend was looking after it in his absence; he explained that he had to go back to Marseilles to see his father who was ill.

'Is everything going well?'

'Peters thinks so,' she said. 'And if he's satisfied, it must be. He'll be meeting us tonight. We stay at this place in Pimlico for one night only and then move on.'

'What about Peters?'

'He stays separately. We join up for the flight out.'

Resnais laughed at her. 'You won't like that much, will you?'

Madeleine looked out of the window. Neat suburban houses, set in identical plots of garden ran past the window.

'This is a job,' she said, without looking at him. 'Maybe the most important one we've ever done. It isn't time for making your stupid jokes.'

He only laughed again. They booked into the hotel. When they were alone, Madeleine opened her suitcase and took out a nightdress. Resnais watched her.

'Ah,' he said, 'what a pity you don't like me, chérie. I suppose you expect me to sleep on the floor?'

'No,' Madeleine glanced up at him briefly, 'in the chair. We should stay here for about an hour. Then we can go out and get something to eat. Peters has told me where to go. He'll meet us there.'

She took a French magazine out of her case, sat on the bed and started reading. Resnais lounged in the scuffed armchair and wondered if his dog was missing him.

It was six-thirty when Eileen arrived at Eaton Square. Kelly had sent a cable telling them to expect her. The Portuguese butler opened the front door, took her case and said, 'Welcome home, Madame.'

'Thank you, Mario. Everything all right?'

It was not a serious question. The house was perfectly run by a large staff; Logan paid top wages but he required faultless service and, in spite of a shortage of domestic workers, it was typical that he got what he demanded. There were fresh flowers, boldly and beautifully arranged in the hall; hot-house roses in her bedroom and a maid waiting to take her coat and prepare a bath for her. For years Eileen had lived in this style and after the first reaction from her old, easy-going Irish life, she had taken it for granted. It was part of being married to a very rich, exacting man. She had decorated and furnished the house herself, successfully resisting the suggestion that the interior decorator who had done Logan's office suite should take charge of arrangements. He had been delighted with the result. He had a natural eye for quality, and her taste was exactly what he wanted. Elegance and luxury, but no touch of ostentation. A magnificent Irish Chippendale desk was her father's wedding present to them. It was the kind of generous, unrealistic gesture that Logan didn't appreciate, especially since the old man was short of money. He would have preferred to buy his own desk and not be milked for loans in later years that were never going to be repaid.

Eileen went upstairs to the top floor. There was a little white painted gate, secured by a safety latch. Its purpose was to keep Lucy from toddling to the stairs and falling down them, but it always seemed to Eileen as if it were meant to keep her out.

She opened the nursery door and went in. It was a pink and white room, overdecorated and clinically neat. Toys were ranged along one wall, repeating the colour scheme; pink and white fairies danced in friezes round the room. The nanny was sitting down, sewing. When she saw Eileen she got up, smiling and distant, as if she were welcoming a visitor.

'Oh, good evening, Mrs Field. Did you have a good journey – we weren't expecting you back so soon.'

'No, it seemed pointless to stay on. I could have been there for ages. Where's Lucy?'

'She's asleep,' the nanny said.

Eileen walked to the night nursery door and opened it. She didn't look at the older woman or say anything. She went inside.

'Please, Mrs Field,' she heard the voice behind her. 'Don't wake the child. Surely in the morning...'

'She's not asleep,' Eileen said. 'Close the door please, Nanny.'

She switched on the light and the little girl sitting up in the pink and white bed held out her arms.

Eileen was in her room unpacking when there was a knock on the door.

'Madam! There you are now, I'm sorry I was out!'

Bridget Hagan's family had worked at Meath for generations. Her father was Eileen's groom when she was a child. She was a sturdy, cheerful girl of twenty-six, and she had worked for Eileen for five years.

'You're looking tired,' she said. 'Did you have a horrible journey? Let me do that, Madam; I'll put everything away.'

'It was tiring, Biddy. And I don't like flying anyway. Today's your day off, isn't it?'

'Sure and there's the Prince of Wales waiting to take me out tonight! I can go off any time. Shall I get some tea for you?'

'No thanks. Biddy, I'm going to need your help. I'm giving Nanny notice tomorrow morning.'

Bridget's face cracked into a huge smile.

'Thank God for that! Wait till Mario and Marianna hear about it! The old hag – won't she be mad?'

'Biddy, will you help me look after Lucy? I'm not going to get anyone like her again. I want the baby to myself.'

'High time too, Madam,' the girl agreed. 'What about Mr Field – what'll he say?'

Eileen hesitated.

'He's very busy in Iran at the moment. I haven't bothered him about it.'

'Don't you worry,' Bridget said. 'I'll do everything I can for Lucy. I've always wanted to get me hands on her and the old gorgon wouldn't even let me in the nursery!' She smiled at Eileen and started unpacking and hanging up her clothes.

She didn't feel hungry, but Bridget fussed over her, bringing a tray into the library. It was a small, comfortable room, with an air of casual elegance that costs so much money to achieve. There were photographs of herself and Lucy and a big portrait study of Logan, which was often reproduced in newspapers. Seven years of marriage to a man who had become a stranger. He had another woman now, a woman who could share his passion for business and stand on equal terms with him. Eileen had never been his equal or his partner; she had come low on his list of priorities and accepted it; she wasn't sure how high even Lucy rated when it came to Imperial Oil. He could never have said, like James, 'If you need me, I'll come back.'

It would have been easy to cable, to call the lover in the wings onto the stage. Easy to follow the habit of seven years and leave the initiative to a man. But this time she wasn't going to do it.

Nothing shamed her more than the realization of what she had allowed Logan to do with their child. The fussy, elderly mother-substitute with her rigid routine, the spotless nursery and the regimented toys. The deliberate exclusion of the mother from real contact with her child.

All that was over. James had said she had guts and she was glad to find that he was right. The guts to face life on her own and to fight Logan for the custody of Lucy.

She finished her coffee and went upstairs to the second-floor bedroom. Logan insisted on a king-size bed. He had given her a magnificent Poussin landscape two years before. She wondered whether he had given Janet Armstrong pictures or jewellery. More likely share options. She would appreciate them more. She got into bed and within minutes she fell asleep. It was just eleven o'clock.

In a cheap Indian restaurant, less than a mile away off Victoria Street, Madeleine, Resnais and Peters sat round a table, planning the kidnapping of Lucy Field.

For five years Colonel Ali Ardalan had been the head of the Iranian Secret Police – Sazemane Attalat Va Amniyate Keshvar – the dreaded SAVAK. He had begun his military career in Army Intelligence, where he distinguished himself against the Kurdish tribesmen who were fighting a guerilla war for self-rule on the Iraqi border. His father had been in the same regiment as the Shah's father, the army sergeant who had deposed the last Qajar emperor and taken possession of the Peacock Throne. Ardalan belonged to one of what were known as the thousand families, the old Persian aristocracy; it had taken a generation before they felt comfortable serving the upstart Reza family. Ali had no such reservations. He admired the Shah for his courage, his fervent nationalism and his ability to weld the people together in personal loyalty to him.

The Colonel had spent some months in England on a course at the Military Academy; he had liked Sandhurst and admired the English. He was an open-minded man, keenly intelligent and ready to learn anything which he felt could be used to Iran's advantage. He was a soldier and a patriot. He believed that the safety of his country and the personal safety of the Shah were above all other considerations. Since his appointment as head of SAVAK he had perfected a system of espionage and counter-terrorism which was the admiration of similar services throughout the East. His enemies described him as a monster of cruelty and repression; his torture chambers were places from which few suspects came out alive.

He knew everything about everyone in public life; his shadow fell upon Ministers and civil servants, on the armed forces, the diplomatic service, the universities. The intellectuals and the moderates shuddered when the name Ardalan was mentioned. He was a close friend and adviser of the Shah and the only man who could have access to him at any time, night or day. He was married, with a second wife and three young children. They lived together in a large, well-guarded house on the outskirts of Tehran. In private life, he was a quiet man, modest in his personal needs. He had gathered together all the available information about Logan Field; this was a routine precaution before anyone was allowed an audience with the Shah and Ardalan insisted upon it, regardless of who was involved. He knew that Field's wife had gone back to England, because all European-owned houses were under supervision and James's houseboy was in police pay. He also knew that Field was having trouble with the Minister Khorvan. The Colonel did not trust either of them. The Englishman was trying to exploit Iran's huge natural oil resources and the Minister was indulging his left-wing tendencies by impeding the negotiations. Ardalan knew all about the demand for a refinery because the Shah himself had told him. It would be interesting to see if Imperial Oil could be bullied into agreement. The Shah had no objection to Khorvan imposing the harshest terms on any European company. Ardalan had none either, so long as the motive behind the manoeuvre was purely in the interests of Iran and the Shah. He was not sure that this applied to Khorvan, but he knew the Shah too well to say so at that moment. If the Minister succeeded, the Shah would be pleased. If he failed and the negotiations broke down, then it would be proper to question his motives. Ardalan didn't trust the Minister and he didn't like him personally. He was having him very closely watched, but he hadn't told the Shah this either.

The Colonel was on his way to his office at Niavaran. He drove in a bullet-proof army car and they never used the same route in succession or left at the same time. On that morning he instructed his driver to take a way through one of the poorer districts of the city by way of diversion. From there they could proceed to his office. Since no one knew which way he was travelling, the Colonel felt himself safe from ambush. It was not a prospect that worried him, although he took precautions. He was a brave man and unafraid of violent death. They were driving through a narrow back street when their way was

47

barred by a small crowd. A police motorcycle was parked against the wall. The driver jammed his hand on the horn and the people began to scatter. The Colonel was in civilian clothes; he wore English suits and white shirts with a discreet tie. He leaned forward and told the driver to slow down. He always said that nine-tenths of an intelligence officer's equipment was a talent for doing jigsaw puzzles, and the tenth part was instinct. Instinct made him curious, and his curiosity made him stop the car to find out what had happened.

His driver called through the window to the crowd. A moment later the cycle policeman came up. The Colonel opened his window and asked what had happened.

'A man has been murdered,' the policeman reported. 'His body is inside the house.'

'Ah,' said the Colonel. Tehran had a low murder rate; crimes of violence were rare, though the incidence of burglary was high. The Colonel opened the door and got out. He said one word to the policeman, 'SAVAK', and the man cringed.

'Show me the body,' he said. The inside of the house was dark. He heard the sound of a high, female wail of grief. In a little room at the back the policeman stopped and opened the door. Ardalan recognized the slaughterhouse smell. There was blood all over the floor and he stopped carefully to avoid staining his shoes. The dead man lay on his back; he wore only a greasy shirt, and a woman crouched in the corner. Ardalan told her to be quiet and the crying stopped. He bent over the body. Above the terribly gashed throat, the face was unmarked, the eyes open. The Colonel looked for a full minute at the dead man.

'His name?'

'Habib Ebrahimi, sir.'

'What have you discovered?'

The policeman stammered, 'Nothing yet, sir. The woman is his wife. She couldn't tell us much. Nobody knows who did this.'

'The woman is afraid,' Ardalan said. 'This is not the place to ask her questions. Send for a car. They are to bring her to Niavaran. I will talk to her. For the moment touch nothing. My men will come down and search the house. Are there any signs of robbery?'

'No, sir. He and his wife lived in this room. There are

48

families in the other rooms. Nobody heard anything and nothing has been taken.'

'Send the woman to me,' the Colonel said. 'And tell her she has nothing to fear. I am sorry for what has happened and I want to give her money. Tell her that.'

He went out into the street and the crowd gave way for him. The policeman opened the door of the car for him and saluted. The Colonel sat back, told the driver to go on, and sniffed at his pocket handkerchief. He used a strong cologne and it drove the smell of sticky blood away as he breathed into the handkerchief.

The one-tenth instinct had not failed him. Nor would the other nine. A man called Habib Ebrahimi had been butchered in a mean little room in a poor quarter. The name was of no significance to the Colonel, but he had instantly recognized the face. It was the waiter who had served him at the oil company's reception for Minister Khorvan. The same waiter he had seen hovering round the Minister and Logan Field. It was not coincidence. He knew that. It was a piece in a jigsaw puzzle. Half an hour later he was sitting in his office, talking very patiently and gently to Habib Ebrahimi's wife.


Peters had hired a Ford Cortina from a car-hire firm at Victoria. He drove to Eaton Square a little after nine that morning. Madeleine looked rested and she was smartly dressed in a dark blue suit, with a coloured scarf over her hair.

'They ought to come out soon,' she said. 'I don't think it's very warm; I wouldn't take a child walking in this wind.'

Peters looked at her and for a moment he smiled.

'You're not English,' he said. 'They believe in fresh air.'

Time passed; a delivery van from an exclusive grocers came to the door and a box of goods was taken down the area steps to the entrance below.

Peters saw it was ten past ten on his watch. A traffic warden was patrolling the street, checking the cars. Peters's hand grabbed Madeleine's knee. His fingers bit into her leg so hard that it gave no pleasure.

'Look!'

The door of Logan Field's house was open. A man wearing a white jacket backed down the short steps, carrying the top half of a pram. Holding the handle and taking the minimum of weight was a middle-aged woman in a brown coat and hat. The pram was gently set down on the pavement; the man-servant went back into the house. The woman went round and straightened the covers. A small girl, wearing a pink beret and coat sat upright, a cover over her legs. She was holding a white teddy bear.

'That's her,' Peters said quietly.

Madeleine didn't answer. She saw the woman, the pram and the little girl.

He went round and got into the driver's seat. The pram was moving down the street towards them in the direction of Belgrave Place. Peters started the engine and sped past them. At the top of the road he turned and followed them, driving carefully now.

'We'll follow,' he said. 'I guess they'll go to the Park. Then you can start the operation.'

The nanny moved at a brisk pace. It relieved her feelings to walk quickly, steering the pram. She crossed the busy road to the rear of Buckingham Palace and headed for St James's Park. It was her favourite walk. That morning the crowds of tourists irritated her, gawping at the scarlet uniformed sentries, staring mindlessly at the Palace windows, although the Royal Standard was not flying and any fool knew the Queen was not in resi-dence. The child was very sensitive to her moods; she knew when to ask questions and when it would provoke an angry command to keep quiet. There was a little plastic bag full of crumbs in the bottom of the pram. For twenty years the nanny had been bringing other women's children to the lake in St James's Park and showing them how to feed the birds.

She found a vacant seat and sat down; her back ached and she had tired herself walking so fast.

'Nanny,' Lucy Field ventured. 'Get out?'

'In a minute,' she said. 'Just wait a minute, like a good girl.'

She couldn't believe what had happened. She had gone down to see Mrs Field, prepared to make her position plain and expecting unconditional surrender. She really couldn't have her mothers walking in and waking up the children at any hour, and she really felt Mrs Field should have shown more con-sideration. She hadn't been given the opportunity to say any-thing. She was given a month's money and told very politely that Mrs Field was taking the child away and she could leave in the morning. She was thinking back on the scene, wishing she had come out of it better. The little girl sat mutely in the pram, waiting to be lifted out.

'What a beautiful child,' a woman's voice said.

The nanny looked round, startled. She hadn't even noticed that someone had sat down beside her. Normally she enjoyed talking to people and it pleased her when Lucy was admired. The woman was young and spoke with a foreign accent. She was well-dressed and she smiled at her.

'So pretty,' she repeated. 'Do you look after her?'

'Yes,' the nanny said. Resentment was boiling up in her. To be turned out of the house... In twenty years no other mother had ever dared.

'She's a credit to you. How old is she?'

'Three,' she said. 'I've been with her since she was born. Here, come to Nanny dear; you can have a little run but don't go near the water.' She lifted the child out and brushed her pink coat down. 'Play just here, dear, where I can see you. Show Teddy to the lady.'

Madeleine Labouchère held the toy for a moment. She smiled encouragingly at the little girl, who smiled back. She was rather a small child for her age, pale and slight by comparison with the fat, spoiled children of the Lebanese rich. She seemed to be subdued.

'She's a dear little thing,' the nanny said and her eyes pricked. She was going to miss Lucy. And the splendid house, the easy life with servants to wait on her. She was going to miss it all. She brought a handkerchief out and blew her nose.

'I don't know how she'll manage without me. I've been the only mother she's ever known, poor little mite.'

'Oh dear,' Madeleine said. 'Are you leaving then?'

'Yes.' The nanny sniffed and blew her nose again. She wanted sympathy. 'I've been given notice. Just like that! The mother's decided to look after her herself! Huh – I wonder how long that'll last.'

The hands clasped round Madeleine's bag were gripping tight.

'How awful for you,' she said. 'When are you leaving?'

'Tomorrow,' the nanny said. 'I told her this morning, I'm

not going to be treated like that after all I've done for that child. I'm going first thing tomorrow, I said. She didn't like that, I can tell you!' It was so easy to turn the truth around; she was almost convincing herself that this was how it had happened. 'She wouldn't have dared do it if Mr Field had been there! He trusted me completely.'

For one panic-ridden moment Madeleine had thought that Logan had suddenly come back too. She opened her hands and there were wet sweat marks on the leather purse.

'I expect she'll get another nanny,' she said. 'But it's very hard on you.'

'Oh dear no.' The sarcasm was heavy. 'Says she's taking Lucy to Ireland! That dreadful place, I ask you – going to look after her all by herself. I hate the Irish. We ought to let them get on and murder each other, that's what I say. *She*'s Irish. Now Lucy, don't wipe your hands on your coat!'

Madeleine got up. The little girl stared at her; she had large blue eyes, with a hesitant look. Ireland. Unconsciously she used Peters's rare expletive. Jesus Christ on wheels. Ireland. The mother was in London, the nurse was leaving. The child was going to Ireland. The whole operation was falling apart.

'I must be going,' she said. There was a gun in her handbag. It had come in Resnais's brandy flask, wrapped in plastic. For one wild moment she contemplated shooting the woman and grabbing the child. Now a couple were walking towards them; they had rounded a bend in the path without Madeleine seeing them. She hadn't a chance. She waved to the little girl and walked away. When she was some distance up the path she began to run to where Peters was waiting with the car.


'We found this,' Colonel Ardalan's assistant said.

It was a strip of paper about two inches long, torn from a larger piece. It seemed to be the top of a newspaper. There were six figures written on it in pencil. They were faint and the paper was very crumpled.

'It was in the trouser pocket,' the policeman said. Ardalan smoothed the paper down with two fingers and looked at it.

'And that was all?'

'Yes, Colonel. There were a few household things, another suit of clothes and the wife's possessions. Nothing much. They were just ordinary poor people. He was employed by the Hilton hotel as a waiter and I asked the personnel manager about him. He said as far as he knew the man did his work and that was all.'

Ardalan was smoking a thin cigar; he looked at the end of it and then rubbed it out in the onyx ash tray.

'His wife said he was a clever man,' the Colonel remarked. It had taken a long time to get the woman to talk beyond a frightened mumble. When she offered this information about her husband, Ardalan had been impressed. Clever in what way? He knew about politics, she said. He had tried to talk to her but he said she was too stupid and couldn't understand. She had dropped her head in shame. These things were not for women, but he had been very angry. He went to the cafés and talked with other clever men. Three nights before he died, he had come and woken her up. He was excited and she thought he was going to beat her. But he only said bad things about the Minister Khorvan. What kind of things? Ardalan prompted her gently. Her husband had called the Minister a traitor. The Colonel had given her an encouraging smile. She was a pretty girl in her mid-twenties; the hand holding the black chador near her mouth was trembling.

She owed her life to Habib's appropriation of the bed. He made her sleep on the floor and so the murderer hadn't seen her when he crept into the room. She had crouched in the darkness, too terrified to cry out, while her husband struggled and fell out of bed. She hadn't see them cut his throat; she heard a horrible gurgling noise and then the killer slipped away.

Ardalan gave her a sum of money and sent her back in a police car to her family who lived on the other side of Tehran. He looked at the piece of paper and the jumbled figures. Six, all running into each other.

He lifted his telephone, pressed for an outside line and slowly dialled the figures. He heard the number ringing. It went on for some time until he hung up. He copied the figures out on a memo sheet and handed it to his assistant.

'Get someone to find the address for this. I believe Habib Ebrahimi was involved in some kind of subversion. There is to be a full investigation. Start at once.'

Peters left the boarding house that midday. He checked into

a respectable middle-class hotel in Cromwell Road, said he was staying for one night en route for New York, and booked a table in the restaurant for two friends for dinner. He spent the afternoon in his room, thinking. He had listened to Madeleine, not asking a question till she had told him everything. She had mentioned her idea of making the grab on the spur of the moment and he had frowned. 'Thank Christ you didn't do anything like that,' he said. She hadn't wanted to go back to Resnais. She wanted to stay with Peters.

'What was the kid like?'

'Oh – rather a miserable little thing. Typical upper-class child. Listen – if we don't act immediately we'll lose the chance!'

'We're going to act,' he said. 'But not till we've worked out how.'

He had sent her away and gone off alone to his hotel to think of a new plan. Madeleine was right. If they delayed, the child would be gone to Ireland. And there was no provision made for their escape from there. Whereas the organization had fixed the route out of England. All he had to do was use the telephone when they were ready.

At seven o'clock they met in the lounge of the hotel. He shook hands with Resnais and kissed Madeleine on the cheek. He was dressed in a suit and silk roll-necked sweater. He looked a typical American in transit, entertaining two foreign guests. They had a drink each and talked about nothing; three other couples were using the lounge. By twenty-past seven they took their seats in the restaurant. At that hour it was almost empty. Four diners were scattered around at distances from each other. Peters ordered the set menu and a bottle of wine. Resnais leaned across to him.

'What are we going to do? Nothing will be as easy as our original plan.'

'Taking a child is never easy,' Peters said. 'Madeleine mightn't have been able to get away with it.'

'I could,' she interrupted. 'That old woman didn't want to be bothered with the child. She would have let me take her.'

It had been such a simple plan; the less complicated the manoeuvre the better. Peters had always used the shortest route to any target.

Madeleine was to make an acquaintance with the Fields'

54

nanny; two or three meetings in the Park. A way of becoming familiar to the child. A request to take the little girl out of sight for a moment, just to walk with her, show her something. Peters and the car would have been waiting. The message would have been planted in the pram. 'Lucy Field is safe. If you want to get her back unharmed *do not go to the police*. Go home. We will contact you.' It was so simple it was disarming. There would be no struggle with a frightened little girl being hustled into a car by strangers. She would know Madeleine and go with her freely. And by the time the frantic nurse returned to Eaton Square, a further message would be telephoned, repeating the warning not to go to the police but to contact her employer Logan Field and do exactly what he said. It was unthinkable that a responsible employee, faced with a threat to the child's life, would have done otherwise than she was told by the kidnappers.

'*Merde*,' Resnais said, repeating it angrily. '*Merde de merde!* Everything has to be changed. What are we going to do? Cancel it?'

Peters looked at him. He waited while the waiter set the first of three uninteresting courses down before them. A halved grapefruit with a sticky cherry in the centre.

'We're going to take her tomorrow,' he said. 'I'll tell you how.'

## 4

The telephone line between Tehran and London was clearer than usual. When James Kelly got through to Eileen he could hear faintly but distinctly. It was five o'clock his time and he had booked the call at eight that morning. He had spent a long day at the company's office, going through the figures with Logan, the chief mining engineer and the accountant, who had come out from England.

Money bored Kelly, who had not been trained in its business application. He had no flair for complicated calculations and cash flow remained a mystery which he had to pretend to understand. He dealt in people and situations; there was a residue of Foreign Office snobbery in his approach to balance sheets. Logan had a brain like a calculator; he not only understood figures but he enjoyed them. His attempts to manipulate the figures so as to justify the additional investment were fascinating, if obscure, to James.

He didn't share Logan's belief that Khorvan was serious. He was sure that this was a piece of Iranian face saving, an exercise in mischief, a gamble even; anything but a proposal which had to be met or lose Imshan.

Logan had brushed his reassurances aside.

'The bastard is out to get us,' he said that morning. 'I felt it in his office and I haven't changed my view. He thinks the cost of the refinery will smash the deal. It's my guess *he* suggested it. I've got to think of some bloody way round it before we go to the Shah.'

Kelly had felt superfluous at the meeting which went on all that morning and into the late afternoon. He had managed to excuse himself, without Logan really noticing, so he could get

56

home in time for the call to London. Hearing Eileen's voice made him happy.

'How are you? How was the flight?'

Banal questions which had to be asked, part of the ritual of communicating through the telephone, when what he really wanted was to say how much he missed her. And how much in love he was. He could imagine her while they talked. He had a poor visual memory, but Eileen's face was perfectly clear in his mind.

'I think I'll go over and stay with my father. He hasn't seen Lucy for ages. Biddy can come with us.'

'You go over to Meath,' he said. 'Get the ball rolling first with the solicitors and then go home. It'll do you both good. You're sure you don't need me to come back?'

'No,' her voice was grateful. 'No James. It's sweet of you, but I can manage perfectly well. I've made up my mind and it's not as bad as I thought.'

James hesitated. 'Can I say something?'

'Of course. Anything.'

'I love you,' he said. 'I'm not trying to rush you, but I just want you to know. Goodbye, darling, and God bless you. Will you ring me when you get to Meath?'

'I will.' He could hear that her voice was unsteady. 'I promise I'll call as soon as I can.'

But in spite of talking to James, and having her father's instant support, Eileen couldn't sleep that night. There were moments when old habits asserted themselves and she argued that what she was doing was unnecessary. There was no real need to uproot Lucy from her home; she didn't have to wage war on Logan. She had been his wife for seven years. There must be understanding and flexibility left after all they had been to each other. He wasn't a cruel or vindictive man. Just because he had fallen in love with someone else it wasn't a reason for believing him incapable of decent feelings.

And then her instincts shouted down the logic. When it came to his child, Logan had excluded her ruthlessly. He had shown no sensitivity; he regarded his daughter as his property. His obsessive love for her had condemned the little girl to a stulti-fying regime and denied her a full relationship with her parents. He would never let Lucy go and no arguments or appeals would persuade him. Much of his protective love for Eileen had been diverted to the baby; she realized that too. There was no virtue in being weak or sentimental. Logan was incapable of being either.

She gave up the attempt to sleep, switched on her light and read for most of the night. At eight the next morning she was woken by Bridget with coffee and the newspapers. She felt worse after the few hours of uneasy rest, but at least her mind was made up.

'I have some business to do today,' she told the maid. 'Then I'm going back home with Lucy for a few weeks. I'd like you to come with me.'

'That'd be grand, Madam.' Bridget looked delighted. She had left under a cloud of family disapproval. She didn't mind going back as Mrs Field's personal maid. 'I'd love to go home. When will we be going?'

'Tomorrow,' Eileen said. 'I'll get our tickets through Mr Field's office. They can send them over.'

At the bedroom door Bridget hesitated. She looked at Eileen sitting up in the over-large bed. There wasn't a trace of envy in the girl's nature where Eileen was concerned. She didn't notice the handmade nightdress, the beautifully appointed room with all its overtones of luxury, the tray she had brought up from three floors down. All she saw was how pale and unhappy poor Mrs Field looked, with great dark rings under her eyes as if she hadn't been to sleep at all.

'There's nothing wrong, is there, Mam?' she lapsed into the familiar Irish.

'I'll tell you about it when we get to Meath,' Eileen answered. She managed to smile at her. 'Don't worry, Biddy. I'll be all right.'

The nanny left at midday. Peters and Madeleine were stationed in the hired car at a place in the road where they could see the front door of the house. They saw the taxi come up and the woman go down the steps with a manservant carrying two large suitcases. Lucy Field had not come out for a walk that morning, nor had anybody else left the house. Peters lit a cigarette while he waited for the taxi cab to move off.

'In a way it's worked out better,' he said. 'We had to gamble on the nurse not going to the police. Sure as hell the mother won't. She'll have Logan Field back here on the next flight.'

'The risks are greater,' Madeleine Labouchère said. 'That house is full of people.'

'You're not nervous, are you?' he looked at her briefly.

She shrugged. 'A little. If anyone interferes we're going to have to shoot them. So long as you realize that.'

'As a last resort,' he said. 'Resnais will do his part and we'll walk out without any trouble. Don't go anticipating it. This isn't a commando raid.'

'I wish it were,' she said. 'I'd feel a lot easier.'

Peters looked at his watch. It was ten minutes past twelve.

'Okay,' he said. 'We've got three hours to get to the field. Resnais has just walked round the corner. Let's go.'

It seemed as if the butler had been waiting by the front door for them to ring. Madeleine had scarcely stepped back from pressing the bell when the door opened. Mario saw a well-dressed woman and a tall American.

'Yes?'

'Is Mrs Field in?' Madeleine smiled and stepped forward. She had authority with servants, having been brought up with them. Mario gave way and they walked into the hall.

'Yes Madam. Who shall I say?'

'Mr and Mrs Lyons, from San Francisco.'

'If you'll wait in the drawing room, please, I'll call Mrs Field. I think she's upstairs in the nursery.'

'Oh, then we'll go on up.' Madeleine hooked her arm through Peters's. 'I haven't seen Lucy for so long – I'm sure she's grown.' She gave a dazzling smile at the butler and started up the stairs. He heard her laugh and say to her husband, 'My dear – what a lot of stairs! No wonder Eileen keeps her figure.' He had a feeling that they should have been shown into the drawing room, but he didn't see how he could have prevented the lady when she was so determined and seemed to know Mrs Field very well. An English butler wouldn't have hesitated; Mario didn't have the tradition of that intimidating breed behind him. He decided that there was nothing to worry about and went downstairs to the basement. He wanted to gloat over the hated nurse's departure with his wife and Bridget Hagan.

Eileen had Lucy by the hand. The child missed her morning walk. She pulled gently at her mother.

'Park,' she said.

'I'll take you this afternoon, darling,' Eileen said. 'You're coming down to lunch with me – that'll be fun, won't it? We'll have a lovely lunch together in the dining room...'

She opened the door of the day nursery and moved onto the landing. The little white gate stood open. She heard the voices first. They were low and they came from the floor below.

'It's at the top of the house. All the better.'

That was a man speaking, a man with an American accent, talking very low.

'We'll just take the kid and walk out.'

Eileen stood very still. She felt a pull on her hand and looked at Lucy; the child was trying to drag her forward out of the doorway. *Take the kid*. Panic rushed up in her, blind and horrified. *Take Lucy*. Logan had sent someone to take the child. There was no time for reason, panic won. She swung Lucy into her arms and ran back into the day nursery.

'Mummy...' the little girl began to wail, sensing terror in her mother.

Eileen rushed through to the night nursery; her instinct was to put Lucy somewhere safe, to interpose solid wood between her and whoever Logan had sent to take her. She put her daughter on her bed.

'Lucy – darling, stay there. Stay quietly there, like a good girl. I'll be back in a minute. Here, take Teddy...'

There was a key in the outside of the door; she had never noticed it before. She slammed the door and locked it. When she turned round, Peters and Madeleine Labouchère were in the room. She didn't say anything or even cry out. She stood flattened against the door behind which she had locked the child. Peters brought his right hand out of his coat and pointed Resnais's smuggled pistol at her. He spoke very quietly. Madeleine had shut the door behind them. They were enclosed in the pink and white room with all the fluffy toys standing at attention.

'Mrs Field? Don't make any noise please. Just stay quite still and listen. Then you won't get hurt.'

'What do you want?' Her voice came out in a whisper. 'Who are you?'

'Get away from that door,' Madeleine ordered. Her tone was

sharper than Peters's. She saw the frightened woman guarding her child as an enemy, nothing more.

'No,' Eileen said. And suddenly she heard herself loud and clear, 'No. You're not going to get my child!'

Peters took a step towards her. She saw the muzzle of the gun coming closer and she felt nothing but panic for Lucy. The nursery windows were wide open, protected by iron bars painted white so that the little girl couldn't climb up and fall out. The key bit into her palm.

She moved so quickly that neither of them realized what she had done. The key flew through the window and vanished into the street below.

Peters grabbed her by the shoulder and pulled her away from the door. She gave a wild cry and started to struggle. He jammed the gun into her neck. Madeleine wrenched at the nursery door. She swore furiously in Arabic.

'It's locked! The key...' She swung on Eileen. 'Where's the key?'

'She threw it out of the window,' Peters said. He had his hand over Eileen's mouth.

'Shoot her,' Madeleine said. 'Shoot her and we can break that door down!'

'No,' Peters said. 'We can't get the child. If we kill her the whole operation falls to pieces. It's a full murder and kidnapping. We've got to change the plan.' He spoke in Arabic. He handed the gun to Madeleine. 'Do exactly what I tell you. We're going to take the wife instead.'

He spoke to Eileen; he held her tightly round the waist, pinning her arms to her sides.

'Listen, Mrs Field. It's quite likely your child is on the other side of that door, listening to us trying to get in. I'm going to take my hand away. If you cry out or make any noise, my friend will start shooting through that door. Do you understand?'

He waited a moment and then released her. She stared at him and then at the girl, aiming her gun at the nursery door. There was a sound from the other side of it.

'Mummy...Mummy!'

Eileen gave a cry that was a moan of fear and anguish that only they could hear.

'Don't...don't, for God's sake.'

'We don't want to hurt her,' Peters said. 'Or you, unless we have to. You've got to come with me, Mrs Field. You've got to do exactly as I tell you or my friend will go on firing through the door until she kills your child. Or seriously wounds her.'

Eileen swayed for a second. Peters caught her by the elbow. 'We're going to walk out of here; we're going downstairs and into the street. My friend will wait here for exactly three minutes and, if there is no disturbance, she'll follow us. No harm will come to your child. Just so long as you cooperate.'

'Logan didn't send you,' Eileen whispered. 'He wouldn't do this...who are you?'

'You're in the hands of the Palestine Liberation Army,' Peters said. 'We're taking you as a hostage.' He spoke to Madeleine. 'I'll leave the door open. Listen carefully. If you hear anything unusual, open fire. Give us three minutes by your watch. Then if everything has gone quietly, come down.' 'Now,' he said to Eileen, 'are you ready?'

She pulled away from him. The moment of panic had passed. She felt numb and cold with terror. All she could see was the woman, pointing the gun at the door.

'Lucy,' she heard the woman call out softly, 'come here, come to the door...'

Eileen grabbed wildly at Peters. 'No ... no, no ... I'll come with you. I'll do anything.'

He guided her out to the landing, gave her a push when she hesitated and turned back.

'You won't,' she begged. 'Please, you won't do it...'

The girl gave her a look of contempt.

'You'd better cooperate. I have another clip of cartridges in my pocket. I'll use them all.'

She went downstairs ahead of Peters. He had no gun, no means of forcing her to go with him. Upstairs, her child was a foot away from mutilation or death. On the first landing, she met Bridget coming up. The girl stood back for her, and Eileen passed without a word.

Mario was in the basement, engaged at the area door by Resnais, who was asking for directions to an address in Eaton Place. He had kept the Portuguese talking for several minutes. There was nobody in the hall. Peters moved beside her and opened the front door. Eileen stopped.

'Please,' she whispered, 'please call her down. I beg of you. . .'

He opened the door and they stepped out into the sunshine. Resnais was coming up the area steps. Peters took Eileen by the arm.

'Just keep calm,' he said. 'Nothing will happen to the child so long as you do what I tell you. Over here.'

There was a Ford Cortina parked on the opposite side of the road. Peters opened the back door and told her to get in. Resnais came round the other side and got into the driver's seat. Peters sat watching the front door of the Fields's house. It opened and Madeleine Labouchère came out. She came over to the car. Peters spoke to her in Arabic.

'Everything all right?'

'Yes,' she said. 'The child was crying. I shut the nursery door. Nobody will hear from downstairs.'

'Good,' he said. 'Telephone down and tell them to meet us at Orval instead. Then go straight to Heathrow and get on a plane. Get rid of that gun. We'll meet at the rendezvous.'

Resnais put the car into gear and it moved off.

'My friend is going to wait around,' Peters said to Eileen. 'I've told her to go back into the house and kill your child unless you do what we tell you. She won't hesitate.' He saw her lean forward for a moment, covering her face with her hands. 'Sit still,' he said. He was paying little attention to her. There was nothing she could do. And with Madeleine left behind, nothing she would attempt. The child was locked in her nursery. Her mother, watched by a maid, had gone out. Something had to be done, but he wasn't sure what. The servants had to be reassured that the locked door was an accident and the only person who could do that was Eileen Field. They shouldn't delay for long. It was twelve-twenty-five. Resnais was driving in the direction of Baker Street. Peters saw a telephone box. He told the Frenchman to stop.

'Mrs Field. . .' He looked dispassionately into the haggard face. 'Nobody must know you've been taken. I want to impress this on you. The safety of your child depends on it. And your own safety.'

'I don't care what happens to me,' Eileen said. 'I don't care what you do to me. Just leave Lucy alone. . .' Tears were spilling down her face.

'You'll have to telephone home,' Peters said. 'Make up some story that'll satisfy your staff. Say the door was locked accidentally and put someone in charge of your child; tell them you're going to be away for a while. I shall be right beside you, so don't try anything funny. Wipe your face.' He gave her his handkerchief. 'Okay. Now get out.'

They were side by side in the telephone box. Eileen dialled her own number and he put in a coin.

'Watch it,' he said. 'Don't try anything.'

'I won't,' she turned to him, holding the receiver, 'All I want is for Lucy to be safe.'

She asked to speak to Bridget. Terror cleared her mind. She thought quickly and with desperate cunning. Ireland. The safety of Meath House.

'Biddy? Listen, I've got to be away for a few days. Yes, it's that business I told you about. Don't worry, I'll get it sorted out. Lucy's locked herself into the nursery. No, no – don't panic, it's quite all right. She slammed the door and the lock jammed. Just get a locksmith right away. Of course, I'm sure. Everything's fine. But I want you to take her to Meath. The tickets are being sent over this afternoon. Let my father know you're coming and I'll be following in a day or so when I've cleared all this up. Yes, Biddy dear, it is about Mr Field. I'll explain it all when I come over. Tell Mario I've gone out of London for a few days and I'll be going direct to Ireland. There's nothing to worry about and I'll see you both soon. Look after Lucy for me.'

She hung up and began to sob helplessly. Peters gave her a moment to recover.

'Okay,' he said. 'You did okay. Come on.'

People were passing in the street outside. He put his arm around the weeping woman and guided her back to the car. Resnais watched them. He noticed that their prisoner had beautiful legs. He hadn't had time to examine her properly.

'Right,' Peters said to him. 'Drive for the field. And go steady. We don't want to be stopped for speeding.'

He lit himself a cigarette. Eileen was leaning back beside him, with her eyes closed. Looking at her, he remembered the woman who had been on the aeroplane from Tehran. From the

moment he walked into the nursery that morning, he had a
sense that he had seen her before. And not just in the photographs he had studied for the kidnapping of her child.

Janet Armstrong was booked into a suite at the Hilton.
Logan had met her at the airport and driven her to the hotel.
He thought she looked sleek and elegant, wearing a white suit,
with her silvered hair glinting in the late sun. He had ordered
flowers for her and she noticed them with pleasure.

'This looks like a florist's – Logan, you are wonderful.'

She came and kissed him on the mouth. He held her
greedily. Even a touch and desire exploded between them.
She pulled back from him and laughed.

'Who's been suffering from night starvation? Give me a
moment, darling. I'd like a drink first.'

There was no fuss about her; she was as direct as a man. It
was an attitude that profoundly excited him.

'I've ordered champagne,' he said. 'After all we've got something to celebrate.'

She sat down while he opened the bottle; she slipped off her
shoes and pulled her legs under her. Logan gave her a glass and
she raised it to him.

'To you,' she said.

'To us.' He sat beside her, one hand resting on her ankle. She
knew that he wasn't going to waste too much time on talking.
He wanted sex and this was not the moment to say she was
tired. She realized with surprise that this was the first time she
hadn't been completely natural.

She had refused him on other occasions if she didn't feel like
going to bed, but not now. He was determined to force the issue
for both of them. She understood him so well that she sensed
the self-defiance in his attitude. He wanted her to celebrate
with him, to show that she was as untouched by conscience as
he insisted that he was himself.

She wriggled her foot and he gripped her ankle and began to
massage it.

'You look tired,' Janet said. He did. There were deep lines
either side of his mouth and his eyes were tired. 'What's happened with Khorvan?'

Logan put his glass down.

'I don't want to talk business now. I want to talk about you and me. I'm going to get a divorce.'

She sipped her champagne.

'Are you sure, Logan? I love you, but I don't want you to do anything you'll regret.'

'It couldn't go on,' he said. 'Eileen faced me with it and I told her. Things have been going from bad to bloody worse for months. I'd had enough of it anyway.' He poured into his glass and it frothed over.

'That's lucky,' Janet said.

'I want you to marry me,' Logan said.

Janet looked at him calmly. It was the most important moment of her life and she felt the frozen calm of the great gambler as the ball drops into the numbered slot that means a fortune.

'Only if you're sure you love me,' she said.

'For Christ's sake,' he said angrily, 'you know bloody well I do. Come here.'

An hour later, Logan woke. She was already up, dressed in a long jersey dress that showed her figure. She stood by the bedside and smiled down at him.

'You're a marvellous man, Logan. The most marvellous lover a woman ever had. I'll marry you, darling. Just don't try and get away from me!'

'It's after seven,' he said. 'I've asked Kelly to have dinner with us and bring Paterson. I told them to come here.'

'That'll be a gay little gathering,' Janet said. She sat on the edge of the bed and held his hand. 'Kelly can't stand me; he doesn't like women with minds of their own, and Paterson bores me. He never stops talking finance.' She brought his hand up and kissed it. 'They'll sit there looking stuffy and disapproving. I thought we'd spend the evening alone.'

'They're good men,' Logan said. He wasn't offended. If Eileen had criticized any member of the company, he would have been irritated. As far as Janet was concerned, they were all part of the family.

'Kelly's done a fantastic job out here. And I need Paterson more than anyone else in Imp at this moment. Go and run a bath for me, darling. Then I'll tell you all about it.'

He got out of bed and stood naked, stretching. Janet watched him openly admiring. He had a good body, well-muscled and without surplus fat. He looked a middle-aged man at the peak of fitness and virility. Only his face showed that something fundamental had happened to him since he had left England. He looked every year of his age. Janet saw this too. She came and embraced him from behind, leaning against his shoulder. It was a moment of rare tenderness between them.

'I'm going to have a lot of children with you,' she said. 'I'll go and run your bath now.'

Apsley Field was normally used by racegoers. It was a small, privately owned airstrip within five miles of Newmarket and during the morning a dozen light aircraft had taken off with passengers for York, where a major race meeting was being held that afternoon. The pilot of the chartered Piper Aztec was not one of the charter firm's own men; he had motored down at nine o'clock, checked in with the office and satisfied them of his flying credentials. He was waiting in the small outer office, drinking coffee and chatting to the girl typist who sat outside. The director of the charter firm hadn't been pleased to see him. He objected to an outside pilot being brought in, but the fee for hiring the plane had been increased by a third on condition that it was flown by a pilot known to the passengers. Times were getting tighter in the charter business; the number of owners and trainers rich enough to fly themselves round England to the races was decreasing.

The pilot explained that he always flew his clients. The wife was shit-scared of flying, as he put it, and she wouldn't go up with anyone else. They were rich enough to pay him whatever he asked and he flew them and their friends to racecourses all over England and France.

'Why don't they have their own bloody plane, then?' the director said.

The young man shrugged.

'They have but it's in the middle of its bloody C of A. I'll just check the ship and see if she's ready, then I'll hang around. They didn't give me an exact time. Just told me to be ready. Typical.'

He settled into the outer office with the typist and passed the time smoking and making a series of easy-going passes at her.

He seemed a nice, relaxed type; couldn't care less about anything. She was beginning to fancy him, when one of the ground staff came up and called him.

'Your load has turned up.'

'Right. 'Bye sweetheart. Next time I'm round this way I'll buy you dinner. Okay?'

'You've missed most of this afternoon's meeting,' she said.

'They're staying overnight. Their nag's running there tomorrow. 'Bye!'

'Take these,' Peters said to Eileen. 'Just walk alongside me and don't do anything to attract attention. We're going on a trip. So watch yourself.'

He hung a pair of binoculars on her shoulder. She stared at him, holding on to the leather straps with hands that shook.

'Where are you taking me – what are these for?'

'Never mind.' He had hold of her arm and he was walking her briskly across the airfield. A small Cessna took off a hundred yards away from them and buzzed into the sky like a red bee. He saw their pilot coming towards them; the man waved.

'Mr Harris? She's over here, sir. We're all ready.'

Resnais was behind them; she heard him whistling. During the journey from London she hadn't heard him speak once. Peters knew the pilot. He was a freelance and the organization had used him several times to ferry people and guns. He didn't belong to any political party. His only concern was money, and provided he was paid enough he would undertake anything. The original passenger schedule was for two men, one woman and a child. Now the child was missing. He looked briefly at the woman. She looked grey with fear. The reason didn't concern him. He spoke quietly to Peters.

'You're one less.'

Peters didn't answer and the pilot shrugged. He led them to the small six-seater plane; an airport mechanic was waiting for them. Eileen saw him watching her. For a second she was tempted to tear herself free of Peters and scream for help. As if he read her thoughts, he hurried her to the steps. The mechanic had moved away. The few seconds' hesitation had cost her the chance. She climbed up ahead of Peters and went inside the plane. He pushed her into a seat and sat beside her.

'Fasten your belt,' he said. She didn't move; it was too late now. Too late to save herself. He leaned over and pulled the webbing safety belt round her, buckling it tightly. The Frenchman sat behind them. Eileen held tightly to the seat arms as the engines revved and caught and the plane began to taxi to the runway. As they took off she hid her face in her hands. Peters watched her, anticipating hysteria or collapse. He had seen that look exchanged with the mechanic and guessed that she was a hair-line away from calling for help. But shock had slowed her reactions, paralysing the will to resist. It wouldn't have lasted at their original destination, the airport at Nice, with Customs and Immigration and people surrounding them. She would never have gone through without raising the alarm, whatever he threatened. His organization had been geared to carrying a child of three who had been added to Madeleine's false passport. Now the details had been changed. Ostensibly the plane was bound for York, where it would stay overnight and return the following day. There was no radio at Apsley Field, so that once airborne the plane's movements would be unnoticed. Twenty-five miles behind Nice, in a small valley at Orval, there was a field where the British had landed agents and supplies in the latter stages of the war. Peters had simply changed instructions to the pilot and Madeleine would have phoned through to alter the arrangements for meeting them on landing. The car which should have taken him, Madeleine, Resnais and Lucy Field away from Nice airport would now be diverted to the secret landing field and a supply of petrol brought to fuel the plane for its return journey. He turned to Resnais.

'Come and sit here for a minute.'

They exchanged places. Resnais eased himself into the seat beside Eileen. He buckled the safety belt and turning round deliberately looked at her. She seemed sick and frightened, but she was attractive in spite of it. It amused him to frighten her still more. Eileen saw the appraising look and the slight smile on his mouth. She edged against the wall of the plane to avoid touching him.

'I am Resnais,' he said. 'I shall be looking after you.'

Peters came back; for a moment Eileen thought he would leave the Frenchman where he was and take the seat behind them. She didn't realize it, but she gave the American a look of agonized appeal.

'Thanks,' he said. He stood over Resnais and the Frenchman got up and resumed his former seat. Peters didn't look at Eileen Field. Resnais had been upsetting her and he was irritated. It wouldn't help to have an hysterical outburst during the flight. He spoke over his shoulder to Resnais.

'Did you bring that flask with you?'

'Yes. It's here.'

'Give it to me.'

He unscrewed the top and passed it to Eileen.

'It's brandy; drink some.'

'I don't want it.' She shook her head and turned away.

'It isn't drugged,' Peters said. 'It'll steady you. Do as you're told. Drink it.'

She sipped and then swallowed. He took the flask and put it to his mouth.

'Where are we going?' she asked him.

'France,' Peters said. 'That's all you're going to know, so don't ask any more questions. And the pilot's working for us, so you needn't try anything there. You can just relax, Mrs Field. Make the best of it. So long as you're sensible, nobody will hurt you.'

He spoke with calmness. The brandy had helped her; she wasn't so sickly white. He didn't know whether she believed him and he didn't care. In a way he admired her quickness in saving the child. It was just unfortunate for her that she had been so brave.

## 5

Colonel Ardalan read through the report a second time. It was brief; it informed him that the telephone number found in the murdered Ebrahimi's trouser pocket had been traced to an apartment block on Torshab Road. The apartment had been rented by an American archaeologist called Peters. He had been living there with a woman and had left the previous week, paying his rent up to date. So far as the landlord was concerned the American had been an ideal tenant. The neighbours told the investigator that he had entertained few visitors; most of them seemed to be Iranians, but one woman remembered seeing a car with diplomatic plates. There were no noisy parties, nothing during his tenancy which had aroused suspicion. It was all very neat and tidy. Too neat and tidy. It looked as if this unknown American had gone out of his way to avoid attention. Ardalan blew smoke rings and played with the sheets of typed paper. His only visitors were Iranians. Except for the car with diplomatic plates. He rang down for his assistant and ordered his car to be brought round. Half an hour later they were sitting in the flat of the neighbour who had seen the diplomat's car.

She was a woman in her mid-thirties, already too fat, with four children shouting in the background. Ardalan was patient and polite. He could see that she was frightened and could easily be persuaded to say anything. He asked her when she had seen the car; her answer was vague. Some time in the last two weeks – maybe less. It hadn't stopped by the flats; she was looking out of the window – her flat was on the ground floor – and she had seen it draw up far down on the opposite side of the road and a man get out. She was surprised when he crossed over and came into the flat.

'Naturally,' the Colonel agreed. 'You were curious. How do you know he went to Peters's flat?'

'Because I opened my front door and saw him go upstairs. I heard the American's voice. He said something like, "Hallo, Homsi. Come in."'

'Homsi,' the Colonel repeated. 'Thank you. That's very helpful. Do you remember if this man ever came again – or had been before? Did you recognize him?'

'No,' the woman said. 'I'd know him again if I saw him. He only came that one time. So far as I can tell.' She glanced nervously at Ardalan, who smiled at her. He had a way of reassuring people. He stood up.

'You've done well,' he said. 'Very well. Now you understand one thing. You mustn't speak about this to anyone. You may tell your husband that we have been here but what you told us is to be kept secret. Otherwise you will both be in great trouble. You understand that?'

She nodded, too frightened to speak.

'Great trouble,' Ardalan repeated. 'But if you are silent and do what I tell you, you will be rewarded. Tell your husband so. We are going now, but I shall come again.'

In the car on the way back to his office he turned to his assistant. His name was Sabet and he had graduated from civilian police work to Ardalan's special political branch.

'Homsi,' the Colonel murmured. 'What nationality does that suggest to you?'

'If it was Al Homsi, a man from Homs, he could be Syrian.'

'Syrian. Yes. I think it could be Syrian. They are always involved with terrorism. How stupid to use a car with diplomatic plates.'

'People get careless. He didn't think anyone would notice.'

'The woman said he only came once. I think it was sooner than she remembers. Otherwise she wouldn't have such a clear picture in her mind.'

'She says she can identify him,' Sabet said.

Ardalan smiled.

'We will go through our list of members of the Syrian Embassy. We will see if we can find this Homsi.'

Logan and James Kelly were on their way to the Ministry of

Economics. Their appointment with the Minister Khorvan was at ten-thirty. To Kelly's relief, Janet Armstrong was not with them. The financial director, Ian Paterson, was sitting in front with the driver. The two-tone blue Rolls Royce slid through the traffic down Shah Reza Avenue; it was baking with heat at that hour. The air-conditioning was full on inside the sealed car.

'Half the cost,' Logan said. 'We can start with that.'

Kelly saw Paterson's face in the driver's mirror. It looked grim and disapproving.

'He'll turn it down,' James said. He felt gloomy himself and irritable. He had put in a call to London early that morning and been told that Eileen had gone to Ireland. He didn't know the number and had no way of finding out. He could only hope she would contact him. He was prepared to quarrel with the Minister because he couldn't vent his feelings on Logan. Or that bloody woman, stuck up under all their noses. He really hated Janet Armstrong and he hadn't been trying to hide it. Whenever he saw her asserting herself in the meetings, which Logan insisted she attend, James's temper began to seethe. She was so sure of herself, so competent. He couldn't fault her opinions either and this angered him more. Logan spent every evening out of the house; he hadn't suggested bringing Janet there and James was thankful for that much tact. But he came back in the small hours, and twice he didn't return at all. He looked tired out and taut with nervous tension. By comparison the woman looked triumphant and serene.

'He'll turn it down,' he repeated.

Logan looked at him, frowning.

'So you've just said. All right. He turns it down. This is a bloody poker game. He wants to get the top out of us and we know we can't pay it. Not until we've had more time to work on the figures. So we play for that time.'

'No amount of time will make that a viable proposition.' Paterson, an outspoken Scot, turned round in his front seat. 'It can't be done,' he said. 'And no Board would sanction it. We'd be paying them for the right to bring their oil to the surface, and getting nothing out of it ourselves.'

Logan leaned a little forward.

'You let me worry about the Board. We're not going to lose this field, no matter how tough the deal.'

'I was thinking,' Kelly said, 'that in view of the importance to Western economy, we might consider asking for joint American and English subsidies.'

'We daren't bring in the Americans,' Logan said. 'Or we'd risk losing the deal to Exxon. As for getting anything out of our present government – you must be joking! When have they ever supported business interests? The bloody civil service thinks profit is a dirty word; wouldn't be any better if we had the other lot in power either. I'd go to Japan before I started farting round Whitehall.'

He hunched himself back into the upholstery. His expression was truculent. Kelly decided to let his condemnation of the civil service pass unchallenged. He knew Logan in this kind of mood and nothing was going to get him out of it until he saw Khorvan.

'In fact,' Logan said suddenly, 'that might not be a bad idea. Japan is starving for oil. They are totally dependent on oil and haven't got a barrel – and they've got plenty of money. They might be the people to enter into agreement with us over Imshan.'

Kelly didn't want to admire him but he couldn't help it. Logan had this genius for throwing off ideas, for seeing a solution which was so simple it was ridiculous someone else hadn't thought of it first. But they never did. It needed Logan's unique combination of ruthless logic and dashing inspiration. Ian Paterson had twisted round in his seat again and was looking at his chairman, his mouth pursed up. He could hardly be described as a man given to quick enthusiasms.

'Japan might be a possibility,' he conceded.

Logan ignored him. He was furious with Paterson for emphasizing the difficulties which he already knew. The reference to his dependence upon the Board would rankle for a long time. Democratic processes like voting at board meetings didn't appeal to him. His authority and his methods usually assured him of getting his own way. Kelly had seen him once chairing an Annual General Meeting during the second Arab–Israeli war and been mesmerized by his approach to opposition. The rare smile, the genial wit, and above all the overbearing sense that he knew what was best, had silenced critics from the floor and given him a complete mandate to meet the crisis as he thought fit. He was a different man from the brusque, autocratic chairman of the giant oil company, or the husband of Eileen, not quite a gentleman, at home in Eaton Square. There were so many facets to him, none of them appealing to Kelly, and yet he was fascinated. He could afford to be, without that unpleasant feeling of being patronized. He was going to marry Logan's wife. He didn't know how long it would take; he was just certain that it was going to happen.

The car drew up outside the Ministry and they got out. In his first-floor office, Khorvan told his secretary to keep them waiting. He had a cup of Turkish coffee he wanted to finish; also he was hoping to irritate Logan Field by the discourtesy. He wondered what solution, if any, they had thought of to his impossible proposal. A refinery costing another three hundred million dollars. Khorvan smiled as he drained the tiny silver cup. Actually, he thought it was a better idea than the high standard of township and amenities which were already in the terms. His people didn't need swimming pools and recreational centres. They wouldn't appreciate luxuries which were unrelated to their experience of life. Food, money and a woman. That was the basic requirement of the Iranian worker. Add a corner of land to till, no matter how dry and back-breaking, and you had satisfied the peasant. It would take years of re-education to change the attitudes of his people and Khorvan despised the instant methods practised by the West. All that resulted was waste and corruption. America had poured out billions in foreign aid after the last war and only intensified the envy and contempt of those they imagined they were indoctrinating. Khorvan believed that the slow process of Marxist socialism provided the only solution to the underdeveloped peoples of the world.

He had sent a message to the Soviet Trade Secretary, telling him to delay the departure of the Russian technical team which had been hanging around Tehran for weeks, hoping that negotiations between the Government and Imperial Oil would come to grief. When his demands were not met – and he knew that Logan Field was capable of bluffing till the last moment – he could gently re-introduce the Russians. He hoped profoundly that Logan Field could be induced to offer him a bribe. That would establish the purity of his motives when he exposed the offer to the Shah. He intended to hint that a gift might influence him. He pressed the buzzer for his secretary. The same beautiful girl came in; she was not Khorvan's mistress, although the idea occurred to him when he wasn't too busy. He admired her elegant dress, and saw the expectant gleam in her eyes.

'Send in the gentlemen from Imperial Oil,' he said. He lit a cigarette and stood up, holding his hand out to Logan Field. Chairs were disposed for them and Logan took the one nearest Khorvan's desk. Kelly sat next to him, with Ian Paterson on his left. Khorvan smiled politely at Logan.

'My apologies for keeping you,' he said. 'I was very occupied. Tell me, how is your beautiful wife?'

'I'm afraid she had to go back to England,' Logan said. 'Our daughter wasn't well.'

'Oh?' The Minister looked annoyed. He had accepted an invitation to the party James was giving for him and he had expected to find Eileen there. Her absence was quite irrelevant, but it gave him an opportunity to be offended. James felt his muscles stiffen in anticipation. Logan shouldn't have mentioned it. He hadn't thought to warn him.

He heard Logan say smoothly, 'Of course, she's coming back to be at your party, Minister. She wouldn't miss the chance to entertain you.'

'I look forward to meeting her again.' Khorvan bowed his head politely.

'And now,' Logan said, 'my colleagues and I have been examining your proposals. Ian, have you got the folder? I'd like you to keep this, Minister, and after our meeting this morning perhaps you'd find the time to study the financial breakdown in terms of the investment as a whole. I must say now that we haven't been able to meet your demand for the total cost of the refinery.'

Khorvan leaned back; it was as if a shutter had closed on them.

'Equally,' the strong voice went on, 'we've come up with an idea for cost sharing between the Iranian government and ourselves. Ian, you're the financial expert. I leave this part of it to you.'

Kelly watched Logan; he lit a cigarette, leaving his massive gold case on the Minister's desk. He had never appeared more relaxed. His retrieval of the mistake about Eileen had been instant and faultless. Kelly had spent a lot of time over the last three years trying to understand Logan Field. He had seen his bad temper, his intolerance and arrogance; his gift for coping with difficulties. But until now he hadn't appreciated how Logan glittered in adversity. He was like a great actor seizing and subduing an unplayable part. Combined with his ability to assume a role was the cold-blooded nerve of the born gambler.

Imshan was in jeopardy; the greatest coup of Logan's career was menaced by the hostility and greed of the Minister. This was Logan's view and the more he observed the Minister's tactics the more Kelly was unhappily inclined to agree. But Logan was neither worried nor discouraged. What Kelly saw that morning, during the slow, frustrating negotiation which all knew was already doomed to fail, was a man enjoying every moment of the game. It might well be that Khorvan had met his match.

'There are three with names that sound similar in the Embassy,' the Colonel said.

Sabet nodded. 'A trade attaché, a passport officer and one of the military staff. I went back to see the woman again and she described the man she saw as being very thin with a full head of hair. The military attaché is short and fat; the passport officer is bald.'

'So it looks like trade, then,' Ardalan remarked. 'We mustn't make a mistake. We have photographs of all three on our files – show them to the woman and see if she can identify any one of them. The name Homsi might not be genuine. We have to consider that. But we have an interesting situation, don't you agree?'

'Very interesting,' Sabet said.

Ardalan passed him a cigarette.

'A man is murdered for no motive and that means the only motive was to shut his mouth. He is some kind of political activist and he happens to be passing drinks at a reception given for the Minister of Economics and the chairman of Imperial Oil. He carried the telephone number of an American archaeologist living in Tehran. The archaeologist blends so well into the background that he is unlike any Americans I've ever known. His friends are Iranian. And one Syrian from the Embassy. Go and take those photographs over to Torshab Road. I want an answer today.'

Sabet went out and Ardalan finished his cigarette. It was a jigsaw puzzle without pieces. His difficulty was to find the pieces before he could attempt to solve the puzzle. It might well be that the visitor to the apartment that night was not a Syrian. That left him with the American Peters and the girl who was living with him. Police records cleared them both. Neither had any suspect connections. Peters came from France via West Germany. West Germany. Ardalan didn't know why this worried him, but it did. He rang through to the aliens section and asked for the report on Peters to be sent up. There would be nothing in it; he had already read the single sheet through. An archaeologist, intending to help with the Iranian dig at Persepolis. There were dozens of foreigners participating. The paper was laid in front of him. Everything was in order. Peters had left Munich on March 28th. *Munich.* That was what had set off the alarm bells in his mind. There had been reports of a top-level Palestinian terrorist meeting in the city. Interpol had been alerted; the watch on airports and Israeli Embassies had been increased for some weeks in expectation of bomb attacks. March 28th. It was the right time. The Colonel sent for the details of Madeleine Labouchère. Aged twenty-five, French citizen domiciled in Paris. Nothing suspicious there. Only her relationship with the American. The Colonel was frowning, tapping each finger in turn against his thumb. He wondered how long Sabet would be. At a quarter to four the assistant knocked and came into the office. He placed a blown-up photograph, obviously the work of a hidden photographer, in front of the Colonel.

'Saiid Homsi, trade attaché. She identified him at once.'

For a moment Ardalan said nothing. He looked up at his assistant and down again at the photograph.

'There was no doubt? No doubt at all?'

'None,' Sabet said. 'I showed her all three photographs and asked her to point to anyone she recognized. She chose Homsi without looking at the others. "That's the man who came here." That was what she said.'

'Trade attaché,' Ardalan murmured. 'The head of espionage

78

in an Embassy usually hides in the passport section. Very well. We will have to talk to this Saiid Homsi.'

'How?' the assistant asked. 'How, without causing an incident?'

Ardalan leaned back and rubbed his forehead with one thin hand. Black hairs grew profusely on the back of it and crept under his sleeve.

'There is only one way,' he said. 'And I have to satisfy myself that it is justified. Then I will get the authorization. Until then we will set a non-stop watch upon Homsi.'

The villa was built on a rock; it was poised above the sea, surrounded by a two-acre garden, ringed on the shore side by a ten-foot wire fence. It was a long, low building, dazzling white, shaded by palm trees and giant pines. A huge purple Bougain-villaea sprawled over the front wall. They had locked Eileen into a room on the first floor overlooking the sea. The landing at the field in the country had been a nightmare. The little plane bumped and shuddered and she was thrown violently forward; the seat belt saved her from being flung out of the seat. She had given a scream of terror and felt the American grab her. She was dragged out of the plane, trembling and dazed, hustled by Peters across the grass at a run which brought her stumbling down, her high-heeled shoe turning under her. He had been extremely rough in his handling of her; he almost threw her into the back of the car. The Frenchman jumped in on the other side. A man was in the driver's seat and they swung off onto the road. The American leaned over and took something from the driver. She heard them speaking in a language she couldn't understand. He sat back and pointed a gun at her side. There was no expression on his face.

'If you make any attempt to attract attention or do anything stupid, I'll kill you. Just sit dead quiet. You understand?'

'Yes,' Eileen whispered. She had tried to identify the coast when they left the country roads and started on the road by the shore. It was very warm and the sea was the bright Mediter-ranean blue; there were palm trees. They came into a big resort. Beach umbrellas and sunbathers, people sitting on the terraces of smart hotels.

Several times they stopped by traffic lights and as the car

halted the gun was rammed into her side. She recognized a large, magnificent hotel on the left. It was the Negresco; she and Logan had stayed there twice soon after they were married. They were driving through Nice.

They arrived at the villa some twenty minutes later. The tall gates swung open and they drove up a drive lined with palms. When the car stopped the Frenchman got out first. He stretched in the sunshine and yawned. Peters nudged her.

'Outside.'

He had put the gun away. When she stood in the drive she felt as if she were going to faint. She clung to the car door for support and the Frenchman put an arm round her waist.

'Come inside,' he said pleasantly.

Peters came up beside them.

'Leave her alone,' he said. He took Eileen by the arm. The villa was cool and spacious; the ground floor was open-plan and luxuriously furnished; an expensive modern abstract covered the far wall. The American walked her up a marble staircase and along a corridor. The room was simply furnished, with a bed and a chest and a single armchair. There was mesh over the window. He came inside with her and let go of her arm.

'You'll stay here,' he said. 'There's a bathroom through there. Make no trouble and nobody will hurt you.'

'Wait...' Eileen turned to him. 'Wait, please. What are you going to do? Why have you taken me?'

Peters closed the door. He searched through his pockets and brought out a flattened packet of cigarettes. He lit one.

'You look beat,' he said. 'Sit down.' She sat on the bed watching him.

'What do you hope to gain?' Eileen said. 'I don't understand. I've never even been to Palestine.'

'We haven't got anything against you,' Peters said. 'We were going to take your child. She wouldn't have come to any harm. We're reasonable people.' He drew on his cigarette. He didn't offer one to her.

'Reasonable? You call kidnapping a little child reasonable? You'd have shot me in that car, if I'd made a sound, wouldn't you?'

'Yes,' he answered. 'We have a job to do and nothing must interfere with it. As far as you're concerned, Mrs Field, it was your bad luck to be there and get taken instead. We're not interested in you, but we can use you. Alive or dead won't make any difference, so don't get clever. I'll bring you something to eat.'

He went out and she heard the door being locked. She got off the bed and stood looking round her. She went to the window first. It opened inwards, secured by a catch on the wall. The mesh covering it outside was rigid and showed a view of blue sea with a curve of coastline bending from the right. It was impossible to see below. Eileen went into the bathroom leading off the bedroom and found another window, also protected. This showed the same line of coast continuing round. The house overlooked a bay and the right-hand promontory connected with the mainland. There was no skylight in the bathroom, which was small and plainly equipped. From the glimpse she had caught of the interior, the room chosen for her was in the servants' quarters of the villa. She paused by the bathroom mirror, shocked by her appearance. She looked haggard and dishevelled; there was a streak of dirt on her face, smudged by tears. She washed in cold water. There was no soap and no towel. She dried herself on the bedcover. The room was very hot and airless and she lay on the bed exhausted. She was almost asleep when she heard the door open. The American came in carrying a tray. He put it down on the dressing table.

'You'll get three meals a day,' he said. 'And if you need anything, you can ask Madeleine. She'll come up and take this away.'

Eileen sat up.

'If that's the woman who threatened to murder my child, don't you send her near me. I wouldn't ask her for anything!'

Peters shrugged.

'Suit yourself. Resnais can come up to you.'

Alarm flared in her. She didn't know why, but she didn't want the Frenchman coming into that room alone.

'No! No, not him. You're in charge of this – I hold you responsible.'

Peters had no intention of wasting time with her. To him she was dehumanized, an object rather than a person. He meant to put the tray down and go out. The use of that one word stopped him. Responsible. He looked at her.

'I'm not responsible for anything about you, Mrs Field, except seeing that you don't escape. And you're in no position to dictate who comes up here and who doesn't.'

She got off the bed and faced him.

'You've kidnapped me,' she said. 'You've dragged me here by force and you're holding me for some purpose that I know nothing about. By the grace of God, it's not my little girl that's locked up here. How exactly would you have treated her?'

'As fairly as we'll treat you,' Peters said. 'So long as you behave yourself.'

She turned away from him. The eyes were so cold. For a moment she had been angry enough to challenge him, but there had been no response. It was like confronting a machine. She began to cry.

'There's no soap,' she said. 'And no towels. I had to dry with the counterpane. I've no clothes, not even a comb! I don't want your food – I won't eat anything!'

'Suit yourself,' he said again. He went out and locked the door. She cried for some time, until she had worn herself out. There was a carafe of water on the tray and she was very thirsty. She drank most of it, leaving the food untouched. The outburst had relieved her; she felt clear-headed and personal fear was minimized by the immense relief that she had saved Lucy. Logan wouldn't have expected her to act so quickly. Throwing the key out of the window had been an instant reflex. Everything she had done since they confronted her in the nursery was dictated by the need to protect her child. She had gone out of the house, driven through the streets, entered the plane; when the American mentioned Madeleine, she had instinctively connected the name with the woman who had threatened to empty her pistol through that nursery door. His admission that it was the same person hadn't sunk in for a time. But now she knew it meant that there was no more danger to Lucy. They were all together in the villa. She had no one to fear for now but herself. Eileen went back to the tray. Her stomach knotted against the idea of eating. There was cold meat, butter and bread, piled on one plate. Probably there was no one besides the three kidnappers in the villa. Then she remembered the driver. The Palestine People's Army. That was what he had said. Arab terrorists. The driver had been very dark-skinned, certainly not European. She forced herself to eat the bread and butter. She had a vague idea of conserving her strength without knowing why. She believed herself to be quite calm, and in one sense she was. In another, her whole body was quivering with shock and in spite of the heat she felt clammy and cold. She went to the window again and hooked her fingers through the mesh. It was fixed to the outside wall and it didn't yield a millimetre when she tried to pull it. They had made their preparations very carefully. Which meant that Lucy's kidnapping had been planned some time ahead. But why Lucy? Why her? Facing the bright blue sea through the steel mesh, Eileen understood that the reason was in her marriage to Logan Field. And through Logan, Imperial Oil. But why? Why? The question hammered at her, making her head ache. What had Logan or the company done, or what could the terrorists hope to gain by holding her? Their original target had been Lucy. There was a clue there. A child held as hostage. But against what? It must be money. She heard the door open again and swung round. The woman stood inside. She was casually dressed in a white shirt and dark blue trousers. She looked like a smart holidaymaker.

'Have you finished?'

Madeleine was a French name, but she wasn't French. The eyes were green, but there was a dark tinge in the skin that was stronger than sunburn. Eileen remembered her at Lucy's door, calling the little girl to come into range.

'I told him not to send you up here,' she said. 'Get out! Take your filthy food and get out!'

The girl laughed.

'You won't be so full of fight in a few days. Think yourself lucky you're not shut up in the cellars. That's where I'd have put you!'

Eileen looked at her; the sneer was fading on the girl's face as she met the contempt and disgust of the older woman.

'You'd have murdered a child,' she said slowly. 'You'd be capable of anything. You're not even a woman.'

She turned back to the window. Without knowing it, she had said the one thing to which Madeleine was vulnerable. She had denied her identity as a female. She didn't see the blaze of hate directed at her as the girl took the tray and went out. To be less than a woman was the ultimate insult to a Lebanese, however liberated and equal with men she thought herself to be. Peters had told her to bring the prisoner soap and a towel. An impulse of feminine spite had made her ignore this. It irritated her that he should pay the woman's needs any attention. Let her do without the amenities. There weren't any luxuries in the refugee camps. She went back downstairs, dumped the tray in the kitchen and found only Resnais in the lounge. He looked up at her and grinned.

'How is our charming guest?'

'Insolent! And arrogant!' Madeleine settled into one of the white sofas. The owner of the villa was an Algerian millionaire with strong terrorist connections. He had a passion for white.

'I'll deal with her if she gives any trouble,' the girl said. Her expression was vicious and sulky. Resnais watched with amusement. Women never surprised him when they displayed cruelty. The idea that because they bore children they were more compassionate and squeamish than men was a myth. Women were capable of absolute savagery provided that the motive was strong enough. There was a thread of female dislike between Madeleine and the hostage which had nothing to do with politics.

'Where's Peters?'

'Out on the terrace.'

'I don't think that room is safe enough,' she said. 'I think we should put her down in the cellars.'

The Frenchman lit a cigarette.

'She must have really made you angry,' he said. 'I wonder what she said?'

Madeleine swore at him and jumped up. He watched her go out in search of Peters and his laughter followed her.

James Kelly's solicitors had never heard from Eileen. That was the first result of a series of telephone calls which he undertook after days went by and he heard nothing from her. This in itself worried him badly. She had promised to protect herself and Lucy. All he knew from their London staff was that she was away and staying in Ireland. A second call to Eaton Square elicited the telephone number of Meath House and began the incredible frustrations of attempting to link one erratic line of communication with another equally unpredictable.

James's anxiety was based on his fear that she might have decided to try for a reconciliation. He had no reason for supposing that Logan would agree, or that the influence of Janet Armstrong was not stronger every time they met. It was just a nagging fear that his hopes were going to be disappointed and because of the distance between him and Eileen there was nothing he could do. Ireland and its telephone system defeated him for a full twenty-four hours. He had agreed to take the call at any time; if Logan was in the house it couldn't be helped. James doubted if he would have noticed or cared. All his energies and concentration were bent upon the problem of reaching a solution which would safeguard their concession at Imshan. Paterson, the finance director, had already been despatched to Tokyo to sound out the Japanese oil importers. A favourable response would bring Logan himself flying out.

Time was not on their side; as Logan pointed out in one explosive meeting, there was a Board meeting scheduled for two weeks' time in London. Something had to be presented to them which would pass; if the present situation became known, there would be opposition that might even defeat Logan's persuasive powers. They had to have some indication of solid financial support from the Japanese before a whisper of the outrageous demand for the refinery reached London.

Equally the Iranian government had to be reassured that Imperial Oil was working on the problem and was optimistic of an acceptable solution. Added to which the British Embassy in Tehran had informed James privately, through the unofficial channel open to an ex-Foreign Office member, that the Russian technicians were still in the city and were remaining on advice from Khorvan himself.

That night the party in honour of the Minister was taking place at James's house. He had left the office after lunch to supervise the arrangements; he was asking Logan what explanation could be given for Eileen's absence, when Logan took a call from Tokyo and there was no question of interrupting him. James had a flair for giving parties; he had learned the art in Embassies abroad, when his help had been enlisted by various official wives. He had an instinct for entertaining people which caused a lot of envy among his bachelor colleagues. It was often said that James didn't need a wife to make a party go. He had decided to give the reception in the garden; a lot of extra plants and potted shrubs had been brought in; there were two big tables set under the trees, crates of whisky, gin and champagne, and quantities of fresh fruit juice for the teetotal among their Iranian guests. As a compliment to the guest of honour, the flower arrangements were in the Iranian national colours of green, red and white. As a bonus, and again through the good offices of the British Embassy, James had organized a display of fireworks as the climax of the evening. He had checked everything and decided there was time to have a leisurely bath and change even before Logan returned, when the houseboy told him there was a telephone call.

Imagining it might be the call to Ireland, James raced back to the house. It was an unfamiliar voice, heavily accented.

'Mr Kelly? Good evening. My name is Saiid Homsi. I am from the Syrian Embassy.'

James scowled. He had no contact with the Syrians and no wish to establish any. He had really thought it might be Ireland...

'Yes?' His tone was not encouraging. 'What can I do for you?'

'I think there is something I can do for you,' the caller said. 'I have some very important information for your Mr Field.'

'In that case,' James said, 'I suggest you speak direct to him.'

'Unfortunately I cannot do that. It might be dangerous. I need your help, Mr Kelly.'

James hesitated. Dangerous. He didn't like that word.

'I don't understand,' he said. 'Can you explain, please. Do you want me to pass a message to Mr Field?'

'No,' the man said. 'No, I have to speak to him myself. Believe me, it is very important. I have something to tell Mr Field and the matter is very personal. Very delicate. Would it be possible to meet him at your reception this evening?'

'Mr Homsi, I don't believe we've met. What is your position in the Embassy? And why can't you make an appointment with Mr Field in his office?' James was listening carefully; he spoke calmly, trying to decide what to do. Orientals loved intrigue, but this was extreme.

'I am a trade attaché here, Mr Kelly. I am not an important

86

person. But my message for Mr Field is important. I cannot be seen to approach him; all of us are watched here by Colonel Ardalan's men. What I have to tell Mr Field can only be whispered in his ear in a public place like your party. May I present myself tonight?'

'Yes,' James said. For a moment he had hesitated. 'Yes, please come. Introduce yourself to me and I will bring you to Mr Field.' He heard a murmured 'thank you' and then the line buzzed clear.

By the time he was ready to receive his guests he had thought of a dozen possibilities for the extraordinary call and rejected them all. He wished profoundly that it had no connection with the Syrians. They were the least welcome Embassy in Tehran and the object of the Secret Police's suspicion as a headquarters for subversives from within.

He was surprised to learn from the servants that Logan had not returned to change. The explanation was obvious but it infuriated him. He had gone to bring Janet to the party. Entertaining her, and seeing her in Eileen's place, was going to tax his good manners very hard. When Logan's car swept up to the front door twenty minutes before the party was due to begin, he deliberately went to the table and got himself a drink. When he turned round Janet Armstrong was advancing on him. She looked very cool and smart, wearing a long dress of pale green; he saw a handsome emerald and diamond brooch on her shoulder and guessed it came from Logan. Logan was behind her.

'Congratulations,' she said. 'It all looks marvellous. Doesn't it, Logan? You certainly manage well without a wife!'

James gave her a look of plain dislike.

'What will you have to drink? Logan?'

'Scotch,' was the answer. 'Soda and plenty of ice.'

Janet came back and hooked her arm through his.

'I'll have the same,' she said.

James gave the houseboy the order and a waiter came forward with the glasses on a tray. A silence hung over the three of them. James made no attempt to break it. To hell with his diplomatic training. He hated the woman and he despised Logan for flaunting their relationship. Logan either didn't notice or couldn't be bothered to make conversation. Janet faced James and smiled. She knew he disliked her, although she had no idea it was more than a male antipathy towards a successful woman. His opinion didn't interest her. He was extremely clever and Logan thought highly of him but he wasn't her type. He was too much of a gentleman. She liked a little roughness round the edges. She hugged Logan tightly for a moment and then let him go. They had been to bed before coming and she felt very close to him.

'It's a lovely evening,' she said. 'I'm sure the party will be a great success.'

Logan would expect her to carry the situation and she was too self-confident to be outfaced by James.

'I expect it'll be a bit of a drinking marathon, so I'd better eat some of those delicious things over there.'

She walked over to the table and began to pick among the canapés. James went over to Logan. He had decided to tell him about the telephone call and give him the choice of meeting the man or not. Logan listened, sipping his whisky.

'What the hell can it be? We've never touched the Syrians with a ten-foot pole. Have you any idea, James?'

'None,' James said. 'But if you're going to talk to him you'd better be very careful. This might be some game thought up by Khorvan; something they could use with the Shah to discredit us.'

'Trafficking with subversives – could be. But if I don't talk to him I might be making a mistake. And he doesn't seem anxious to compromise himself either. Otherwise he'd have come to the office. I'd better talk to him and find out what it's all about.'

'All right,' James said. He could see Janet walking back to them. 'But I think you ought to safeguard yourself. I've asked Ardalan tonight. He loves parties; he came to the other one. I'll mention this to him. That way no one can accuse you of going behind the Government's back.'

'Right. Do that. If this is some trick of Khorvan's, it'll blow back in his face.'

Janet came and stood beside him. James saw the first car coming into the main drive.

'Have you heard from Eileen?' he said.

'No,' Logan answered. 'And I don't expect to. Janet will look after Khorvan. But the news from Tokyo is very encouraging.'

'Oh?' James showed no enthusiasm.

'Paterson called this afternoon – you were there, weren't you? Anyway he said he's had strong reactions from the importers. He's seeing the Deputy Prime Minister the day after tomorrow. If he gives his blessing, I'll fly out and see the Prime Minister next week. I'm bloody hopeful, James. I think we're going to pull it off!'

'You will if anyone can,' Janet said. They stood together to receive the guests. It seemed to James as if Eileen Field had never existed. He decided quite calmly, while talking to a director of the Bank of Iran, that he really hated Logan.

Soon after seven he saw Colonel Ardalan in the crowd. He had brought his pretty wife with him; Iranians tended to leave their women at home when attending European parties. James went up to him and the two men shook hands. They had met on many occasions and James found the Colonel an attractive personality. It was difficult to believe the stories about his methods.

'A charming party, Mr Kelly,' Ardalan said. His wife nodded and smiled. She didn't speak good English and was shy of exposing it.

'Thank you,' James said. 'Could we have a word in private – just over here.'

They stood together under a plane tree, which Iranians called chenar; there was no one near them.

'Something rather unusual has come up,' James explained. 'My chairman felt you ought to know about it. He's very anxious not to do anything contrary to the wishes of the Government.'

'Naturally,' the Colonel said. 'Please let me help in any way I can. What is this unusual occurrence?'

'I received a telephone call,' James said, 'from a man calling himself Saiid Homsi. Says he's a trade man at the Syrian Embassy.'

'I've heard of him,' Ardalan said mildly. 'What did he want?'

'To come here and speak to Mr Field. Privately. He said he had something to tell him. Mr Field felt he'd better see the man and find out what it's all about, but we wanted you to know.'

'I appreciate that,' the Colonel said. 'I wish more of our

European expatriates showed such good sense. And good will.'
He smiled at James. 'My function is to protect the State, Mr
Kelly. I am also happy to protect our friends, whoever they
may be. Syrians are dangerous people. Let Mr Field see this
man and then if you will tell me what he wanted, that would be
the wisest way.'

'We'll do that,' James said.

Colonel Ardalan laid a hand on his shoulder for a moment.

'I hear rumours,' he said, 'that your negotiations for Imshan
are not proceeding smoothly. I hope you won't be discouraged.
His Imperial Majesty wants a British firm to develop the oil
field.'

'I am very happy to hear that,' James answered. 'Minister
Khorvan drives a hard bargain. We are trying to meet his
terms.'

'I hope you succeed,' Ardalan said. 'I see him over there,
talking to the lady in the green dress.'

'Yes,' James said. 'She's the chairman's assistant.'

'I don't see Mrs Field,' the Colonel said.

'She's in England.' James moved away, the Colonel following.
'As soon as this man Homsi makes himself known, I'll take him
over to Mr Field. I'll let you know what happens.'

'I will be obliged,' the Colonel said. He went back to join his
wife. The party was going under its own impetus. The garden
was crowded with people and there was a roar of conversation.
People were eating the food and waiters with trays of drinks
slipped in and out. James stood aside and listened. It was a
success. Logan had Khorvan in a group composed of Janet
Armstrong and the assistant resident director; the Minister
was laughing. The first hour was the most important. If they
were bored, the Iranians left early. If they stayed on for the
buffet supper, then it meant they had enjoyed the party and
might stay until the early hours. There were a number of
women and some of the senior Iranian officials had brought
their wives. There were couture dresses and lavish jewels; the
new rich among them adored to make a display of wealth and
the wives glittered like Christmas trees. It pained James to see
some of the British Embassy ladies looking dowdy; he thought
how Eileen would have redeemed them all had she been there.
The steely elegance of Janet Armstrong didn't count with him.

There was no grace about her, no natural style. He felt a little tug on his left sleeve.

'Mr Kelly? Good evening.'

It was a slight man, very swarthy with bright black eyes.

'I am Saiid Homsi.'

James had planned the manner of Field's meeting with the Syrian. It couldn't take place in the open with dozens of highly placed Iranians as witnesses. He didn't waste any time.

'Come with me, please,' he said. He went into the house with the Syrian following. The drawing room opened onto the garden. James turned to the man.

'Wait in here. I'll tell Mr Field. He'll come in a moment.'

He gave Logan the message in a quick aside. He saw Khorvan watching him and he eased himself into Logan's place.

'Minister, I haven't had time to do more than welcome you. I hope you have everything you want.'

'Everything, thank you,' Khorvan said. He was enjoying himself. The food was excellent; he loved the rich, spiced tit-bits which were a feature of Iranian parties, and the beautiful setting had put him into a genial mood. He disliked Logan Field but he found him stimulating. They had spent some time in semi-friendly sparring; Khorvan was very sensitive where his own feelings were concerned. The slightest condescension or tactlessness would never be forgiven, but Logan had trod with feline delicacy over this thin crust of self-esteem. Khorvan would never like him, because he was almost a symbolic enemy, but he enjoyed his company.

'Everything,' he repeated to James, 'except that I miss my hostess. I am very disappointed not to see her.'

James hoped that Janet had heard. A fractional change in her expression satisfied him that she had.

'Mr Field said their daughter was ill, and she couldn't leave England. I am sorry to hear it.' Khorvan was needling him a little and James knew it. The absence of Eileen Field was only important in that it gave him an excuse to carp at his host and put him on the defensive.

'We all miss her,' James said loudly, hoping that this too went to its target.

His attention was claimed by a beautifully dressed, exotic Iranian girl, married to one of the few Persian aristocrats still in public life and herself the heiress to a vast fortune. Her father owned one of the largest mines in Iran. Substantial gifts of 'A' shares to influential ministers and a part holding to the Pahlevi Foundation had saved the mine from being nationalized. She was vivacious and attractive; she spoke French and German fluently and perfect English. She was bored with her husband and had often indicated to James that she found him attractive. If it hadn't been for Eileen, he would have taken up the challenge. While he flirted with her, he wondered what was happening with Logan and Saiid Homsi in the house.

# 6

'I've brought you towels. And some soap.' Peters put them on the bed. Eileen was sitting in the chair; the bedside lamp was on. It was quite dark outside. The room was stiflingly hot.

'Thank you,' she said. 'At least I can wash properly.'

He took something out of his pocket and dropped it on the heap of towels. It was a man's pocket comb.

'You can have this,' he said.

'I'm so terribly hot,' Eileen got up slowly. She moved as if she were exhausted. Peters didn't mean to, but he balanced on the edge of the bed. He didn't intend to stay and talk.

'Do you have to have that mesh over the window? It looks high enough and I promise you I'm not going to jump out. It stops the air from circulating; I feel suffocated in here.'

'The mesh was put there for the child,' Peters said. 'To stop her falling out.'

'Would you have really kept her locked up in here?'

'No.' He took out a cigarette and lit it. 'She would have slept here. Madeleine would have looked after her; she'd have had the run of the garden. We meant to treat her properly.'

It was all so logical, and at the same time so inhuman. She didn't argue with him and the split-second impulse to spit her condemnation in his face was quickly mastered. She felt as if she were groping in total darkness whenever she talked to him. It wasn't so much a dialogue, however brief, as an exploration of a species quite unknown to her. And unlike the woman he showed her no personal hostility.

'Could I have one?'

He looked surprised for a moment. Then he got up and offered her the cigarettes. He gave her a light.

'Would you tell me something?' Eileen asked him. Peters waited. 'Why have you kidnapped me?'

'I can't tell you that. It's nothing personal against you.'

'It must be something to do with my husband. Why can't you tell me?'

Peters looked at her and drew on the last of his cigarette.

Madeleine had said she was arrogant. She had spent a long time with him on the terrace, arguing that they should imprison the woman in the cellars and insisting that she was the type to give trouble. Peters hadn't agreed with her then and he saw no sign of it now. There was nothing about Eileen Field which antagonized him personally. She had saved her child at her own risk and he gave her credit for courage. She wasn't being truculent with him, whatever Madeleine said.

'It *is* to do with your husband. That's all I can tell you.'

She picked up the comb and used it. One tooth was broken. It was his own comb. He noticed that she had pretty hair, which waved naturally round her face. She looked at him and shook her head.

'And if he refuses to pay the ransom – whatever it is?'

'He won't,' Peters said. 'But the little girl would have been better.'

'That's a filthy thing to say,' Eileen said slowly. 'Don't you have any feelings? Don't you see that to use a little child for a purpose, ransom or anything else, is the lowest, most despicable thing anyone could do? I'm not trying to argue with you, because thank God you didn't get her. I can't understand how you could *say* a thing like that!'

'We have a different set of values,' Peters answered. He wondered whether she could be brought to understand them if he did explain. It was a Liberation Army axiom that no opportunity to put their case should be neglected. There were cases where prisoners had become converted and asked to join in the struggle. She was intelligent and courageous; she didn't remind him of the mindless rich women he had known in the States, creatures of such superficiality that they wouldn't have survived Eileen Field's experience with enough wit to ask a question. She hadn't whined or grovelled. And the room was like a bake oven. His own clothes were sticking to him.

'You see a little girl,' he said slowly. 'I see a whole people. Thousands of children, not one child. Children without food or shelter, or hope for the future. I see their families, living with

94

disease and dirt in hovels made of packing cases. To do something about that, I would have snatched your child, Mrs Field, and I don't see anything wrong in it. So long as she came to no harm.'

'If, if she did come to harm – if she got ill or had an accident – you'd still be able to justify it?'

'The end would justify it,' Peters said.

'That old lie about the Jesuits,' Eileen answered. 'It's been made the excuse for every crime under the sun. Tell me, what happens to me if my husband refuses to accept your terms? Supposing he won't give you the money – what will you do with me?'

Peters got up.

'I'll leave you these,' he said. He put the cigarettes and a box of matches on the bed.

'I shouldn't have asked that,' Eileen said. 'You don't have to answer. I can imagine. Please, couldn't you take that wire off the window?'

He went over and tested it, as she had done earlier. He knew that the drop below was fifty feet to the rocks, and that the sea boiled round them in a strong undercurrent. There were no pipes or ledges on the outside walls. Nothing but a suicidal drop.

'Okay,' he said. 'I'll have it taken out tomorrow.'

'Thank you,' Eileen said. 'Would you tell me your name?'

'Peters,' he said. 'Do you want anything else?'

'Something to read,' she said.

'I'll see what there is,' he said.

When he had gone, Eileen ran to the window. She pulled at the wire mesh. Once that was down, at least there was a possible way out. She could see the sea below and guessed that there must be a sheer drop or he wouldn't have agreed to take the mesh away. The encounter had left her taut with nervous tension. He had been neutral, giving the few necessities without making her beg for them; there was a disturbing lack of personal animosity towards her. She would have found it easier to fight him if there had been. He wasn't going to treat her cruelly or indulge in petty persecutions. But if the order came through he would take her out of the room and shoot her dead. She knew that without any doubt. As a young girl her experience of men had been limited to the jolly young Irishmen with whom she had grown up, friends in the hunting field, partners at the rowdy horse show parties and the lavish balls where throwing bread rolls and squirting siphons of soda were a ritual part of the entertainment. Men had been in love with her and she had flirted happily with many of them. If Logan Field hadn't come to Ireland to look at a property owned by their neighbour, she would have married one of the gay young men who slid down the banisters at parties and known nothing different. There was no one in her experience comparable with the man who had kidnapped her. She had travelled widely with Logan when they married first; a month in the United States had brought her into contact with Americans from many different groups. They had been friendly, hospitable and easy to like. She could even recognize Peters as a physical type. Tall, showing traces of Scandinavian ancestry, physically very strong; he had the loose, easy way of moving that was typically American. She remembered saying to Logan that they made Englishmen look jerky by comparison.

He didn't waste words; he had cold eyes, very blue, and when he looked at her there was no expression in them. Not antagonism, or suspicion, nothing. She had felt instinctively that to be aggressive would gain her nothing. It hadn't been easy to master the impulse to fly at him with her nails, when he talked about what they had planned to do with her child. She had stayed calm and, by so doing, she had wrung a major concession from him. The wire was coming off the window. She wondered how high above the sea the window was. If it was possible to climb down even part of the way and then drop... she was a strong swimmer. The bed sheets and the counterpane. The towels he had brought her. It might be possible to make a rope. She went into the bathroom and splashed her face with cold water. The heat was sticky and close. She had never resorted to cunning in her life; it had never been necessary to wheedle and manoeuvre with a man to get something out of him. It was strange how quickly adversity instructed.

She lit one of the cigarettes Peters had left her. She needn't have done that. They weren't a necessity. She paused, struck by the thought that Logan wouldn't have left her the cigarettes, if he had been Peters. He certainly wouldn't have taken the wire off the window. Not because he was inhuman or enjoyed being harsh. But because he was a total realist. Prisoners lived with bars and didn't smoke. She turned the cigarette over in her fingers.

The cold eyes, the impersonal approach to her. She remembered how rough he had been when they landed, the gun pressing into her side through the drive to the villa. She didn't know why, but she shivered. She mustn't antagonize him. She must be quiet and dignified, because it seemed to have the best effect upon him. She must thank him when he brought her food, and appear to be quiescent, waiting for news of her release.

And that release would come. It must. Thinking how best to outwit Peters had brought only critical thoughts of Logan to her mind. She felt ashamed and petty. Jealous still of his choice of another woman, of the dismissal of all their years together and the happiness that both of them had known. She finished the cigarette and took her dress off. She lay down in her slip on top of the bed, propped up on the pillow. It was too hot to sleep. She remembered their first meeting and closed her eyes, willing herself out of the stuffy room with its implications of nightmare back to Clonagh Castle nearly eight years before.

The son of the house had wanted to marry her. The family were their neighbours and her father's oldest friends. Their name was Louth and the title went back to the twelfth century. They had a magnificent house with an original Norman keep, and a bank manager in Dublin whose patience was coming to an end. Clonagh was up for sale and the Fitzgeralds had been invited to meet the prospective buyers, a very rich Englishman who they hoped to persuade. Eileen was twenty; her dress was made by the dressmaker in Meath and was five years out of fashion. She had no idea how beautiful she looked the night she met Logan Field. She only knew that he dominated the room. Beside him her own father, even Lord Louth, who was a considerable personage in the country, and certainly his son, her suitor, seemed like a group of out-of-date ghosts, with their insular jokes and their endless talk of horses and neighbours. The Englishman had shamed them by his knowledge, his range of interests and his authority. She had felt him as a physical presence and when they were separated at the dinner table, she had seen him looking down towards her.

Logan hadn't bought Clonagh Castle. He didn't like Ireland or the Irish, only she didn't discover that till after she was married. He had met her and made up his mind. Within a month they were engaged and within three they were on their honeymoon.

She was back in the room again, with the ugly bedside light burning and a mosquito whining overhead. They had been deeply in love. She had been shy and untutored; he had been patient and tender until she understood his passion and could meet it. It couldn't go for nothing. Love might die but there were always traces left. If he were in danger at that moment, if positions were reversed, she would have given anything, done anything, to rescue him. He was a strong man, a powerful force, excited by obstacles. She had been part of his life, even if not the major part. Thoughtless and ambitious above all, but in his way he had loved her very much. With hindsight, she admitted that she had forced the issue of their marriage into the open. Had she stayed quiet, there might have been no crisis, no breakdown. Logan would get her out. She didn't doubt it for a moment.

She fell asleep and started a long, incoherent dream about climbing out of the bedroom window on a rope that had no end towards a sea that came no nearer. And suddenly it stopped and she was falling. She woke from the throes of finding herself struggling violently in Peters's arms and being borne down onto the rocks.

'I don't believe you,' Logan Field said. He had taken a step towards the Syrian, but Homsi didn't retreat. He shrugged, both his palms turned upwards.

'I am only a messenger, Mr Field,' he said. 'A go-between. I can assure you these people seized your wife three days ago. And they mean what they say.' He shook his head a little. 'Naturally this is a great shock to you. I do sympathize.'

'I don't believe it,' Logan repeated. 'My wife's in England. If anything had happened to her, I'd have been told at once!'

'Apparently it was done in such a way that nobody knows she is missing,' the Syrian said. 'The terrorists want this kept completely secret. That is one of their conditions. You must tell nobody. I advise you to do as they say. They are a very dangerous, extremist group.'

'I'll find her,' Logan said. 'I'll get every police force in the world on to it.'

'The moment you go to the police or say anything, she will be killed,' Saiid Homsi said quietly. 'Make inquiries by all means, Mr Field, but if you want your wife alive, you must be very, very discreet.'

He watched the Englishman; the man had lost colour and his hands were clenching and opening. For a moment Saiid had feared he might be punched to the ground when he first gave Field the news.

Logan turned to him.

'You're hand-in-glove with them,' he said. 'Syria supports these bastards; everyone knows that. You're no bloody innocent! You tell me where she is and I'll see you get more money than you've ever dreamed of. Cooperate with me and get my wife out of danger and I'll pay you any price you ask!'

'Unfortunately,' Homsi said gently, 'I can't be any help. I don't know where Mrs Field is being held and I couldn't assist in a rescue. It isn't a question of money, Mr Field. This is a problem even you can't solve by signing a cheque. These people aren't interested in a ransom.'

'What do they want then? What's the deal?'

'They haven't told me that,' Homsi answered. 'All I know is that Mrs Field is in their hands. They want you to know this and to be ready to hear their terms for releasing her. They will tell me more in the next twenty-four hours. That's all I know.'

'Jesus Christ,' Logan muttered. 'I still can't believe it.'

'I think you will find,' the Syrian murmured, 'that it is unfortunately true. I will go now, Mr Field. If you will contact me the day after tomorrow, I will have more news for you. That gives you time to check on their information. If you find Mrs Field is safe and well at home, nobody will be more pleased than myself.'

He opened the door to the garden and walked into the crowd. Logan didn't move for a moment. Then he went to the table where James kept a tray of drinks and poured himself a whisky. He drank it straight down and then picked up the telephone. At that hour there was no delay in putting a call through to

London. He sat by the phone waiting for the operator to ring back. He didn't have another drink and slowly the shock was wearing off. At one moment he had almost attacked the Syrian. There was something so hypocritical in the dark face, so maddening in the precise polite English that Field wanted to punch and pummel him into a bloody mess. When the phone rang he seized it and shouted down the crackling line.

'Mario? Mr Field here. Is my wife there? What? When? Oh, for Christ's sake, speak up. The line's impossible. When did she go? And Lucy – Bridget took her. Have you heard from her – from Mrs Field? I see. All right. No, never mind.'

He dropped the receiver. She'd left the house on Wednesday. They understood she was going to Ireland. Lucy had been sent in advance with the maid. They'd heard nothing from her since. That was three days ago. Three days. The Syrian had said she was taken three days ago... He heard a noise and looked up. James had come into the room.

'Logan?'

He was sitting in the semi-dark.

'I saw Homsi come out. What happened?'

James switched on the lights and saw Logan's face.

'My God,' he said, 'what's wrong?'

'Get me a drink, would you,' Logan said. 'Not too big, I've already helped myself.'

'What's happened?' James said. He put the glass down in front of him. 'What did he tell you?'

Logan rubbed both hands over his face; they were greasy with sweat.

'He said he'd been approached by an Arab terrorist organization.' He spoke quietly but it sounded as if he were only just keeping control. 'They had a message for me and he was acting as the go-between. It seems they've kidnapped Eileen. Anyway that's what they claim.'

He wasn't looking at James Kelly.

'I've just been through to London. She's not there. They say she's gone to Ireland. If this kidnap threat is true, that's just the place they'd grab her. I'll have to go back and make sure.'

'You won't need to,' James Kelly said. 'I've booked a call to Ireland. It should come through any time. Then we'll know. Who are the people who say they've got her?'

'Homsi didn't give a name. He just said they were very dangerous extremists. Black September by the sound of it. Do you believe it, James? Do you believe they've got her?'

'Syrians don't play games,' James said. He felt physically sick. 'What do they want? What's the ransom?'

'Not money,' Logan said. 'The bastard told me that. They've given me twenty-four hours to check that she's missing. Then they'll tell me their terms. If I go to the police or let anyone know she's gone, they'll kill her.' He looked at Kelly. 'I still can't believe it,' he said. 'I can't take it in.'

The noise of the party outside came through the garden doors as a pleasant murmur. Logan finished his drink.

'Why were you telephoning Ireland?'

Kelly ignored the question.

'When do you contact Homsi again?'

'Tomorrow. James – what am I going to do? I tried bribing him to help but he didn't want to know. In Christ's name, what do they want if they don't want money!'

'They wouldn't pick on you for that,' Kelly said slowly. 'You're not that rich. It's something else. Don't try buying Homsi again. He might be tempted to take money from you and that could wreck the whole chance of negotiating with these people. I know the type. One move that looks as if you're trying to pull something and they'll murder her. They're not criminals. They're fanatics. Go to Homsi tomorrow and for Christ's sake do exactly what he says. I've got to think up some reason to satisfy Ardalan; I promised to let him know what Homsi wanted.'

'Make some excuse, think of something,' Logan said. 'You don't think if we contacted Interpol and explained...'

'No,' James said. 'No. Say nothing and do nothing. It's too dangerous. I'll tell Ardalan some story.'

'Why doesn't that bloody Irish call come through? I'll get on to them.' Logan reached for the telephone. Kelly stood by while he shouted at the international operator.

'It's no good, Logan,' he said. 'You stay here and wait for it. I'll go and see Ardalan.'

'No,' Logan stood up. 'I've got to rejoin the party. We don't want to upset the Minister.'

'Of course,' James said. 'I'd forgotten about business for a moment. I must get my priorities right.'

On the way to the garden door Logan turned back.

'Coming apart at the seams isn't going to help Eileen,' he said. 'Talk to Ardalan and then you wait for the call. Let me know the moment it comes through. She may be perfectly safe, staying with her father.'

Kelly watched him push his way through the crowd, moving towards Khorvan. Janet Armstong's green dress looked white in the fading light. The garden was illuminated with lights discreetly placed among the trees and shrubs. As soon as it was dark the firework display would begin. Logan had left the doors open and there was a steady flow of talk and laughter; glass tinkled as something was broken. He could see Khorvan talking to Logan; Logan seemed to be laughing.

Kelly sat down. He looked for a cigarette and couldn't find one. It was a reflex and he made no further effort, although there was a box on the desk. A dangerous extremist group. Logan was clinging to a secret hope that somehow Eileen was safe; he thought the telephone call might prove the Syrian wrong. Kelly could understand this. He wished he could have shared that hope. But he knew that it was vain. Eileen Field was not in Meath House. The men who had sent Homsi to her husband didn't make mistakes. They would demand impossible terms for her release; he couldn't even guess their nature. There would be days of negotiation; perhaps weeks. He knew the pattern. Until the last moment they would preserve the hostage alive. They had a code, brutal and pitiless but predictable. If they got what they wanted, they wouldn't sacrifice the human pawn. But one infringement of the rules by Logan, one suspicion that he was trying to hold something back and Eileen would be murdered. Executed, in their terminology. He remembered the horror of a photograph of a German diplomat, ritually shot through the head after a similar kidnapping had failed to gain its object.

For a moment he felt sick and overcome. An ugly thought came to him. Logan was distressed and shaken. But supposing the price they asked was something that he didn't want to pay. He stepped out into the garden to find Colonel Ardalan. He had already thought of an explanation for Homsi's visit. Nobody must suspect that anything was wrong. His talk with the Colonel was interrupted by a message that his Irish telephone call was coming through.

Colonel Ardalan had enjoyed the party. He was a gregarious man who liked meeting people; the firework display had been a great success. He drove home with his wife and sat on his terrace, smoking and sipping whisky after she had gone to bed. He didn't believe a word of James Kelly's explanation. It was all very glib. The Syrian had some rare Coptic manuscripts which he thought Logan Field might be interested in buying. He had understood, correctly, that Field was a collector of antiquities and Logan got the impression that the items were prohibited for export. He had no intention of involving himself with a dubious purchase and had told Homsi to look for another customer.

It was a very probable explanation and in different circumstances the Colonel would have believed it. There was a flourishing illicit trade in rare antiquities for which no export licence was available in certain countries, notably Greece. Anything of exceptional quality commanded a high price.

Ardalan had listened politely and thanked Kelly for telling him. He even added a mild caution that the Syrian might offer something really tempting at a later date. He had noted the absence of both men after Homsi's interview. When Logan Field rejoined the party he didn't look as if someone had offered him a smuggled manuscript. And James Kelly's hand was shaking when he shook it as they said goodbye. Ardalan never failed to detect fear; and that was what he saw in the eyes of both Logan and Kelly. He finished his whisky. The pieces of the puzzle were assembling. One key piece was the Syrian. The second, and equally important in its solution, was Logan Field.

'Darling,' Janet said, 'aren't you going to come in?'

Logan had driven back to the hotel; he had gone as far as the lift with her and she was taken by surprise when he kissed her briefly on the cheek. He hadn't seemed in such good spirits for the last half of the evening; knowing him so well, she detected a forced note in the friendly sparring with the Minister.

'Not tonight,' he said. 'I'm tired out.'

The lift was coming down, the red eye winking on the indicator.

'There's nothing wrong, is there? You don't seem yourself.' She put one hand on his sleeve.

'No, of course not,' Logan said. 'I'll ring you tomorrow before we go to the office.'

The lift doors slid back and she stepped inside. He had turned and was walking away before they closed.

Eileen had never arrived at Meath House. Her father had been curt and uncommunicative on the telephone. Logan had mastered the impulse to shout at the old sponger that his daughter was missing and in great danger. He didn't seem worried by her absence. Logan suspected furiously that the old man was too busy spoiling his granddaughter to think of anything else. He had hung up. He didn't look at Kelly. The hope had been a flimsy one, but until he followed James in to speak to his father-in-law he hadn't admitted how much he had clung to it. 'She's not there,' James had said and handed him the telephone.

Logan drove back through the empty Tehran streets. The last half of the party reminded him of the classic nightmare in which the dreamer is isolated from contact with everyone surrounding him. The evening had begun with making love to Janet; he had come to the party in a mood of high optimism. His personal life was exciting and the difficulties of securing Imshan might well be surmounted by a deal with the Japanese. He had never felt more in command of the future than when he arrived at Kelly's house. He closed his eyes during the drive and all he could see was Eileen. It couldn't be true. She couldn't be shut up in some blacked-out room, at the mercy of fanatics who would kill her without hesitation. Her face floated free in the darkness, the face he had thought so beautiful he had commissioned Merton to paint her. She couldn't be helpless and afraid, perhaps even ill-treated. He sat up with a jolt, unable to bear his imagination's choice of possibilities. What did they want in return for her? What was the price they would ask through Saiid Homsi? Twenty-four hours. A full day and a night before he would know. If it wasn't money it was going to be something political. Something advantageous to the cause of Arab fanaticism, with which, next to outright Communism, he had the least sympathy of all. The lights were on when he went into Kelly's house. The moonlit garden and the jasmine scent reminded him of the evening he had told his wife he wanted someone else. There was no evidence of the party; everything had been cleared away. James came out of the sitting room as he went to the stairs.

'Do you want a whisky? It might help if we talked about it.'

'No, thanks,' Logan said. 'We know what the score is now. That little bastard told the truth. They have got her. All I can do now is wait to hear the terms.'

James stood in the doorway; he had been drinking since the party ended.

'Whatever it is, you'll pay?'

'Don't be a bloody fool,' Logan said.

He went upstairs and Kelly heard the bedroom door shut. He stayed in the hall for a few minutes, finishing his drink. Money would have been easy. He knew Logan wouldn't hesitate whatever they asked. He could have given them money; Imperial Oil would subsidize if it went beyond his personal capacity. He had been drinking but his mind was clear. Only the pain was dulled. Logan was ready to do anything to save his wife. James had been telling himself that in the hope that he could still a growing sense of doubt. Logan wouldn't sacrifice her, no matter what he had to do. It was irrelevant that they were breaking up, that he was in love with someone else. He might be a ruthless bastard whom James disliked as a person, but he wouldn't hesitate. He went back into the room and poured another whisky. He didn't think of going to bed. He had to get drunk before he fell asleep in the chair.

The window mesh was taken down by the Algerian who had driven them from the airfield. He didn't look at her and he didn't speak. He prized the wire away from its battens on the wall, picked up his tools, spat as he passed Eileen and went out, locking the door. She ran to the window. Now she was able to lean out and to see the distance from the sea below. She could have wept with disappointment. The villa was built on a rocky protuberance. Down below her was a sheer wall of rock and then a jagged outcrop, round which the sea foamed and battered in a powerful undercurrent. She waited, trying to judge the exact footage to the ground. It was obviously beyond knotted bedsheets and a jump into the sea. Peters had known what he was doing when he had the protective mesh taken down.

She pulled herself up and leaned further out, looking for anything which might serve as a hold if she tried to climb down. She didn't hear him come up behind her. He caught her by the waist and dragged her back into the room. She twisted round, struggling, and he pinned her arms behind her. For a brief moment they faced each other and Eileen felt the impact of his body.

'What the hell were you doing?' Peters said. He moved her away from the window. She was breathless and he was holding her tighter than was necessary. He let her go suddenly. 'What were you doing leaning out like that?'

Eileen faced him defiantly.

'Looking down,' she said.

'You won't get out that way,' Peters said. 'There's not a toe hold and it's fifty feet, so forget it. Otherwise I'll have the wire back on.'

'How do you know I won't jump out?' she said.

Peters looked at her.

'I don't,' he said. 'That's up to you. All you have to do is wait.'

She turned away from him.

'I'm going mad shut up in here,' she said. 'Isn't there any way I could have some exercise?'

'No,' he said. He pointed to the bed. 'I brought you some books. Try reading.'

There were three books, the biggest she recognized as a best seller, written by one of the popular purveyors of sex and sensation.

'You've told me nothing,' Eileen said. 'Hasn't my husband been contacted?'

He lit a cigarette.

'I guess so.'

'But you've no news? Or you just won't tell me!'

He saw her turn quickly away and realized that she was crying. She had lost a lot of weight; he noticed that when he held her. She had felt very slight. She looked as if she were sleeping badly and often the trays came back with most of the food untouched. He had said so to Madeleine, who disgusted him by suggesting that she be left to starve for a few days as a hint not to sulk. When he came in and saw her at the window, he had thought for a second that she was going to jump. Ten days could be a long time when you were a prisoner. He remembered the times he had been in jail himself.

Eileen turned and faced him; she wiped her eyes.

'Has he said anything? I can't believe there's no news.'

'So far as I know,' Peters said, 'he's negotiating.'

'Negotiating?' Eileen got up slowly. 'I don't understand. What have you asked him for? Why couldn't he just say yes?'

'Why don't you take a look at those books,' Peters said. 'You'll know when there's any news. And don't go hanging out of that window again.'

She picked up the second book and the third. A travelogue about an expedition to Katmandu and a novel by someone whose name she didn't know.

'Do you want anything?' Peters said.

'I haven't a change of clothes,' she said. 'I feel filthy dirty. I haven't even a toothbrush.'

'Madeleine will get some things for you,' he said. 'I'll tell her.' She didn't look up at him.

'Thank you for the books.'

'There wasn't anything else in English. Except some smut magazines. I didn't think you'd want those.'

He left and she heard the door lock.

Negotiating. It was a word she had heard Logan use so often. Dealing, bargaining, pulling something off. Negotiating with the terrorists. She had a vision of him sitting in his office off Cheapside behind the tycoon sized desk with its batteries of telephones and intercoms, negotiating for her life. Giving a little, holding something back; going through the business routine while she waited in the stuffy little room, with people who were under orders to kill her if he didn't give way to their demands. It was an unfortunate word for Peters to use. It explained the ten days without a decision. She couldn't believe it. Logan must know that she was in mortal danger; he had no way of knowing that she was not being ill-treated, kept in some hole underground. But, she reminded herself, her reaction was hysterical. In all cases of kidnapping and hi-jacking and all the other modern means of extortion by terror, negotiations had to take place. As to how the money was paid. In what denomination. How the hostage would be released. It always took time. A little time, but not ten days, for the love of God. She remembered Logan in moments of crisis. They had been in Paris, in the apartment on the Rue St Dominique when the Arab sheikdoms stopped their oil exports to the West. She had seen Logan with his back to the wall then. They had been entertaining when he got the news of the sheiks' action. It was in the middle of a cocktail party in their elegant drawing room, with the Austrian ambassador and his wife as guests of honour and some of the most influential people in French political and industrial life as their guests. Logan had been called to the telephone. When he came back, he walked over to her, smiled and suggested they should select a few friends to dine at Maxim's afterwards. It was not until they came home at one in the morning, after a successful dinner party and a brief visit to Régine's fashionable night club, that Logan had told her what had happened.

'They've shut off the oil,' he said. 'The bastards have got us by the short hairs.'

'What can you do?' she had asked him.

'Negotiate,' was his answer. 'Deal with them, give as little as possible and hope to Christ they back off.'

He had gone to bed with her that night, made love and fallen instantly asleep.

She wondered whether he had taken the news of her abduction with the same ruthless calm. She picked up the sex novel and it fell open as always at a well-handled page full of graphic sexual details. She didn't mean to read it. It brought Peters to her mind. There had been a moment while he was pulling her away from the window, when there was something sexual in the way he held her. She had felt it instinctively and fought against him. He had let her go so quickly that it was an indication that he too was aware of it and had been taken by surprise. She tried to close the memory out of her mind. It frightened and disturbed her; it added a dimension of danger to the already terrifying situation of her captivity. He reminded her of a powerful animal; he moved very quietly and he gave the impression of tremendous force, ready to be let loose. She had seen the ugly, merciless side of him when she was kidnapped. It was unrealistic to forget that because he had shown her a little humanity and brought her a few books. Whatever had flared up between them because of the rough physical contact, it had to be forgotten, buried. She had to think of Logan, rely on him to rescue her. He wouldn't gamble with her life; he wouldn't wheel and deal with organized terror. It had been wrong to doubt him and lose faith. She picked up the book on mountaineering and began to read it. The Algerian brought her food that evening and she didn't see Peters again for two days. When he did come, he brought Madeleine with him.

He hadn't told her the reason; it didn't seem necessary to explain. He unlocked the door and Madeleine walked through it. Eileen was sitting in the upright chair; she alternated between the bed and the chair, trying to read, sometimes just dozing in the heat. When it was cool, in the early morning, she walked up and down the narrow space between the walls, trying to exercise. When she saw the Lebanese girl she got up.

'Well,' Madeleine said. 'She looks all right to me.' She turned to Peters. Her manner was aggressive. 'All this about her not eating – I don't see anything wrong with her!' She looked at Eileen with open hatred. She had expected to find her cowed and dishevelled. Instead she was in full control of herself and her look of contempt was stinging.

'Why have you come here,' Eileen said. 'Keep out. I'll have nothing to do with you!'

'You shut your mouth,' Madeleine shouted at her. She swung round to Peters. 'Are you going to let her talk to me like that?'

He looked angry; the spectacle of Madeleine bristling like a cat annoyed him. He wasn't going to tolerate a scene between two hostile women. He had expected Madeleine to show more self-control.

'Shut up, both of you,' he said.

Eileen looked at him.

'That creature would have murdered my child,' she said. 'I'm going into the bathroom until she gets out of my room.'

It was Madeleine who moved, blocking the way.

'You do as you're told, you "trainee" or by Allah I'll deal with you!'

Eileen stood still; the other girl's fists were opening and closing; she was coiled like a spring, waiting to lash out at her. She turned and walked back to the chair. She spoke to Peters.

'What do you want?'

'You said you wanted clothes,' he said. 'Madeleine – for

Christ's sake, stop behaving as if you were in a bazaar brawl!'

'How dare you say that to me?' she blazed at him in Arabic. 'Didn't you hear her insult me?' She turned to Eileen. 'As for you,' she said, 'remember one thing. Your husband isn't in any hurry to redeem you. Maybe he doesn't want you back. And when we know for certain, Madame, I shall be the first to come and see Resnais do his job. And you can guess what that is, can't you?' She put her head back and laughed. 'We'll see how high and mighty you are then!'

Peters came up to her. He gripped her arm and it hurt.

'Go downstairs,' he said. 'Go on. Get out! I'll talk to you later.'

He hurried her to the door and pushed her outside. She slammed it after her. He put a slip of paper and a pencil down on the chest of drawers.

'Make a list of what you want,' he said. 'Just the necessities. I'll see she gets them for you. And don't take any notice of what she said.'

'He hasn't answered, has he?' Eileen said. 'It's two weeks now and I'm still here.'

'I told you not to listen to her,' Peters said angrily. 'She hates you and she'd say anything.'

She looked up at him.

'Is that Frenchman the executioner?'

'Get on and make the list,' he almost shouted at her. He went over to the window and looked out while she wrote. He was furious with Madeleine. She reminded him of a wild animal when she spat the threat at Eileen Field and taunted her with Logan Field's delay. It had been cruel and spiteful and these were qualities that repelled him in a woman. Of the two women, it was their prisoner who had come out best in the exchange. He wished above all that Madeleine hadn't told her about Resnais.

Eileen came up behind him.

'Here it is,' she said.

He brushed against her as he turned. She stepped back quickly.

'Don't let her come up here again,' she said quietly. 'Please.'

He went without answering. He found Madeleine waiting on the terrace. She had a drink in her hand and she was sullen, the explosive temper only just under control. He gave her the piece of paper.

'Go into Nice tomorrow and buy those,' he said.

She took it from him, looked at it for a moment and then threw it in a crumpled ball onto the terrace floor.

'Clothes! Toothbrushes and soap and all the little luxuries? Have you gone mad? I'll see her damned in hell before I get her any of them!'

'I am responsible for her. You'll buy them,' Peters said, 'and that's an order.'

'Oh no, it's not,' Madeleine shouted. 'You've just gone soft! Madame has everything brought up on trays – you come telling me she isn't eating – what does it matter if the bitch starves! She has to have a change of clothes – where is she, in a luxury hotel? What do you think happens to our women in Israeli prisons? What's got into you, Peters? You stood and let her insult me, instead of smashing her face in to teach her some manners! Do you fancy her for yourself? Is that what it is?'

He slapped her sharply across the face. She didn't flinch and no tears came into her eyes. She called him a name in Arabic.

'I won't do it,' she said. 'And you can't make me! Get them yourself!'

That night he moved out of her room. She hadn't believed it at first when she came upstairs and found he had left her. She loved him and she was wild with jealousy because her instincts detected that he was losing interest in her and that however she exerted herself to please him in bed, her hold on him had weakened. Now it had gone altogether. She looked at the empty bed and though the physical blow hadn't made her cry, she did so then. She was too proud to go after him, although she padded down the passageway until she saw a light under one of the unused bedroom doors and knew he had moved in there. He had left her and she knew it was because of their quarrel and her refusal to buy a few necessities for Eileen Field. She saw his concern as weakness; while he talked about responsibility, Madeleine dismissed this as an attempt to delude her as well as himself. He had never felt responsible for an enemy before. He hadn't shown the same softness towards the stewardess in the airliner, who had lain bleeding from a bullet wound in the back, or for the terrified passengers.

Only for this woman, this hostage taken against a vicious capitalist plot to undermine the Arab strength; for a representative of the class he was supposed to hate and had sworn to annihilate. Smooth hands and skin, rich clothes, a house with servants and luxuries. Madeleine had burst out of similar circumstances, eager to prove herself by hard work and rough living, proud that she was as capable as any man. For a woman like Eileen Field she reserved her most brutal contempt. Peters should have felt the same. He should have been repelled by a useless parasite whose only value was in her relationship to one of the capitalist tyrants they were dedicated to destroy. She couldn't understand or forgive his tolerance towards the prisoner. The only explanation for it was so painful that it throbbed like a wound. He was attracted to her. Perhaps he didn't realize it, or wouldn't have admitted it, but Madeleine knew. Something about that woman had touched a responsive feeling in him. If it were purely sexual, it would have been tolerable. Rape wouldn't have worried Madeleine; she wouldn't have objected if her man had satisfied an urge to have the woman and then kill her. But it was more than that. She was a person to him. She had feelings, needs. She went back to her room and wondered how she could risk showing Peters that he was betraying himself and everything they both believed in. Even if she did, she couldn't be sure to get him back. But at least she had to try.

They were eating lunch on the terrace. It was prepared by the surly Algerian who seldom spoke except to Madeleine. Resnais had spent the morning swimming. He was in a mischievous mood. The atmosphere between Peters and the girl was tense and this irritated him. The villa was beautiful, the food and wine very good, and the weather magnificent. His thoughts were not occupied by anything except occasional anxiety for his dog in Paris and he intended phoning through to make sure it was all right. He decided to pass the time by goading the Lebanese girl. If she hadn't been so jealous of Peters and the hostage, she might have been pleasant to him. He knew Peters had left her room.

He had been days without a woman and it would be a nuisance having to pick one up from outside. He knew Peters would forbid it if he found out.

'Why don't we go into the town this evening?' he said to Madeleine. 'If Peters will spare you for an hour.'

'She can go,' the American said. 'I've no objection.'

'Why don't we all go?' Madeleine said. 'We've been shut up here for too long. It's getting on our nerves.' She glanced at her lover; it was a plea for reconciliation. She saw that he had completely ignored it; he didn't even look up at her. Anxiety made her persist. 'We could go and have dinner somewhere. We don't have to sit here playing nursemaid. Ahmed can keep watch on her. Let's have a little fun tonight.' She leaned over and laid her hand on Peters's arm. She loved him so much that it was a pain and she wanted him more than ever before. 'Please,' she said, not caring that Resnais was watching them, 'let's go together.'

'You go,' Peters said coldly. He moved his arm and her hand slid off. 'I'm not leaving her to some goon like Ahmed. We're here to do a job.'

'He's right,' Resnais said. 'Just suppose Ahmed felt lonely and decided to pay the lady a visit . . . You come out with me, Madeleine. Peters can watch over her.'

It was a cunning choice of words. Madeleine reacted as if she had trodden on a snake.

'Watch over is right,' she snapped. She spoke to Resnais. 'You know the wire's been taken off her window? I saw it the day before yesterday. Isn't that crazy?'

'I didn't know that,' Resnais said. He looked at Peters. 'Why?' He asked the question softly; the situation was no longer amusing him. 'Isn't that dangerous?'

'No,' the American said. 'There's a fifty-foot drop to the rocks. She was half-suffocated in there.'

'How do you know she won't throw herself out?' Resnais said. 'I think you should have consulted us about this. The wire should be put back.'

'She shouldn't be up there at all,' Madeleine broke in. 'I've said from the beginning. . .'

'I know what you've said,' Peters interrupted. 'Just because it's a woman and you've got some spite against her. From now on, Madeleine, you'll keep your mouth shut about how she's to be treated. Otherwise I'll shut it for you.' He turned to Resnais. 'You're right about the wire; I should have told you.

But I'm in charge of the operation and responsible for her safety. You can take my word, she won't escape. Or try to jump out. She's not the type.'

The Frenchman shrugged.

'If you're satisfied.'

They separated for the afternoon; Madeleine, sullen and silent, went to the rocks to sunbathe, Peters called for the car and went out, and Resnais lounged in the shade in the garden. The situation was no longer funny. Now there was friction between the three of them, with himself and the Lebanese girl drawing together in opposition to the American. He had never worked with Peters before but he knew his reputation. The girl was typical of the fanatic Arab female; so far as he was concerned she was wasted out of bed. He despised liberated women. A man like Peters was only effective because he was immune to human weakness. And that included small humanities like removing a safeguard because it was making their prisoner uncomfortable. He remembered the hi-jacking of the Lufthansa, the world headlines over the deliberate killing of the steward and the photographs of the shot stewardess and passengers being taken by stretcher from the aircraft. Peters and Madeleine had been responsible for that; there were stories about the American's activities in Chile, which were chilling enough to be legends. Now he and the girl were falling out over Eileen Field. Their relationship was disrupted and their common loyalty didn't bind them.

He stretched in the lounging chair, raising his arms above his head. Up there, on the first floor, was the cause. Peters hadn't let him go near her since they arrived. She had something, that was evident. He had felt it when he sat near her in the plane and murmured that he was going to look after her. It had amused him to frighten her. She was the class of woman with whom he felt sadistic. He had a mistress in Marseilles who was refined and well-educated; it excited them both when he debased and abused her. He didn't share Madeleine's personal motives but he wouldn't have objected in the least to keeping the wife of the chairman of Imperial Oil in a cellar which was underground and haunted by rats. He had never felt that the rich deserved anything else. He couldn't see her window; it was hidden by the pine trees. He wondered what it was about her that was turning Peters into a human being. The American wouldn't like it but he felt he should go and see for himself.

The telex came through from Paterson in Tokyo; Logan had been in the office for an hour when it arrived. Janet was with him. He had phoned as he promised and she sensed the same tension. She didn't make the common feminine mistake of asking what was wrong a second time. She met him at the office, not as mistress but as a colleague. Whatever was worrying him, he wasn't ready to tell her about it and the worst thing she could have done was to press for answers.

Janet thought of herself as a cool woman; even admitting that she loved Logan, she insisted on her individuality and freedom from dependence. She was surprised at the extent to which his off-key attitude had shaken her. She hadn't slept and it needed a real effort to assume her executive personality. Surprise gave way to irritation, not with Logan but with herself. Loving a man was one thing, but to be tempted into an emotional scene was a weakness she couldn't excuse. If he had a problem, he would discuss it when he was ready. Equally she could have reserved some crisis in her life from him.

When the telex arrived, Logan got up and came over to her. 'It looks as if the Japanese are ready to come in! Listen. "Deputy Prime Minister Tomo Funasaka requests your presence at conference with Prime Minister to discuss possible financing of project. Signs extremely encouraging; importers meeting again today. Suggest you arrive Tokyo day after tomorrow. Paterson." If that bloody Scot says anything's extremely encouraging, it must be in the bag!'

He threw his arm round Janet and suddenly the strain was gone. They were together; she understood the meaning of that telex in terms of Imshan and he could feel the same excitement in her.

'Darling,' he said, 'isn't it great – I feel sure we're going to work something out now. Do you want to come out with me?'

'Just try and leave me behind!' she said. 'I wouldn't miss it for the world.'

Logan switched on the intercom. His Iranian secretary came through.

'Send in Mr Kelly and Mr Phillipson right away.'

He turned back to Janet. Her response had been just right. She loved the game as much as he did.

'If I can get them to agree to a government loan in return for a guaranteed supply of oil, we can make up the total cost of building their bloody refinery without cutting too deep into our own profit margin. I reckon we'll just be able to do it.'

'Are you going to inform London?' Janet asked him.

'No,' Logan said, 'I'm not going to tell anyone, except Kelly, Phillipson and you. And I don't want Khorvan getting a sniff of it either. Otherwise he'll dream up something else by the time I get back. You make the bookings for us, darling. I don't trust the staff here. Ah, come in James – Phillipson – sit down. We've got some good news.'

Kelly had a hangover; he ignored Janet and sat watching Logan. Confidence, authority, a controlled excitement. He had completely lost the look of drawn apprehension since last night. For a moment, disorientated by a blinding headache, Kelly imagined that the good news he was about to hear concerned Eileen.

'This is the telex that's just come in from Ian Paterson.' Logan passed it to James. He read it and without speaking handed it to Phillipson, the deputy resident director. He heard an exclamation of approval. Logan was addressing them.

'Tomo Funasaka is supposed to be the policy maker. If he supports something, the Prime Minister usually goes along. I'm going out immediately and taking Janet with me. I believe this has to be kept as quiet as possible, so she's making the bookings outside the office and I don't want anyone in the building to know where I've gone. As far as they're concerned I've taken off for a week.'

'What about London, sir?' Phillipson asked.

'Say nothing,' Logan said. 'I'll telex them from Tokyo when I've got some kind of a deal going. It may take a few days.'

James didn't contribute anything and Logan didn't seem to notice. The discussion was brief and he heard Janet making suggestions about revised cash-flow projections. It was a concert of voices, coinciding with the hammers in his head. Phillipson making the right noises, but not contributing too much. He knew how to handle men like Logan. There'd be a future for him with Imperial Oil. And the woman, with her masculine mind, playing the asexual role. Logan, generating his own excitement at the prospect of turning Khorvan's attack on them into a triumph. He was leaving Tehran immediately to conduct negotiations with the Japanese. On his own admission he could be away some days, a loose term which could encompass up to two weeks. Logan was dismissing them. James got up.

'Could I see you for a minute – in private?'

'Yes. Janet – you don't mind, do you?'

She smiled at Logan and went out of the office. Kelly faced Logan. He genuinely didn't know why Kelly wanted to speak to him alone. It was incredible, but quite true. He had forgotten about his wife.

'You have an appointment with Homsi today,' James said. 'What happens to that? What happens to Eileen while you're in Japan?'

Logan didn't hesitate. His mind switched direction. James could see it happening.

'I'll see Homsi as arranged. I'm going to contact him this morning and fix a meeting. If there's anything immediate to be done, then you can handle it for me. My guess is, we'll have quite a negotiation on our hands.'

'Would you mind telling me which negotiation you have in mind?' Kelly lit a cigarette. His headache seemed to be improving.

Logan leaned back in his chair.

'Both, if you want me to spell it out. And I might as well spell out a few other things. I am going to do everything to get Eileen released. Whatever they want, I'll give them. You asked me a question last night. I thought you were pissed so I let you get away with it. You asked if I'd pay the price, no matter what. I said yes and I'm saying it now. Though why it's any of your bloody business, I'm not sure. I'm seeing Homsi today and then I'm going to Tokyo. Nobody else can go instead, it's got to be me. Everything depends on it. Without a Japanese deal we can pack up and go home and leave Imshan to the Russians. While I'm away, you handle the ransom, whatever it is. I may be back in a few days. Is that clear?'

James got up; he put out his cigarette in the ashtray on Logan's desk.

'Perfectly clear. You go off on business and leave me to bargain for Eileen's life. Most people wouldn't do it for you. But I will. I'll do anything and everything I can for her while you fart around Tokyo looking after fucking Imperial Oil. And you'll have my resignation this afternoon. If there's one thing I won't work for, it's a prize shit like you.'

'You're in love with her,' Logan said. 'So you ought to be glad of the chance. Now get out of my office. I've got work to do.'

When the door closed, it slammed. Logan swore, not so much at Kelly, but at the circumstances. He had realized the situation with Kelly when he heard about the call to Ireland. It hadn't disturbed him because beside the issue of Eileen's disappearance it was unimportant. But he had stood there, accusing him, and suddenly making Logan defend himself. To himself. A prize shit. That had stung; the contempt implicit in the term had stung him even more.

Kelly thought he should stay and negotiate with Homsi. But this was unrealistic; he had no doubt about that. He was going to hear the kidnappers' terms and set the deal in motion, leaving Kelly to tie it up. At the worst he was a telex away and a plane flight if he was needed. But nobody else could sit round the table with the Japanese government and secure investment backing which would give Imperial access to the richest oil-field in the world. If it was a question of priorities, and this was the essence of Kelly's condemnation of him, then he insisted he had got them right. He wouldn't help Eileen by sitting in Tehran; if he delayed, the Japanese would take offence and the seriousness of their approach would be questioned. There was nothing else he could do but go. Nothing.

He told his secretary to get him the Syrian Embassy. A moment later he was speaking to Homsi. He arranged to meet him in the Bank of Iran where the State treasures were on display. It was suggested by the Syrian as a place where they could meet without being conspicuous. There were always crowds of tourists looking at the Iranian crown jewels. He hung up before he could be asked a question. Logan called for coffee and settled down to work. He never found it difficult to close one problem out and concentrate upon another. The telex from his finance director had driven Eileen out of his mind; she would have remained in the background until it was time to see Homsi, not because he was inhuman or unconcerned about her, but because for thirty years his business had always had first claim. It was as much a reflex as a decision that booked for Japan, regardless of other responsibilities. It had never occurred to him to do otherwise, until James Kelly questioned it. And now the question was in his mind and he was having to fight to answer it. He couldn't think clearly and he pushed his work aside. He was going to Japan. That was an irreversible decision. He wouldn't permit Kelly to make him feel guilty to the extent of changing that. But until he had seen the Syrian he couldn't apply his full concentration to anything else. He had to know what they wanted. Then he could agree to it. Having agreed, he could go to Tokyo without scruples. James Kelly could set what was needed in motion. And he wouldn't take the resignation seriously. Kelly was in an emotional state. When he had something to do towards helping her, he would regain his perspective. The terms were sure to be political and, God damn it, as Logan excused himself, Kelly was an ex-diplomat who was ideal as an intermediary until he got back. But it seemed a long morning till he was ready to take the car to the Bank on Ferdowsi Avenue.

# 7

Peters had never bought clothes for a woman before. He hesitated outside the little boutiques, which were all that Nice offered. The toilet articles were easy. He had been pressured into buying a bottle of cologne by the assistant in the chemist's shop; he had a hairbrush, comb, a plastic bag with a toothbrush and paste and a sponge. He disliked strong scent but the cologne, which he hadn't wanted to buy, was fresh and clean. He remembered how hot that upstairs bedroom was. Even without the mesh over the window, it caught the full afternoon sun. Perhaps the cologne was a good idea. Inside a boutique, he caused confusion by asking for a size twelve in a dressing gown; there was a long caftan which would be useful and this was finally wrapped for him, the French sizing having been established. He found a blouse and a light cotton dress which weren't too expensive, and went back to the car. He had been disgusted by the prices; the sales girls irritated him by their attempts to foist things on him which were unsuitable. He drove back feeling resentful and suspicious that in some way he had made a fool of himself and that everything he had bought was too expensive and wouldn't fit. He couldn't excuse Madeleine's attitude to Eileen Field; it showed her in a mean and spiteful guise which literally repelled him. He didn't want to sleep with her again. He regretted having done so in the first place. She had been a comrade-in-arms then, an equal in the struggle against a capitalist world. He had admired her courage and relied upon her in the hi-jacking enterprise. She hadn't disappointed him. There was no reason why her exceptional qualities should fall away on this mission, leaving a jealous, quarrelsome virago, except that women were generally unreliable and he had been a fool to think she wouldn't prove to be the same. He was in charge of the mission and he needed full cooperation from Resnais as well as from Madeleine. The Frenchman's apparent acceptance of his explanation for removing the mesh from Eileen Field's window hadn't deceived Peters. Resnais didn't like it; he resented not being told and Madeleine had put a suspicion into his mind that Peters was being soft. He eased the accelerator back and the car slid to the roadside. He stopped, found a cigarette and lit it. He was the leader and it was his job to unite the other two behind him. Resnais could be mollified and, if Madeleine could divorce herself from personal relationships with him, he believed she would stop making trouble. Otherwise he would have her recalled. Finishing his cigarette, Peters decided that this might prove to be the proper course, but he had to give her a chance. To be fair to her too. He started the car and drove back to the villa.

Madeleine found Resnais in the hall. She had come in from the rocks; her body was gleaming with sun oil and sweat and tanned a deep brown; the bikini showed big breasts, a little waist and stocky thighs.

'It's nearly as hot as home,' she said.

The Frenchman had one hand on the stair rail and a foot on the lowest step.

'Where are you going?'

Resnais's foot came back to the level.

'I've been thinking about that window. People have been known to climb down bed sheets. I thought I'd go upstairs and look.'

'I'll come with you,' she said.

'I think you should wait here,' Resnais said. 'I want to have a look around. It would be better if he didn't come and find us both in with her. You stay and keep a watch for him.'

Madeleine looked at him.

'You don't trust him?'

'Do you? Isn't that why you're fighting all the time – because you don't like his attitude to the lady?'

'I'm not jealous!' Madeleine raised her voice, 'I wouldn't be jealous of that miserable, stupid. . .'

'Don't shout,' Resnais said quietly. 'You are jealous, my

dear Madeleine, and I respect your instincts. She has changed your man towards you and I don't blame you for being suspicious. So I am going up to take a look at the window. And at her. If there is something between them, maybe I will find out.'

'How?' Madeleine asked him. He stepped on the stair again. 'I may decide to ask her,' he said. 'You stay and keep Peters away till I come down.'

'She'll tell him,' the girl said. 'Don't cross him, Resnais. He's not safe to cross.'

'She'll do what she's told,' Resnais said. He began to walk up the staircase. 'I have a way with ladies. She won't say a word.'

Eileen had fallen asleep; the popular novel lay on the bed, turned downward. The sun was flooding the room and the heat was at the high peak of the afternoon. When Resnais unlocked the door he did so very quietly. It didn't wake her. She was stretched out on the bed, wearing a thin silk petticoat, one hand laid across the cover of the book. He closed the door, transferred the key to the inside and locked it. Then he walked very softly over to the bed. The petticoat was damp with sweat and it clung to her, showing the nakedness underneath.

Madeleine's brown, voluptuous body, almost nude in the flimsy bikini, hadn't aroused him. The pale skin, the slender line of arm and thigh, sheathed in pure silk, with hand-made lace framing both breasts, turned him suddenly hot. He lowered himself onto the bed beside her and, as she woke, he closed his hand over her mouth.

'Good afternoon, Madame,' he said. 'We're going to have a little talk.'

'I know,' Saiid Homsi said, 'how much this means to your company. But after all – it is your wife's life at stake.'

Logan Field had his back to the huge display case. He had made many trips to Tehran and never thought of visiting the crown jewels. He had never been interested in sight-seeing; his collection of antiquities was purely for investment.

'I can't do it,' Logan said. 'By Christ I won't do it!'

There was a subdued glitter in the low electric lights around them, a reflection of thousands of diamonds and precious stones.

Show cases aflame with crowns, tiaras, necklaces, were ranged through the exhibition rooms, deep in the bowels of the Bank of Iran. The men who had kidnapped Eileen Field might just as well have demanded the contents of the treasure vault in hard cash.

'Mr Field,' Saiid said, 'I know this seems impossible. But don't give me your answer now. Think about it. Think what it will mean to your wife if you refuse.'

Directly in front of Logan, protected by bullet-proof glass, was a case containing a huge solid gold globe of the world, completely encrusted with diamonds, rubies and emeralds. There were no sapphires to denote the seas; the stones were considered unlucky by the Persians. Why couldn't it have been money? Every penny, every share, everything he possessed – why hadn't they asked for these . . .? But not Imshan. Not to give up one of the richest oil-fields in the world.

'I can't talk here,' he said suddenly. 'I've got to have time to think.'

'How much time?' the Syrian asked. 'These people are impatient. They want your promise. And they want proof that you are keeping it, otherwise. . .'

'You're asking the impossible,' Logan said. He moved away, pushing past a crowd who were gaping at the Shah's imperial crown. Its value was said to be a million pounds sterling. The Syrian threaded his way after him. Logan had moved to the exit when he caught up. He tugged at his sleeve.

'Give me an answer tomorrow,' he said. 'We can meet here again. In the same place.'

'I'll give it to you now,' Logan said. 'I can't do it. I can't pull my company out of the oil-field.'

The Syrian stood still. There was a grim look on the Englishman's face which worried him. He had expected protests, abuse, even threats, but it sounded as if Field had given a final answer. Saiid was blocking his way out.

'Mr Field,' he said and his voice dropped very low. 'There is something else I have to tell you. I hoped it would not be necessary. Unless you give me a favourable answer by tomorrow, your wife will suffer the loss of a finger. It pains me very much to tell you this. Please reconsider. Every succeeding day that you delay, she will be mutilated further. I don't think you would be happy to receive the evidence. Believe me, it's not an idle threat. I will telephone you in the morning.'

As Logan lunged towards him, he slipped to the side and hurried through the exit. The man whom Colonel Ardalan had detailed to follow him broke from the covering crowd and vanished after him.

People were staring at Logan Field. His attempt to grab the Syrian had been seen and one of the security police on guard in the vaults was on his way towards him. He leaned against the wall for a moment. Then he turned and began the climb up into the street. Outside, in the hot dusty air, he felt an urge to be sick. It was so strong that he grabbed for his handkerchief. The blue company Rolls was waiting by a corner and it began to sail towards him through the traffic. He got inside. He was due back in the office; there was a meeting with the chief consulting engineer and chief geologist. He was still feeling sick. For the first few minutes he didn't know where to go. Kelly's house was the first choice. Somewhere he could be alone; where he could vomit if he wanted to and then somehow face the reality of what had happened in the Bank vault.

Give up Imshan. Pull out of the negotiations with the Iranian Government and go home. Recall his team and close down the exploration. Otherwise they would cut off Eileen's fingers one by one and send them to him.

He leaned towards the chauffeur. The partition was down.

'Go to the Hilton hotel. Then go back to the office and get Mrs Armstrong. Tell her I'm not feeling well. I must have eaten something.'

He had always made his decisions alone. He had decided, impromptu, in the vault, when he told the Syrian that he couldn't do what they had asked. At that moment, his mind had been made up, again by a reflex as natural to him as breathing. He couldn't deliberately sabotage Imperial Oil's interests; he couldn't wreck the chance of breaking the world oil price and saving Europe's economy, whatever the consequences. He had said it and meant it. But he had no defence against that last threat. He had stood alone all his life, neither wanting nor welcoming help. But now he needed it. And Janet, who loved him, was the only person who would do. He went up in the lift to her suite and as soon as he could reach the bathroom, he was sick. Then he poured himself a whisky and sat down to wait for her.

Saiid Homsi drove back to the Syrian Embassy. He was feeling optimistic. Just for a moment he had nearly lost the gamble. His intuitive sense, that most valuable asset to a man in his position, warned him that Logan Field was going to hold out. Threatening to mutilate the wife had been Saiid Homsi's idea and it had been employed at the crucial moment. Europeans had a horror of physical cruelty. To a people long accustomed to mutilation as a means of punishment, it meant nothing. In many sheikdoms thieves lost a right hand, traitors were castrated and blinded. But to the European it was unthinkable. He had been very clever to threaten Logan Field with that. It had probably done more to persuade him than any threat of death. Although no such arrangement had been made, Homsi felt the threat might have to be carried out. He had never favoured the plan to pressure Logan Field by kidnapping his child; he had favoured the outcome even less. He believed that kidnapping and negotiation were too complicated a method of avoiding the threat implicit in Imshan to the power of the Arab world.

He had not been present at the high-level meeting in Munich but he knew that his government had proposed an assassination attempt against the Shah as the surest way of stopping a European company getting their hands on the oil-field. As soon as Khorvan reported to his Russian contacts that the Shah was having talks with James Kelly, the organization had made its plans and set its spies to work. KGB intelligence had been a considerable help in finding out details of Logan Field's family life; his deep attachment to his child was well known. The preparations were made, Peters and his team were briefed, and the operation set in motion.

Syria had been obliged to agree; it was too dangerous to rely on assassination; there had been several attempts in the past, some masterminded by the Russians when the Communist party was outlawed in Iran, but because of the efficiency of Ardalan, none had come anywhere near success. The Shah was encircled by one of the most effective security services in the world. The only vulnerable target was the oil company.

Homsi ordered Turkish coffee and began composing his

report to Damascus. He emphasized Field's initial resistance, but his own view was optimistic; he felt that Field would collapse under the threat of his wife's mutilation. And if he were really hesitating, it might be necessary to show that they meant what they said.

By five o'clock that afternoon, Colonel Ardalan was studying the surveillance report on Saiid Homsi and the companion report on Logan Field. His dismissal of James Kelly's explanation was correct. The story was a lie, concocted out of panic. Whatever the attaché in the Syrian Embassy wanted with Logan Field, it wasn't to sell him stolen manuscripts. The choice of the imperial treasure exhibition showed the true professional touch of Saiid Homsi. A crowded place, where nobody would notice a European and a Syrian in conversation. Ardalan's man had seen the incident when Field apparently tried to strike Homsi. He must have said something very unpleasant to provoke a public loss of self-control from somebody like Logan. Field had left looking ill; he hadn't gone to Kelly's house where he was staying, but to his assistant's suite in the Hilton hotel. She had been brought from the office in the middle of a meeting to join him there.

Ardalan read through the reports and spent some time thinking quietly afterwards. He had switched his intercom to 'off'. Logan Field was a very important man in the Western world. His chairmanship of the big oil company made him a target for intrigue. He was engaged in tight negotiations in Iran at that time and the outcome of these negotiations could have a vital effect upon the political and economic future of the West. Ardalan understood from the Shah that provided the terms were satisfactory Imperial Oil would get the concession. And yet the Russian technical team, with a spearhead of negotiators, was still in Tehran. Therefore they must believe that the door was still open to them. And that pointed to Khorvan. None of this could be linked to Logan Field's encounter with Saiid Homsi. Syria was not involved with Imperial Oil in any way. Its only record as far as the company was concerned was in organizing the destruction of sections of desert pipeline during the first Israeli war.

So why had the Syrian contacted Logan Field? And why

was the Syrian visiting an American amateur archaeologist, whose telephone number was in the pocket of a murdered man? A humble man, a talker round the coffee shops, but a friend of dissidents, and by coincidence hovering round Logan Field at that reception for the Minister. If it were coincidence...

What had begun as a puzzle without pieces was taking on a shape. One thing was certain. Whatever the reason motivating the Syrian government in anything they undertook, it was never in the best interests of Iran. If they had contacted Logan Field, it must be for a purpose that was injurious to the Shah and the country in some way.

Ardalan sent for his assistant Sabet. He offered him a cigarette and showed him the two reports. When he had finished reading them, he asked the assistant his opinion. Sabet hesitated. He didn't want to make a mistake. The Colonel wouldn't forget a hasty or ill-considered view.

'I think,' he said, 'that Logan Field is being pressured by Homsi. Whether this is personal or through the oil company, I don't know.'

Ardalan nodded. 'I think so too. But it's unlikely to be personal blackmail. Homsi is acting for his government. If he is putting pressure upon Logan Field, then Syrian policy is guiding him. We have to know why, in case it concerns us.'

'And you think it does?'

'Yes,' Ardalan nodded again, 'yes, I do. Homsi is involved with an American who is also somehow connected with that waiter at the Hilton who was murdered. The American worried me as much as Homsi. We've had him checked by Interpol. Nobody knows anything about him. He came through Munich at a time when there was a terrorist conference taking place there. There is no proof that he was connected with it in any way. He stayed at a hotel, went sight-seeing, left for Tehran and went to work at Persepolis from time to time.'

He paused and looked at Sabet, his eyes narrowed.

'But I know he was in Munich for that conference. I feel it here.' Ardalan tapped his chest above the heart. 'I can't say this, because it is only my instinct that tells me. I cannot say what I would like to say. Not yet. I have to add more pieces to my puzzle so that it makes some kind of picture. I have to be patient for a little longer and hope that something more comes to hand. Another little piece here and there. Just enough.'

He got up from his desk and Sabet did the same. The Colonel might treat his staff with informality but he didn't expect it to be returned.

'You can't go to His Majesty, then?' Sabet said.

'No, I cannot go to His Majesty with nothing but this.' He pointed to the reports. 'There is not enough there to justify the action I want to take. We will have to wait and watch a little longer. I am sure that my friend Mr Kelly knows exactly what is happening. But he will protect his chairman and the oil company. He will lie as he lied last night. However, I might talk to him.' He stretched and yawned. 'There is a reception at the French Embassy on Saturday. I will see him there.'

Janet sat on the arm of Logan's chair; her hand rested on his shoulder.

'My God,' she said, 'what are we going to do? It's like a nightmare.'

'I don't know.'

He passed his hand over his head, sweeping the hair backwards. He felt comforted by having her with him. She had taken the news calmly; he couldn't have borne an hysterical reaction. She had listened, sitting with her arm around him, got up and refilled the glass with whisky and waited until he had told her everything.

'There is no doubt about it?' That was her first question. 'They have got her?'

'No doubt at all. I'll have to meet their terms. There's no other way. Do you know, I haven't been sick for years...'

'I'm not surprised,' Janet said gently. She leaned down and kissed him. 'You've had a terrible shock. It'll take a little time to get over it. Drink your whisky.'

He had never associated her with tenderness; she wasn't a woman who wasted words or gestures. As a personality she had a diamond brightness; he didn't realize how much she had attracted him simply because she was the opposite of Eileen.

'I've got to work out what to do next,' he said. 'How to explain it to the Board. Christ, I *can't* explain it! It's all got to be done secretly.' He looked up at her. 'How do I pull my company out of Iran without a reason? Ten million spent on exploration. Six bloody months of work and negotiation. A deal coming to the boil in Tokyo. A major breakthrough in oil prices! I'm responsible to my Board – and to the shareholders. Leave aside the wider issues!'

'You can refuse to meet Khorvan's terms,' she reminded him. 'Without Japan you couldn't go ahead with Imshan anyway.'

'And let the bastard win,' Logan said. 'Let him pull the rug from under us.'

'I know you don't want to give in,' Janet said. She got up and took a drink for herself. She turned round and looked at him. 'At the moment you don't see any alternative. If you don't do what these people say, they're going to cut off Eileen's fingers and send them to you, one by one. That's the real threat, isn't it?'

'Yes,' Logan said. His head lowered for a moment. 'Yes. That finished me.'

'It would finish me too,' she said quietly, 'except that I don't believe they'd ever do it.'

The room was very quiet, except for the faint buzz of the air conditioning. Logan looked at her. She was very pale and the tinted silver hair emphasized this; she sipped her whisky.

'The people who've kidnapped Eileen don't go in for that kind of thing,' she said. 'They're fanatics; they're absolutely ruthless and they don't mind getting themselves killed. I won't argue for a moment that if you refuse to do what they want, they'll murder Eileen. But I don't believe they've ever mutilated any victim or ever will. Keeping the West out of the Imshan oil-fields is a massive political stratagem, master-minded from the top. This isn't some crackpot revolutionary movement leading a raid on a kibbutz. This is the Arab world, backed by the Russians. They can't afford to do anything like that to Eileen because of world opinion. Think, if an atrocity like that was known... It's a bluff, darling. Make up your mind what you're going to do, but don't take that into consideration. Homsi just said it to frighten you.' She went and sat down.

'What are you advising me?' He asked the question slowly. She was being practical and thinking clearly. He should have expected her to take an impersonal view.

'I wouldn't dare advise you,' she answered. 'How could I?

If I tell you to be tough, I might be thinking of myself. You'd never forgive me for it. I know that.'

He didn't deny it. He waited. Perhaps she sensed that everything between them was in the balance at that moment.

'So? What are you saying then?'

'Don't be angry with me,' Janet said. 'I'm trying to help you.'

To his amazement she turned to one side and began to cry. He came over to her.

'It's so horrible,' she said. 'So dreadful for you, facing this . . .'

'I've got to give him an answer tomorrow,' Logan said. 'It'll have to be yes. It'll give me time to think it through.'

He got up and brought back two cigarettes for them. He leaned forward, smoking. He had never seen Janet cry; it relieved him. At that moment he felt able to discuss his wife without excessive guilt.

'You wouldn't risk going to the police – Interpol? Surely they could start looking for her without the story leaking?'

'I suggested that to James,' Logan answered. 'He said it was too dangerous. He said I'd have to play it straight across the board with them, if I wanted her released. You know he's in love with her?'

'Then you must bear that in mind when he gives you advice,' she said. 'He'll only be thinking of Eileen; not you or the company. Darling, there's one awful possibility I think you've got to face, before you do anything drastic.'

'That something's already happened to her?'

'No,' Janet shook her head. 'No, I'm sure she's alive now. And probably quite well cared for. What I'm afraid of is that if you give in to them and back out of Imshan, they won't keep their part of the bargain. They'll have got what they wanted and there won't be any witness to stand up and say what happened. Or to identify them. That's what really frightens me.' She leaned towards him. 'I'd do anything to help Eileen,' she said, 'but I just don't see how they can ever let her go.'

'What you're saying,' Logan muttered, 'is that I could throw Imshan away for nothing – that I could play into the hands of Arab extremism by sabotaging Europe's interests, betray my own company, and incidentally finish my career, and Eileen is murdered anyway. Is that what you really think?'

'Yes,' she said, 'I'm afraid it is. I'm afraid she's a lost cause,

Logan. It's the most horrible thing I've ever had to say in my life, but I don't believe you'll ever see her again.'

The telephone rang. She got up to answer it.

'Yes,' she said. 'Hello, James – yes, he's here.' She covered the mouthpiece. 'He wants to talk to you,' she said.

'Tell him to come up,' Logan said. 'He'd better know the position. He's got to deal with Homsi while I'm in Japan.'

She held on to the telephone.

'You're still going then?'

'Yes,' Logan said.

She spoke to James Kelly.

'Come to the hotel,' she said. 'Logan wants to see you.' Then she said, 'What are you going to tell him?'

'The truth,' Logan answered. 'That Imshan is the price. And he's to hold them off while I'm away. This can't be a snap decision. There's too much at stake. Apart from Eileen.'

'You're going to be nice to me,' Resnais whispered. 'Like you are to the American.'

The woman underneath him was so terrified that he misjudged her. He took his hand off her mouth and ripped the flimsy petticoat away.

Madeleine had come to meet Peters as he got out of the car. He had been irritated but suppressed it. He saw her looking at the box with the boutique label on it, but she didn't comment. She put her hand on his arm to detain him and he decided not to shake her off. He had promised to be fair.

'Don't be angry with me,' she said. 'I'm sorry about last night. And today. I don't want to quarrel with you. Come to our room. Let me make it up to you.'

They had walked inside the house; it was cool and white after the outside glare.

'We've got to talk,' Peters said. 'Where's Resnais?'

'I don't know,' she said. 'Sleeping in the shade somewhere...'

The scream was faint but very clear. It rose for a few seconds, sharp with pure terror, and then stopped. Peters flung the girl aside and leapt up the stairs. One push established that Eileen's door was locked. He stepped back and threw his full weight against it. The lock burst. He saw Resnais getting up from the bed and he reached him before the Frenchman was fully on his feet. Peters grabbed him with the left hand, the right smashed sideways into his face. Resnais fell backwards, hitting a chair, which shattered under him as he collapsed on the floor. Peters pulled him upright; his mouth was split and pouring blood. He hit him again. Then he dragged him to the door and threw him into the passage. He shouted for Madeleine. She came running up the stairs. He saw the terror on her face and knew that she had been a party to the rape. She cringed physically as he came near her.

'Get him downstairs before I kill him,' Peters said. Then he kicked the broken door shut and went over to the bed.

No one had ever hurt Eileen; she had no experience of violence. It was unthinkable that a man should have held her down and inflicted agonizing pain on her. She had been stripped, assaulted. If Peters hadn't burst into the room, the Frenchman would have raped her. The shock was tremendous. Her vision swam as Peters bent over her. She was shivering violently and she reacted from pure instinct. She caught him round the neck and held on to him with all her strength, weeping hysterically. He lifted her and carried her into the room he used for himself. He put her into the bed and sat down, waiting for the fit of hysteria to wear itself out. He could feel the trembling in her body.

'Easy now,' he said, 'it's all over.'

'Oh, God,' Eileen whispered, 'don't leave me...please... don't leave me...'

'I won't,' Peters said. 'Tell me what happened.'

'I was asleep,' she said. 'I woke up and he was sitting on the bed. He had his hand over my mouth. He asked me if you were sleeping with me.'

She closed her eyes for a moment and then opened them wide as if she were seeing Resnais and not him.

'I wouldn't say yes,' she whispered. 'He wanted me to; he hurt me. He went on and on hurting me...on my breasts. I couldn't scream...'

Peters pulled down the bed sheet. She had small breasts, beautifully shaped. They were beginning to purple with bruises. The pain must have been agonizing.

'I didn't say it,' Eileen said. 'I wouldn't. Then he said if I told you he'd kill me. He was going to rape me...'

'Did Madeleine come with him?' Peters asked the question. 'Or Ahmed?'

She shook her head.

'No. Just him. I can't stop shaking.'

'You'll be all right now,' he said.

She looked very pale. She was badly shocked and the rigor that was part of it was making the bed shake. Resnais had tortured her to implicate him. He could imagine what he had done to her breasts while he held her mouth closed. He drew the sheet up and covered them.

'Why didn't you say what he wanted?'

'Because it wasn't true. We haven't.'

'No,' he said. 'We haven't. I'm going to get you a brandy and put some ice on your breasts. That'll help the pain.'

He went to the door and yelled for Ahmed. She heard him giving orders in Arabic. The man came up quickly with a glass of brandy and some ice cubes packed into a towel. Peters uncovered her. She made no effort to stop him. She lay and watched him while he wrapped the towel over her breasts. He lifted her while she sipped the brandy. He had held Andrew Barnes in his arms on the dirt and dust of Kent State campus, while the crowd fled for their lives and the acrid smell of gunfire was in the air.

There was no comparison between the dead teacher and Eileen Field; they held nothing in common except a brand of steadfast courage and the role of victim. What he was feeling for her at that moment was a disaster and he knew it. From the moment he brought her to the villa he had been trying not to see her as a person. Above all, as a woman. If Resnais hadn't attacked her as a woman, he might have succeeded.

'Stay quiet, Eileen,' he said. 'I'm going downstairs to deal with that bastard.'

It was the first time he had used her name.

Everything Logan said made sense. James couldn't fault the logic; he sat in the suite at the Hilton, drinking whisky and listening to Logan explaining the full implications of the terms demanded for Eileen's release. Janet Armstrong didn't contribute, but as he heard the arguments he detected her brand of frigid detachment. An easy attitude to take when it was Eileen

133

Field's life at stake. But she had been tactful enough to stay as a spectator in the background.

The company's withdrawal from Imshan was not a decision that Logan could take from personal motives, however strong. The consequences on all levels had to be considered.

James had just sat there, waiting. Logan looked grey and appreciably older. James hoped he felt as ill as he looked.

Imshan was not just vitally important to Imperial Oil. The reduction in oil price would contain the Arab stranglehold on oil for the Western world until oil started to flow from the North Sea and American technology developed new sources of energy. The political factors went far beyond the company's acquisition of rights in a massive oil-field or his own personal commitment to it. These considerations wouldn't have weighed against the threat to Eileen.

James watched him when he said it and didn't believe him. He was being less than honest because he was making a case. James put his whisky down.

If Imshan was developed by the Russians, then it would be a major political defeat for the West.

'There's no guarantee the French and Germans wouldn't get it,' James said, interrupting. 'The Shah doesn't want the Russians either, so it's only Imperial Oil that's the loser. That's what you really mean.'

'Please, James, be reasonable.' Janet spoke for the first time. 'Logan isn't going to abandon Eileen. He'd never do that. He's just trying to find some kind of compromise. He has other responsibilities too. We all have.'

'Speak for yourself,' he said. 'You know there's no compromise with these terrorists. You're just trying to justify letting them murder Eileen. I don't give a bugger about Imperial Oil or the economic situation or anything else.' He turned to Logan Field. 'I promise you one thing,' he said. 'If you let Eileen die, I'll make sure the truth gets out. I don't think there'll be many doors open to you after that. Either of you.'

He was on his way out when Logan stepped in front of him.

'Just wait a minute,' he said. 'All right, I give in to their demands. I pull out of Imshan. Never mind the consequences. Europe doesn't matter, the company doesn't matter, nothing matters but getting Eileen back alive – right?'

'Right,' James said bitterly.

'And then they kill her anyway. Have you thought of that?'

'They won't,' James said. 'They keep their bargains.'

'Not on this level,' Janet said behind him. 'They can't let her go and have the story come out. That's why they've insisted on secrecy! The world mustn't know how the West was blackmailed out of its oil. They'll promise and the minute the negotiations are wrecked beyond recall, they'll get rid of the star witness. My belief is they'll fix up some accident. Then nobody will believe Logan, even if he did try and tell the story. And let's face it, there wouldn't be much point. With Imshan gone and Eileen dead, he'd just ruin his own reputation for nothing. People would think he was covering for having lost the deal.'

'Christ Almighty,' James said slowly, 'you've got a lovely mind.'

'I'm thinking straight,' she said, 'because, believe it or not, I'm not emotionally involved. You and Logan are. In my view the only hope you've got of saving her is to go to the police. And in the meantime play along with Homsi. That's my advice to Logan.'

'I'm going to Japan tomorrow,' Logan said.

'To negotiate the loan,' James said. 'To go ahead no matter what.'

'To keep my bloody options open,' Logan suddenly shouted at him. 'And to make it look good. If I have to screw up the deal, I'll do it when I come back. And that's where you stop calling me and Janet names and take your own bloody finger out. You see Homsi tomorrow morning. Tell him I'm going to scuttle the talks with the Japanese Government. In the meantime he keeps contact with you. And you reassure him all along the line that we're pulling out. Convince him. Try and get a date set for her release. Keep talking.'

'And the police?' James said. 'If you bring them in, she's finished. Mind you, your reputation's safe then. You can stand up as the hero, trying to save his wife from the kidnappers, knowing the first word that leaks out pulls the trigger on her. Bloody clever, Janet. I hadn't thought of that!'

Logan opened the door.

'Get out,' he said.

When James Kelly had gone, she came up to him.

'I didn't mean it like that,' she said. 'You must believe me.'

'I know,' Logan said. 'You're trying to do the best you can. Jesus, I've never felt so tired in my life!'

'You go to bed,' Janet said. 'It's a long flight tomorrow and you've got to have a clear head. I think I should stay here and keep an eye on James. I wonder how long the affair's been going on?'

'What affair?' Logan said. 'What the hell do you mean? Eileen's never been to bed with anyone behind my back!'

'If you say so,' Janet shrugged. They were in the bedroom and he was pulling off his tie. 'But I don't see why you should mind if she had.'

Logan didn't answer. He kicked off his shoes and rolled onto the bed to try and sleep. An affair with James Kelly. Janet was right. There was no reason why he should mind if it were true. But he did. It took him a long time to go to sleep.

Resnais had loaded his revolver and was waiting for Peters. Madeleine was with him. She had stopped the bleeding, helped him to clean up and given him a brandy. He was sitting in the lounge facing the door and she was standing beside him. He had refused to take her advice and go off in the car, leaving her to talk to Peters. It was a brave offer and she rose in his estimation, because he knew she was shaking with fear of what the American would do to her. She had pulled on a shirt over the bikini, as if she felt that seeing her semi-nude would only incense him more against her.

'If he comes down and starts anything,' Resnais said, 'I'll shoot him. So keep out of the way!'

'Listen.' She knelt beside him quickly, all her feminine instincts of survival to the forefront. 'Listen, we can't afford to fight this out. You made a fool of yourself; all right, he beat you up! Ever since that bitch came here she's come between us. It's got to stop now. We have a job to do, Resnais, and instead we're falling out among ourselves. Peters won't attack you again.'

'He'd better not try,' the Frenchman said. His mouth was stiff and swollen. It hurt him to talk. He gripped the gun, hiding it down the side of the cushion. He waited, quivering and vicious like a wounded cat. As a boy his father had beaten him for laziness and stealing. Being small, and growing up in a tough district, he was a natural target for bullies. By the time he was twelve he had learned to use a knife and his threshold of provocation was very low. His graduation from petty crime to full-scale terrorism was not so much a political choice but a natural orbiting to the centre of violence.

'I'll kill him,' he repeated, and he was hoping for the excuse.

They heard Peters coming down the stairs, shouting for the Algerian. They heard him tell the man to go upstairs and keep watch outside the prisoner's room. Then he came through the doorway. He expected the Frenchman to be armed. He knew from his position in the chair, his right hand tucked into his side, that he was hiding a gun. Peters looked at him for a moment and then at Madeleine. He went to a side table, found a cigarette in one of the alabaster boxes, and lit it. He spoke directly to Resnais.

'I'm sending you both back to Damascus,' he said. 'I'll give you a break you don't deserve. I won't say why. I'll send the message through tonight. If either of you goes near her again, Ahmed'll put a bullet into you.'

'You can't send us back,' Madeleine said. 'They'll want to know the reason. We'll come under suspicion!'

'Too bad,' Peters said.

'You bastard,' Resnais said. 'You have her for yourself, eh? Nobody around to see? You are the one who should be taken off the mission!'

Madeleine looked at each of them. One was her lover, the other her comrade. Now much more than personal issues were at stake.

'Resnais was wrong,' she said, 'but it was your fault too. You took the wire off her window without consulting either of us, your comrades. Resnais didn't like it and I agreed with him. He went up to see if it was safe. What happened after was probably her fault.'

Peters looked at her; now it was she who had no identity.

'He tortured her,' he said, 'trying to cook something up against me. Our orders were to keep her safe until we were told different. She wasn't to be hurt. She told me you threatened to kill her, too. What would have happened to our mission then?'

'Let him explain,' Madeleine said. 'Please – we've worked and fought together. He's your brother-in-arms. He has a right to be heard.'

'Okay,' Peters said, 'explain. But first take your hand off that gun.'

Resnais didn't move. The Lebanese girl was right and he knew it. Her plea for a truce touched no chord in him but instinct urged him to comply. He didn't want to be sent back and to have to explain why. He might be believed, but there was no guarantee.

'I went to see for myself if that window was safe,' he said. 'She woke up and started making a scene. I got rough with her, but she asked for it. To you, she's something precious. To me, she's the wife of a capitalist pig and I'm the one who'll shoot her if he doesn't do what he's told.'

'For God's sake,' Madeleine begged, 'let's stop all this. Who is this woman? What makes her so special to you, Peters? I'm not asking for myself now – it's gone too far for that. At any moment we could get an order for Resnais to execute her. What will you say when that comes?'

'If it comes,' the American corrected, 'I'll do it myself. As far as I'm concerned she's in my care. I'm responsible for her and you come under my orders. Both of you. I have no personal interest in her one way or the other. But you're not to be trusted. That's why you've got to be replaced.'

'You're making a mistake,' the Frenchman said. He brought his right hand up and laid it in view on the arm of the chair. If Peters asked for a replacement that would look very bad for him. His complaint against the American wouldn't be believed.

'I made one too,' he said. 'I admit it. I shouldn't have touched her. Wait till tomorrow before you do anything.'

Peters finished his cigarette.

Madeleine said, 'I'm going to get us a drink.' She went out to the kitchen and came back with a bottle of wine. She gave Resnais a glass and handed one to Peters.

'We should be united,' she said. 'We've forgotten our common cause. Let's drink to it now!'

She had a sense of theatre which was less Eastern than Germanic. She chose the role of catalyst and, with the toast, she shamed Peters. He drank and the others did too. He didn't promise anything. He left them to sit on the terrace outside. Before he could decide what to do about them, he had first to examine himself.

It was a beautiful warm evening; the sky was rose and purple with the setting sun. He sat overlooking the sea; from far below there was a hiss and gurgle of waves breaking gently over the rocks. For years he had been committed to violence; the decision taken after Barnes's death during that campus riot had never been challenged. The world was a bloated capitalist corpse. There had to be a burial before the resurrection. He had conditioned himself to kill, just as he was unconcerned at dying. He remembered his mother's reproach, made during one of the futile scenes when he was still at college. How could he claim to love humanity when he wasn't capable of loving another human being? They had known nothing of his devotion and his teacher. They were referring as always to themselves. He was disturbed at recalling it now. He had given of himself in the fullest sense and for a higher purpose than a personal relationship. Suffering in the mass could move him to tears and he had never indulged in personal brutality. That was the weapon of the capitalist enemy; the truncheon-swinging riot police, the sadists in uniform; the cigar-chewing generals and the faceless bullies of the CIA. His adult life had been spent in revenging the murder of Andrew Barnes, in a crusade against injustice and oppression.

From the day she was captured, he could have put a bullet in the back of Eileen Field's head and felt no qualm of guilt because the act was totally impersonal. But now the screen protecting him had crumbled. She was no longer an object in the class war. She had a body and he had held it naked in his arms. He would have beaten Resnais to death for what he had done to Eileen Field. He sat in the darkness and tried to rationalize what had happened. Her courage had impressed him; inevitably then her vulnerability had touched him. He had fallen into the trap of allowing a personal relationship to develop between them. Of talking to her instead of slamming down her food and walking out; of accepting the responsibility which she had thrust upon him that first morning when she faced him in the little room. It was all clear and logical, and he had no excuse for letting it happen. And now he wanted her as well. He wondered whether she knew it, whether she had sensed that even as he wrestled with her by the window, his body had turned traitor and wanted to make love to her instead. Madeleine, with her sharp intuitive sense, had realized what was happening long before he did. Resnais had gone up to the room to prove it. They had drawn together against him because they felt he couldn't be trusted. Now he didn't know if he could trust himself. The truce between them was a false one, but he dared not send them back to Damascus. The Central Committee might send out a new team to take charge of Eileen Field. He couldn't risk that. She mustn't be handed over to anyone else. He could protect her against Madeleine and Resnais.

He got up and went back inside the villa. They were waiting for him, drinking the last of the wine.

'You're right,' he spoke to Madeleine. 'We've all got out of line. We have a job to do but it's got to be done my way. I'm in charge of the prisoner and nobody else interferes with her. If that's understood, we can forget what's happened today.'

'You are the boss,' the Frenchman said.

Madeleine only nodded. Peters didn't stay; he went out and up the stairs. The girl looked at Resnais.

'Do you trust him?'

He shook his head. 'No. He didn't send us back to Damascus because he didn't dare. He's gone soft on the woman. We'll have to watch him very carefully.'

Madeleine stretched in the chair. She turned her empty wine glass over and over. She looked at Resnais.

'I hope the mission fails,' she said. 'I hope Logan Field refuses the terms. I want to see you shoot her.'

'If that's what you want, chérie, be prepared for one thing. I shall have to kill Peters first.'

'I know that,' she said slowly. 'And if you don't, I will.'

Eileen lay still. It hurt her so much to move that she couldn't raise her arms. The immediate trauma of shock was dulled by the brandy. She was still shivering slightly and the ice-packed towel was a soggy mass which she had thrown off. The window was open and she could see a little balcony. It was dark and the sky was clear and bright with stars.

For a long time she had wept, after Peters left and she heard the door lock. She felt brutalized and degraded and more than at any time since her abduction she felt the anguish of being abandoned by the outside world. The days had gone by, interminable, nerve-racking, and nothing happened. No word from Logan. No move to release her. Just Peters coming in, or the Algerian. Hour after hour of solitude, keeping her spirits high with hope. And then that explosion of violence, the outrage of pain and savage sexuality. If she closed her eyes, all she could see was Resnais bending over her. Logan. She cried the name out loud and turned her face into the pillow. Why hadn't he helped her? Why was there not one word, one sign that he was trying to get her out?

James Kelly would have paid the ransom. If it had been James and not Logan, she would have been freed long before. Then, in the despair that shock and isolation brings, she doubted him as well. Nobody knew what was happening to her and their silence proved that they didn't care. They had given her up.

In spite of the pain in her breasts, she dragged herself up and looked at the window. The room was on the same side of the house as the one where she had been imprisoned. It would be equally impossible to climb down. If Logan wouldn't save her, she would have to escape. She would have to find some way of getting out of the villa. Peters wouldn't help her. She didn't even consider that. She didn't want him as an ally. She was shocked and ashamed of the way she had let him handle her body. She admitted in horror that after Resnais's attack she hadn't a resource left with which to fight Peters. And she had to fight him. She had to resist the temptation to give in and let herself depend upon him and look to him for the protection that was not coming from outside. It was going to be difficult. She kept listening for his step outside the door. He was her only friend in a situation of dreadful danger. Without him, Resnais would have raped her. She mustn't think of Peters as a friend. He was a killer, a terrorist like the other two. She pulled the covers over herself and shivered in spite of the heat. When she heard the door open, she shut her eyes and forced herself to pretend she was asleep.

## 8

Logan left for Tokyo at four in the afternoon. It was a long flight with stops in Bangkok and Hong Kong. He had a case full of papers on Imshan to occupy him and two sleeping pills Janet had pressed on him. He had no intention of taking them. He despised crutches of any kind and he had always been able to sleep when he travelled. She had driven to the airport with him, but stayed in the car. He didn't want to draw attention to his departure. He had been surprised and touched to see tears in her eyes when they said goodbye. They had drawn together in the crisis and this was important to Logan. He hadn't much faith in fair-weather relationships. He valued her cool common sense and he needed her sympathy. He leaned back in his seat on the plane and decided that he had never been so much in love with her as he was now.

Champagne was offered. He declined in favour of whisky, opened his case and set out his papers. He had told James Kelly to contact Homsi and demand proof that Eileen was still alive. Janet said he had made the right decision; Kelly looked at him as if he were a murderer. Whatever the outcome, James Kelly was finished as far as a career with Imperial Oil was concerned. Logan had no complaint against him as an employee. He had played a brilliant and vital part in the negotiations and his personal impact on the Shah had tipped the balance in the company's favour. There would be a termination of contract and a substantial compensation. But he was personally unacceptable to Logan. He had decided this, without allowing himself to trace that decision to Janet's remark about an affair with Eileen. He resented James's attitude and his lack of loyalty to the company's interests. When it was all over, he would be told to go.

All over. Logan had read the first paragraph of a memorandum twice without being able to concentrate on a word. There was a cold finality about the way he had expressed it to himself. Janet insisted that there was no way of saving Eileen. He didn't doubt her motives for a moment. She wasn't the kind of woman who would influence him out of anything but an honest opinion. She believed that his wife was going to die no matter what he did. Kelly, condemning him at every step, was sure that Logan had a choice.

In a flash of painful insight, he understood why Janet had been such a source of comfort to him. She denied him the choice and relieved him of the responsibility. He didn't want to lose Imshan. It was hypocritical to pretend that he could throw away the greatest coup of his career, forsake the power and importance of operating the key oil-field in the Western world. The very thought of giving it up caused him such mental agony that he writhed away from it, desperate for an alternative. There must be a way which wasn't the chilling deduction of Janet Armstrong. There must be a hope of saving Eileen and keeping Imshan. He wanted the oil-field because he wanted the power and the success implicit in it. He wanted it for the company which he saw as an extension of himself and to which he was deeply committed. And it was not hypocritical to say that a sense of responsibility towards Western Europe and its oil dilemma was a major part of his consideration.

But no decision could be made until he knew for sure that she was still alive. He settled back to his papers, forcing himself to concentrate. When the hostess came round with the cocktail canapés, he was completely absorbed in his work.

Six miles below and two hundred miles away from the plane as the crow flies, the brother of the waiter Habib Ebrahimi sat brooding in a coffee shop. He was a poor man who worked as a loader at the airport. He lifted heavy crates for ten hours a day for a miserable wage, his back was bowed and aching, and only the dream he shared with his brother brought light into a life dark with poverty. Equality for all, an end to misery and exploitation. He was not clever like his brother. He was content to listen and admire. The meaning of Habib's message was beautiful and clear. But Habib was dead, his wife taken away by the secret police. There was no doubt in the mind of Habib's brother who had commanded the killing. Habib had denounced his betrayal of the people often enough. Khorvan, the traitor. These were the words of Habib and his brother murmured them like a prayer from the Koran.

For some days after Resnais's attack Eileen had been ill. Her breasts swelled up and the pain kept her from sleeping. Shock made her lethargic; she cried copiously and without reason. Peters got her a sedative from the store of medical supplies in the villa. In common with many rich men their wealthy sympathizer was a hypochondriac and there were remedies for everything.

There was no suggestion of moving her back into the little room; as she suspected the window here looked over a sheer drop and she was equally secure. But it was airy and comfortable. Psychologically the new surroundings helped her to recover. By the end of the week she was up and dressed and her spirits had risen. Peters noticed it without realizing that the motive was her determination to escape. It had grown while she lay in bed, depending on him more and more, finding herself fretful when he didn't come. He sent wine in with her food and the quality in those few days when she was ill showed care in the selection. The signs were clear and there were times when she was overcome by panic at her own acceptance of his changing attitude towards her. At no point did she consider asking him to let her go. The locked door and the attention to security told her that this would be useless. She didn't want to expose herself by such a move. And secretly she shrank from the rejection which must follow. If she put herself at his mercy it would be at a price she wouldn't pay. The least part would be her self-respect. She had to do it alone. And since she had been sick, he might well be off his guard.

He came up that morning carrying a portable tape-recorder. 'You look better,' he said.

Eileen denied it.

'I feel awful. I'm dying for fresh air.'

He thought how colourless she looked. He decided he might take her down and let her walk in the garden.

'I want you to send a message to your husband,' he said.

'What kind of message? Have you heard from him? Oh, tell me, please!'

'He wants evidence that you're alive and well,' Peters said.

That message had been relayed through on the radio the night before.

'Of course,' Eileen said. 'How stupid of me not to think of that. He's a businessman. He never does anything without collateral.'

'Sit here,' he said, 'and talk into this mike.'

She shrugged. He had never seen her show bitterness before.

'What am I supposed to say? Please pay them the money or they're going to kill me. He knows that already.'

Peters bent over her. Last night's radio message had been less confident than the earlier reports. Logan Field was not acting in a hurry. He had left the last part of the negotiations with Homsi to a subordinate. He wanted proof that his wife was alive before he would proceed any further.

'Look,' he said, 'you've got a chance to talk to him. Pull out all the stops. It's for your own sake.'

She had sat down and clasped her hands in front of her. She looked up at him.

'I'm not going to beg,' she said quietly. 'And anyway it wouldn't do any good. He could have paid the ransom now if he really cared what happened to me.'

'You're wrong,' Peters said. 'It's not as simple as that. It can't be fixed in a few days.'

'Then it's not money?'

He hesitated. He wanted her to send the message and make it as poignant as she could. Whatever was holding that bastard of a husband back, a frightened plea from her might tip the balance.

'No, it isn't money.'

He saw her glance down at her hands and then up at him.

'God help me if it's something to do with Imperial Oil,' she said.

He slipped the tape into the machine.

'Don't be a fool,' he said. 'Give him a chance. He'll get you back. Now talk into this; give him your name and the date. Make it a personal message, something he'll know is genuine. And for Christ's sake, don't be proud! You can't afford it.'

She took the little microphone on its lead and held it near her mouth. He pressed the switch to record. She did as he had asked; she gave her name and the date. She said she was alive and well and she asked him to get her released so she could go back to Lucy. 'I wish you and Janet well.'

Peters switched off the machine.

'Why did you say that? Who's Janet – what does it mean?'

'You needn't be suspicious,' Eileen said calmly. 'It will just prove I sent the message, that's all.'

'It's too cool,' he said. He was irritated because she wouldn't help herself. 'I'm going to erase it and you do it again. Tell him you're frightened. Tell him you're in danger.'

She got up.

'I told you,' she said, 'I'm not going to beg. If you rub that out, I shan't say anything else. He knows perfectly well what can happen to me. It's just possible he won't care.'

Peters picked up the machine.

'Okay,' he said. 'Have it your way.'

She came up to him as he reached the door and touched him on the arm.

'I know you're trying to help me. I'm sorry. I think I've begun to give up hope. I've been very frightened these last few days.'

'It's because of what happened,' Peters said. He wasn't angry with her any more. She looked wan and miserable. 'It shook you up. Don't give up on your husband. He's doing his best.'

'It's being shut in here all the time,' Eileen said. Her heart was beating very fast. 'If I could just go outside for a few minutes. Sit in the sun...'

'I was going to take you in the garden,' Peters said, 'so long as you promise to behave yourself.'

'I won't do anything,' she said. 'I promise.'

They stayed at the back of the villa, away from the sea. They sat under the shade of a pergola, roofed with vines. She leaned back, looking at the pattern of the leaves over her head, the sunlight fragmented through them. He sat beside her. They hadn't spoken since they left her room.

'Thank you for this,' Eileen said.

'You needed fresh air,' he said. 'So long as you're sensible you can come down every day.'

'Have you ever been in prison?'

'Yes. Twice.'

'It's a very strange experience. You feel completely cut off. As if nobody in the world knew or cared what happened to you. Did you feel like that?'

'No,' Peters said. 'I had friends. I knew they'd get me out.'

He was thinking of a filthy cell in Santiago, where he had been held on suspicion without trial. A bomb explosion had released him. That had been the first time he was arrested. The night he was beaten up in the police station at Kent State was in a special category. He knew what Eileen meant by feeling isolated but he had never experienced it in that sense. He had been isolated from society in the mass for nearly seven years.

'You have plenty of time to think,' she said.

He was leaning back in the chair, his eyes half closed. He was close enough to grab hold of her if she made a move. It was very warm and drowsy under the shade. A large yellow butterfly sped lazily past them, pirouetting on the way to a hibiscus bush. Eileen watched it. She could see the villa through the trees. From her memory of the front when they arrived in the car, there was a wall around it and the gates to the road were down a short drive from the front door. She was wearing the caftan Peters had bought in Nice. Under the long skirts she slipped out of her high heeled shoes. Coming down through the garden she had plotted the way round to the gate in her mind while she walked beside Peters, his hand holding her arm. There was no specific plan in her mind, only an instinct that clamoured for her to take this opportunity because there might not be another. In bare feet she could run fast. He wasn't carrying a gun. The casual dress of shorts and a sweat shirt told her that. If she could reach the gate and the road . . . she was sure there was a villa not more than fifty yards away on the left.

'I'm sleepy,' she said.

He turned his head towards her.

'Go ahead,' he said. 'It's getting very hot.'

She shut her eyes and let herself relax. Her arm was resting near to his; the lounging chairs were side by side. She let it slip onto her lap. She stayed quite still, keeping her eyes closed. The effort was agonizing. She began to count under her breath, marking off the minutes. After she had calculated a quarter of an hour, Eileen opened her eyes enough to glimpse him. He was lying back, his arms folded across his chest, his head turned away from her. She waited for some minutes, watching him. He didn't move. She slid one leg to the side and followed it with the other. One foot on the ground. Again she waited. She couldn't see his face but he seemed to be asleep. The chair didn't creak as she moved. She eased herself upright, watching him in terror in case his head suddenly turned and he should find her poised to run away. He stayed still. Very slowly and carefully she levered herself by her hands until she was half out of the chair with both feet on the ground. She felt as if she were suffocating, her heart beat was so rapid. He seemed to be breathing heavily; his posture in the chair was completely relaxed. She was on the ground. She turned and fled to the right, towards the avenue of trees and the front of the villa.

Peters was not asleep. He thought that she was. He didn't hear her creep out of the chair; he was in the twilight when the mind is blank and the body relaxed. She had almost reached the gates when he turned round and saw that she had gone.

The driveway was gravel and sharp under her feet. The surface was also very hot; as she ran she felt the sting of burning. She was gasping for breath, fighting the weakness of confinement without exercise, seeing the gates in front of her. Twenty-five yards and she would reach them. Peters was superbly fit. He ran like a stag and he caught her as she was wrenching at the locked gates in despair, tears streaming down her face. She started to scream wildly as he pulled her back, holding onto the bars. He heard a car approaching down the road. He slammed his hand over her mouth and hurled her bodily into the bushes out of sight. He held her there, pinned to the ground, until the car had passed them. Then he pulled her onto her feet. She stood, dishevelled and weeping. He pushed her round to the back and into the villa. They went upstairs and he unlocked the door, still holding her.

'You fool,' he said. 'I trusted you.'

She turned in the room and faced him. The reproach was suddenly more than she could bear.

'I had to try,' she cried out. 'Don't you see? He's never going to give you what you want. He doesn't want me back!'

'Shut up!' Peters shouted at her. He slammed the door behind

him and advanced upon her. He was angry enough to hit her.
'Shut up!'

'Tell me what you've asked for,' Eileen said. 'I've got a right
to know.' The moment of collapse was past. She had never had
a chance of getting out. He had known the gates were kept
locked. 'Oh God,' she said, 'I wish you'd get it over.'

'You could have been killed out there,' Peters said. 'If
Ahmed or Resnais had seen you, they'd have shot you dead.'

'That's going to happen anyway,' she said. 'I know it. That's
why I tried to get away.'

'It isn't going to happen,' Peters said. 'You keep on saying
that. I know he'll give it up. Nothing's going to happen to you.'

'Give up what?' Eileen asked slowly. 'What have you asked
Logan in exchange for me?'

He didn't want to tell her; she should have been kept ignorant
either way. But he was losing hope himself because of her
despair.

'Imshan,' he said. 'He's got to pull out of the oil-fields. That's
why it's taking time.'

'I see.' She turned away and sat on the edge of the bed. She
pushed her hair back and there was a streak of dirt across her
cheek from where she had clung to the gates.

'Now I understand why you wanted to kidnap Lucy. He
might have done it for her. But you've asked the one thing in
the world that my husband will never do for me.'

'You're his wife,' Peters said. 'He won't let you die.'

'He wants to marry someone else,' she said and her voice was
flat and calm. 'I came back from Tehran because he'd asked
me for a divorce. You took the wrong person.'

Outside a distant aeroplane hummed like an angry bee. It
was the only sound.

He stared at her. She was sitting very still. The caftan had
been torn when they struggled by the gate. Logan Field wanted
a divorce. They had kidnapped her instead of the child and all
the time she had no value as a hostage. Field was going to dis-
card her anyway. He couldn't believe it. He refused to accept
what she said. There was a slow dejection about her as she sat
on the bed that was unbearable to watch. He came and caught
her by the shoulders.

'You're not lying to me? You're telling the truth?'

'Janet Armstrong is his assistant,' Eileen said. 'That's who he wants to marry. I mentioned her in the message.'

'Oh Christ,' Peters said very low. 'Oh Christ, what a mess.' He was holding her so tightly that it hurt.

'I wish you'd told me before,' she said quietly. 'I've gone on hoping, thinking it was money. He'd pay money for me, I know that. But never Imshan. It's the most important thing in his life. He'd never give it up for anything or anyone in the world. Except Lucy. Never for me.'

Peters looked down at her; her face was upturned, with the dirty smudge on the right cheek and the stains of tears around her eyes.

'How many people know about this?'

'Only the director in Tehran. I told him about it before I left.'

Peters lifted her off the bed. He held her a little way away from him.

'If it's not common knowledge, it doesn't matter,' he insisted. 'Logan may think better of it. He can't live with himself if he walks out on you now. We've got to keep hoping that he'll crack. So long as our people don't find out...'

If Damascus discovered that she wasn't any use to them, he knew what the order would be. Execute her. He had been insisting to himself that if Field accepted the terms, Eileen would be released, but he had begun to doubt that too. Now her life wasn't worth a spent match. He suddenly drew her close to him. He didn't kiss her but for a moment his hand came round and stroked her hair.

'I can't let you go,' he said slowly. 'I can't do that. But I promise you, nobody's going to hurt you. Whatever the outcome, I'll see nothing happens to you. Will you trust me?'

Eileen leaned against him. She felt very tired, as if the will to resist had emptied itself in that attempt to escape. When she reached the gates and found them locked it was the end. Even before she knew that the price for her survival was the one that Logan Field would never pay. The man holding her cared, as her husband did not. He was promising her something which she knew meant his betrayal of his friends and his political beliefs. 'Nobody's going to hurt you.' For almost three weeks she had been holding out against the temptation of all prisoners to form an emotional attachment to a captor who was kind to them. She had lived with fear, uncertainty and physical assault, and somehow kept her courage and her hope. Now all she could feel was his strength and the warmth of his body. He wanted her and she could feel the tension growing in him as he held her. She had no friend in the world left but him. The mental and physical temptation to give in to him was the strongest feeling she could remember. Beyond him was the outside world. She had no contact with it. It had forgotten her. She had lived in the villa, preserved in her isolation and captivity like a fly in amber. Only Peters was real. Peters had saved her from Resnais. He was promising to save her again.

'I'll make it as easy as I can for you,' he was saying. 'You can't get away and you know it now. Do as I tell you and we'll just have to hope it turns out right.'

Eileen lifted her head and looked up at him. The message was clear.

'I've got to go down,' he said. 'I've got to keep the others sweet. They mustn't suspect anything.' He stepped away from her.

'Come back,' Eileen said.

'Only if you want it,' Peters answered. 'You don't have to. It's not part of the deal.'

'I never thought it was,' she said. And she repeated it. 'Come back.'

The party at the French Embassy was to celebrate Bastille Day. There was a reception in the garden. James Kelly had arrived early and he was talking to a group of French Embassy officials. He had been *en poste* in Paris for two years during his Foreign Office career and formed a deep attachment to France. His appreciation of French culture had made him many friends; an introduction to the Ambassador in Tehran had come from one of them as soon as his arrival in Tehran was known. He had come early because he couldn't stand being alone in the house. He had met Saiid Homsi that morning. The rendezvous was in the Bazaar in South Tehran. He had faced Homsi in a dingy little office behind one of the shops selling brassware to the tourists. And he had delivered Logan's demand. Proof that Eileen was still alive or no deal on Imshan would be considered. The interview was brief and the Syrian was just as smooth and hypocritical as he had been with Logan. He had expressed alarm at Logan's trip to Tokyo, but James had reassured him that it was only undertaken to block the negotiations begun by his subordinates. He had added a brief of his own. 'Tell the PLF that I personally will ensure that Imshan comes to nothing, side by side with Mr Field.' The Syrian had smiled a little, showing a gleam of gold teeth, as if he understood how personal James Kelly's motives were. James had gone to the office and somehow got through the day. He didn't want to work; he wanted to call everyone together and tell them that the company wasn't going through with Imshan and they could start packing up to go home.

He didn't trust Logan. He believed, quite wrongly, that Janet Armstrong was influencing him from sinister motives and that Logan was willing to be influenced. He could sense the hesitation, the open-ended option in Logan's mind. He wanted the oil-field; he had already rejected Eileen before there was a choice between them. Above all he was ruled by ruthless logic; even his admirers described him as an arch pragmatist; cat-footed in his ability to leap from one position to another as a situation changed. He was trying to convince himself, not that he couldn't make the decision in Eileen's favour but that it wouldn't help her if he did. James was not inclined to violent feelings. His nature was steadfast and deep in affection, reserved and disinterested in dislike. But for Logan he experienced real visceral hate.

He showered and changed and fled from his house and the torment in his mind to the relief of human company which was not connected with Imperial Oil.

The wife of the First Secretary was chatting to him. She was a charming woman in her late thirties, endowed with a wit and chic which attracted him, and she had managed to make him laugh and relax a little. He felt a touch on his elbow.

'Good evening, Mr Kelly.'

'Good evening, Colonel. Is Madame Ardalan with you?'

The Colonel shook his head.

'Unfortunately she has a fever. Some small thing... She was looking forward to coming this evening.'

The garden was filling with people. The Frenchwoman excused herself and James was alone with Ardalan.

'You look tired, Mr Kelly,' he said. 'Have you been working hard?'

'Yes, fairly hard. Mr Field likes to keep things moving pretty fast.'

The Colonel offered him a cigarette.

'And how are the negotiations going?' He glanced up for a fraction of a second from lighting it and saw the change of expression on Kelly's face. It was only a glimpse, a sudden tensing of the facial muscles, but it told him that the answer wouldn't be the truth.

'Not too well,' James said. 'We're a bit worried about things at the moment.'

'I'm sorry to hear that,' Ardalan said. 'Mr Field must be very anxious. I have heard that he is very enthusiastic about the field.'

'Oh yes.' James's diplomatic training wasn't proof against his terror for Eileen. He abhorred discussing the oil-field and he couldn't hide his reluctance.

'Tell me,' the Colonel said, his black eyes very mild, 'is Minister Khorvan responsible?' He hoped that Kelly wouldn't lie or take refuge in evasions. He knew that Khorvan had tried to block Imperial Oil and had only given way on a direct order from the Shah. If the negotiations were failing, as Kelly indicated, then Ardalan wanted to know if the Minister was to blame.

'Well,' Kelly hesitated, 'I don't think I should commit myself on that. Can I get us both a drink, Colonel?'

'That would be kind,' the Colonel said. He followed James in search of a waiter. They both stood sipping champagne.

Ardalan watched the Englishman for a few moments. He didn't look tired; that was an understatement. He looked as if he hadn't slept for days and there was a drawn, haggard expression on his face when it was in repose. Ardalan had seen a similar look of disquiet on Logan Field's face the night he saw the Syrian. He didn't expect James to tell him anything. He just wanted his opinions confirmed.

'Apart from Imshan,' he said, 'is there anything else that might worry Mr Field?'

'No, not that I know of.'

'I see.' Ardalan sounded disappointed. 'Tell me, has that

Syrian approached him again? People like that can be very persistent.'

'No. No, definitely not. Mr Field wouldn't touch anything illegal. He made that very clear. I see the Minister has just arrived. Would you excuse me, Colonel? I ought to go and have a word with him.'

'Of course. Mr Kelly?'

'Yes?' James said.

'If at any time you need my help, please let me know.'

'Thank you,' James said. 'I will remember that.'

Ardalan saw him edging his way through the crowd towards Khorvan. He watched for a moment, before turning to find someone else to talk to. His prediction to his assistant Sabet was correct. James Kelly hadn't revealed anything, except that he and Logan Field had something very definite to hide.

The garden was filled with trees and ornamental shrubs. It was early evening and quite light, but the shrubberies were thick enough and dark enough to hide a man from view. Among the shadows along the wall of the Embassy garden, there was one that moved.

Yusef Ebrahimi had got into the Embassy grounds with the extra staff brought in to organize the party. He knew, because of what Habib had told him, that Ministers went to foreign Embassies and one of Habib's coffee-shop friends advised him that Khorvan would be going to the French Embassy that night. As if Habib had returned from the dead, he knew that this was the place and the time to exact his vengeance. The traitor and murderer would be in the splendid gardens, drinking and talking to the capitalist enemies of his country. Habib's brother had crouched among the bushes for two hours before the first guests began arriving. He watched from his shelter, looking for the Minister. He felt no fear, only a resolve so strong that it made him tremble. He was a poor man and weak, dust under the feet of the rich and powerful. He had lived his whole life making terms with hunger. When he slept it was the sleep of exhaustion and an escape from the rigours of cruel labour and slave wages. His brother Habib had promised that all this would be changed. He hadn't understood how but he had believed and hoped. He watched from the bushes as Khorvan walked into his view, dressed in his immaculately tailored suit, with diamonds in his cuff links, and it seemed to Habib's brother that blood surrounded him like an aura. He straightened a little and his right hand crept down to his trouser band and found the handle of a long sharp knife.

The Minister was in a sour mood. He had felt unwell the previous day and, in common with many Iranians, he was morbidly afraid of illness. A dozen alarming explanations for his feeling of malaise occurred to him and the reassurances of his fashionable doctor hadn't satisfied him. He preferred to go to London for medical advice. He had an audience with the Shah the following day and this was as much responsible for his symptoms as any germ he had picked up. The Shah wanted a report on the negotiations with Imperial Oil. He was about to give the chairman an audience and he was expecting the Minister to provide full details. The one gift His Imperial Majesty possessed above all others was the capacity to judge other people. Khorvan might feint and dodge effectively with James and Logan Field, and his fellow Iranians; he had no hope of deceiving the Shah. The Shah wanted Imperial Oil to have the concession, albeit on the toughest terms. It was the test of Khorvan's skill to manoeuvre Imperial into a position whereby the company couldn't comply with Iranian terms and the Government couldn't back down on them without a loss of face. Walking this tightrope was difficult enough, but doing it with the tough and resourceful Logan Field tugging at the wire was sufficient reason for having a stomach ache. Khorvan sipped at the orange juice, when he craved a healing draught of Scotch whisky, and made little effort with the other guests. He felt no obligation to be sociable, and when Kelly came up to speak to him he pretended not to notice him. There were four people surrounding the Minister, two of them French, an official from the trade department of the British Embassy, and Kelly. Immediately behind them, the tall bank of shrubs cast an impenetrable shadow. James had waited for some moments without being acknowledged and suddenly lost patience. In the service of Her Majesty's government he had endured bad manners and boredom, but he owed Imperial Oil no such allegiance. As he prepared to turn his back on the Minister, his thoughts were dwelling sourly on the vanished 'gunboat diplomacy' of past decades, when one of the shadows took shape and left the protection of the shrubberies. It became a crouching form, one arm raised. Before Kelly realized what he was seeing, it sprang towards the Minister.

Khorvan was speaking when the knife struck him. His glass fell and shattered, spattering orange juice; he gave a grunting cry and toppled forward. It was Kelly who acted instinctively and grabbed hold of the assailant as he ran for the shelter of the bushes. He struggled briefly with a small, wiry man who kicked and clawed at him, spitting insults in Farsi. Someone in the crowd screamed. The momentary shock had paralysed the on-lookers. Now the woman's cry released them. Seconds later the attacker was seized by other hands and brought to the ground. Kelly knelt down beside the Minister. Khorvan was lying on his back; one of the French officials had opened his jacket and pulled his tie loose. His head lolled to one side. There was a hurried movement among the crowd standing around them and Colonel Ardalan knelt beside James. He turned the Minister's head towards them. The face was a ghastly colour and the eyes were turned up. He laid a hand on Khorvan's chest and then gently turned him on one side. A knife handle was sticking out of his back below the left shoulder blade. Ardalan looked round.

'The Minister is dead,' he said. He got up and went to where the assassin lay, pinned to the ground by two of the guests. 'Take him into the Embassy, please,' he said. 'My men will remove him. I must ask everyone who saw the murder to come with me. If the Ambassador will permit me to make use of a room...'

It was the Ambassador himself who brought the Colonel into the building and placed an office at his disposal. The party was ended and those guests who couldn't assist the Colonel went home. James was the first person to make a statement; there was no change in Ardalan's manner. He was soft-spoken and polite, but it was the head of the dreaded SAVAK who was asking the questions, wearing the face of the amiable Colonel like a rubber mask. James described how the man had run out from the shrubbery, struck the blow, and how he had prevented him escaping.

'That was very brave of you,' the Colonel said. 'The English always keep their heads in emergencies. His Imperial Majesty will be grateful that you caught the assassin.'

'It's a shocking thing,' James said. It was his first experience of violent death and it disgusted him. Equally repellent was his brief glimpse of the murderer being hauled by the hair into a police car. There was a grimace of agonized terror on the man's face that haunted him.

'Who was the man? Why did he do it?'

'We shall soon know,' Ardalan said.

James drove back to his house, past a police guard that had been set up outside the Embassy, with a small crowd of people gathered by the entrance. Khorvan was dead. It seemed incredible; the transition from life to death had been so sudden, as quick as the thrust of a knife blade. His mind shied away from what must be happening to the assassin in the Colonel's head-quarters in Niavaran.

He went home, told his servant he didn't want dinner and sat out in the garden by the fountain with a drink. It was a warm night, scented with flowers; the stars were like diamonds on a velvet cloth above his head and the delicate music of the fountain played at his elbow.

Now that Khorvan was dead, the only obstacle between Imperial Oil and Imshan was gone. He wondered how long it would take for the news to reach Logan in Tokyo. As long as it took Janet Armstrong to cable him. He sat on, his drink forgotten, listening to the water falling into the marble basin. He was a man of thought rather than action; his nature and training combined against a rash or ill-considered act. Loyalty to his superiors was an integral part of his code of life. He had never broken it, even to Logan Field. He went inside to his sitting room and dialled the British Embassy. He was on first name terms with the Ambassador who had been his chief in Madrid. He asked him as a matter of the gravest urgency to arrange for a private audience with the Shah.

The brother of Habib Ebrahimi was subjected to interrogation; that was the wording on the Colonel's report. Long experience of what prolonged physical torture could extract from different types of people assured Ardalan early on that the assassin was telling the truth. He had manufactured nothing. He was the brother of the murdered waiter, Habib Ebrahimi, and he had killed the Minister as an act of private vengeance, believing him responsible for Habib's death. Ardalan had paused there. It was his usual technique before asking an important question. He lit a cigarette and smoked it through.

'Why should an important man like Khorvan trouble himself with a worm like your brother?'

The answer was a mumble. Because Habib had been told to spy on the Minister because he was a traitor who was giving Imshan oil-fields to the capitalists. And so the Minister had had Habib's throat cut.

Ardalan went back and sat down. The room was grey with cigarette smoke, writhing upwards under the lights directed at the prisoner. At last the puzzle made a picture that was recognizable. A major piece had just been fitted into place.

Habib Ebrahimi had been told to spy on Khorvan. His direct connection with the American Peters led to Saiid Homsi. And from him to Logan Field. And from the mouth of Khorvan's assassin had come the proof that linked them all together – Imshan oil-fields. He got up and stretched to ease the tension in neck and shoulder muscles. He spoke to the group of officers standing in the background.

'Take him away,' he said. 'The Shah will want him executed.'

He went upstairs to his office. It was growing light. He had already reported to the Shah by telephone before leaving the French Embassy. Now he had all the information that he needed to take action. An international terrorist group, masterminded by Syria, was intervening in Iran's most valuable economic and political asset. Oil. One assassination had already taken place. It wouldn't be difficult to present the unimportant brother of Habib Ebrahimi as a politically motivated terrorist. A good policeman could judge when it was right to doctor the facts. At eight in the morning he set out for the Palace. His assistant Sabet went with him.

The moment Eileen woke, she knew that he was in the room. It was an instant transition from sleep to full awareness and she lay very still, waiting. She could see the outline of him in the semi-dark; there was a moon outside and the blinds were up. He was standing still, looking towards her. She sat up and turned on the lamp beside her bed.

He didn't speak. He came and stood by her. There was no expression on his face at all and he was fully dressed. A sense of absolute fatality overcame her as she looked up at him and with it a strange excitement and relief. The current was flowing between them, without words and without touch. It was the most powerful pre-sexual experience of her life, those few seconds while she waited.

'If you've changed your mind,' Peters said, 'I'll go.'

'Don't go,' Eileen said.

He sat on the bed and slowly put his hands on her shoulders. 'I won't force you,' he said. 'I'm not Resnais.'

It was Eileen who made the first move. She caught his face with her hands and kissed him on the mouth.

It was an urgent, wordless lovemaking; even so its intensity was matched by tenderness from him. He made love to her and afterwards, when they were quiet, Eileen remembered the words of a friend who had also been a priest. Any fool can have intercourse; it takes a real man to make love. They lay close, their bodies dovetailed, loath to lose contact. For Peters it was a strange experience. Sex and emotion had never mixed before. She was less accomplished as a lover than Madeleine, there were no acrobatics, but there was no comparison in either the satisfaction or the aftermath. He wanted to feel her near him, to touch and kiss. He remembered how other women's desire to cling had jarred upon him. Now he held her possessively until the cycle began again. Passion, exploration, self-loss. Eileen met and matched him as the night passed. It was a different woman who woke in his arms before the dawn. Marriage and childbirth, love and loss, all the human experience of her life with Logan Field was muted. Peters was the reality, the fulfilment she had never imagined could exist. He had made her a part of himself. He woke soon after she did and she felt his hand claiming her breast. She laid her own on it.

'I'll have to go soon,' he said. 'Will you be all right?'

'Yes. You mustn't be seen.'

'I'll be careful.' He pulled himself upright; his fingers twined in her hair, curling it round.

'I'll come back as soon as I can. You go to sleep.' He bent and kissed her. 'You gave me a lot,' he whispered.

'We gave each other,' Eileen said quietly. 'I wish you wouldn't go.'

'Ahmed gets up early,' Peters answered. 'I don't want to take risks. Not now. You do as I say. Go to sleep. I'll come up later.'

She watched him dress and go to the door. He turned and in the pre-dawn light he made a gesture which she couldn't see. Then the door closed and she heard the lock turning. The room was very quiet, the atmosphere heavy and still. Slowly she ran her hands over her body, miming what he had done. Sleep. To make the voyage of self-discovery and then to sleep. It was impossible. Marriage to Logan for seven years. She had thought of herself as a woman, a wife and a mother, a mature human being. A woman whose life ran along a single well defined track. Meath House and Eaton Square. The smart flat in the Rue St Dominique in Paris. Trips abroad. Dinner parties and business entertaining. A little child, immaculately dressed in pink. Not a hair ruffled or a seam out of place. Mrs Logan Field. Whoever she was, Eileen didn't recognize her any more. And never would know her again.

'It's dragging on and on,' Madeleine complained. 'We get messages saying Field has capitulated but no proof! How do we even know it's true? He never lets us near the radio set.'

She and Resnais were sitting in a café in the centre of Nice. They spent a lot of time together. On the surface the atmosphere between them and Peters was friendly, if reserved. None of the three was deceived by it. It was a truce, and waiting to be broken.

'So we only know what he tells us,' Resnais said. 'I'm going to make contact with Damascus myself.'

'No,' Madeleine said quickly. 'Don't do that. It's too dangerous! If he finds out you've talked to HQ behind his back...'

'He's keeping control of that radio link in case the husband backs away at the last minute. Then he'll be the only one to know. He won't carry out the sentence and he'll make sure that I don't.' Resnais lit a cigarette.

'Ahmed says he hasn't slept in his own room for the last four nights. He takes her out in the garden, hidden round the back of the villa,' Madeleine said. 'He brings her wine, cigarettes, books to read. I admit to you, Resnais, when all this started I was jealous. I loved him and I didn't like him being soft with another woman. But it's more than that now.' She lifted the glass of *orange pressée*, and then put it down without drinking. 'He's not just sleeping with her, he's corrupted,' she said. 'He's gone over to the enemy. I've been watching him and he's not the same man. He's not the man I lived with in Tehran and I promise you he's not the man who took the Lufthansa plane. I know he means to let that woman go, even if he has to wreck the whole mission.'

'And sacrifice himself?' Resnais asked her. 'He must know the consequences. Perhaps he plans to defect with her. Give himself up and trade information about the PLF...' He lit a cigarette. 'We'll have to stop him, chérie. And I don't think we should wait any longer. We've held that woman for three weeks. Very soon now, there'll be a decision. Only we won't know it. He can tell us anything – any lie. They can escape together. The next thing we'll know will be when the police pick us up.'

Madeleine swore viciously in Arabic.

'He was one of the great ones,' she said. For a moment her eyes filled with tears. 'He gave up everything for the cause. He was an inspiration to so many of us. And that woman destroys him. I promise you, Resnais, she's not going to get away with it.'

'I don't quarrel with that,' the Frenchman said. 'After all, we are only anticipating events. First, we have to get rid of him. Then we hold her. And I won't interfere with you, if you want to be unpleasant.'

'What are we going to do? Don't try to take him unawares – he's very dangerous.'

'I know that,' Resnais said. 'But so am I. We will arrange an accident and that way nobody will ask questions afterwards. As far as the PLF is concerned, he will have died a hero. And you and I will carry out the mission.'

He put a ten franc note in the bill and folded both under his empty glass.

'We'll go back now,' he said. 'And we must be very friendly to him. Especially you. He must think he has nothing to fear from either of us.'

# 9

Resnais watched Madeleine with admiration. They were eating dinner on the terrace. She had brought out two bottles of wine, sat next to Peters and linked her arm through his. She gave him a warm smile.

'I feel like a party tonight. We've been gloomy and quarrelsome for long enough. I drink to you.' She passed him her glass and Peters had to drink from it. Resnais made his contribution.

'To the success of the mission. I feel very confident it will go our way.'

'It's looking promising,' Peters admitted. 'I had a radio message this afternoon saying Logan Field had agreed to the demands in principle. It may take a week or two before they announce that Imperial's pulling out of Imshan. I think we've got it made.'

'But that's wonderful,' Madeleine exclaimed. 'What a triumph for the PLF – to shut off that oil supply to the West! It's such a pity no one will know.'

'That's the whole point,' Resnais said. 'It's got to be kept secret, otherwise the oil company would dispense with Logan Field and go ahead. They wouldn't care what happened to his wife.'

Peters had been waiting for them to bring Eileen into the discussion. He looked up at them both; he sounded quite disinterested.

'If the deal goes through,' he said, 'nothing *will* happen to her.'

'I want to go into Nice tomorrow,' Madeleine said. She spoke to Peters. 'Will you drive in with me? Resnais doesn't want to come and I'm bored on my own. Please. Ahmed can sit outside her door if you're still worried about that old business. Not that you need to be. Resnais is all right now, aren't you? He's got himself a woman.'

'More than one,' the Frenchman said, grinning. 'There's a very nice little brothel behind the Place Gambetta. Pretty girls and not too much money. Not that you need it.'

He shrugged and leaned back, smiling at them both. The girl was very good. He wasn't surprised by her deceit. He had never trusted a woman in his life, but he admired her acting skill. There was no trace of bitterness or hostility; the violent rupture might never have taken place; she was behaving as if their old relationship would be resumed. And she was leading Peters in the direction he had told her.

'I've been Madame's chauffeur long enough,' he said, 'while you and she were sulking. Now it's your turn to run after her. I'm going off tomorrow to fish. There's a man on the beach who runs a motorboat and takes people out for the day. I'm fed up with sitting around here.'

Peters hesitated. The atmosphere between them had been sour and suspicious in spite of the superficial truce. He needed to keep them neutral at the least. He disliked the feel of Madeleine's body pressed against him, and her scent, expensive gardenia mixed with female sweat, nauseated him. Everything animalistic which had once aroused him now chilled him with disgust. The oiled brown skin, the breasts bursting through the cotton shirt, its ultimate button deliberately left undone, the flashing smile and hot green eyes. He couldn't have touched her after holding Eileen Field. But he needed to keep her quiet. If Resnais were out of the house, there was no danger in leaving Eileen in the Algerian's care. He knew better than to open that door and go inside.

'Okay,' he said. 'We'll go into Nice. When do you want to go?

'In the morning. We can swim and I can do some shopping. Maybe you'll take me to lunch?'

'Maybe. If you don't want to go to the Negresco.'

'Don't be cruel, chérie,' she said softly. 'I haven't been near a place like that since I left home.'

There was a moment, after they finished dinner and Resnais went upstairs to bed, when Madeleine made a genuine move towards him. She had suffered considerably when he left her bed; pride and jealousy had corrupted her love for him into a

163

fiery hate. She despised him for his weakness and raged against him for forsaking the political principles which had brought them together. But worst of all was the knowledge that the woman they had kidnapped, epitome of the spoilt, useless female of the capitalist species, had aroused feelings which Madeleine herself had been unable to touch. She had agreed with Resnais that Peters must be killed and she had spent the evening manoeuvring him into position for the Frenchman. But when the moment came she tried once more; the love which had not completely died in her was crying out for a reprieve.

'I miss you,' she said. She caught his hand and brought it to her mouth; she bit his fingers and kissed the hard palm. 'Come back to me,' she whispered. 'Come to bed tonight.'

She had never begged in her life. She was an independent woman, mistress of herself, capable of withholding or giving her body as she felt inclined. She abdicated everything by slipping down by his knee and stroking it.

'I want you so much. I still love you.'

It was an effort to touch her. An even greater effort not to move aside and escape the caresses that he did not want. He laid his hand on her head and tried to be kind. He knew as he did so that all she would understand was the rejection.

'It's better not,' he said. 'It had started to complicate things. And we can't afford that. We're friends and comrades now. We've got to be content with that.'

She got up and, to her credit, managed to shrug as if she didn't mind. He didn't understand the motive and he admired her self-possession.

'As you wish,' she said. 'I suppose a lot of women have made themselves look foolish over you. So I have joined the club. I'll go up then. But we're going to Nice tomorrow?'

'I'll be ready at ten,' Peters said. 'Goodnight, Madeleine.'

As soon as she had left the terrace he had forgotten her. She hadn't made a scene and he was grateful. It was eleven o'clock. Resnais must be asleep and he would have to give Madeleine time to go to bed. Then he could go upstairs and into Eileen's room. He felt in his pocket for the key.

He had tried to analyse himself and her. Sexual desire was an easy explanation. He had wanted to go to bed with her and this was the motive which had made him attack Resnais and reject Madeleine. Equally she was frightened and lonely and had conceived a masochistic hunger for the man who held her prisoner. It was all very glib and probable, but it wasn't the explanation. There was something much more fundamental than a physical bond or a twisted psychological urge. All the protectiveness in his nature, the single-minded championship of people in the mass, had suddenly narrowed and channelled towards one person. She wasn't the most attractive and certainly not the most beautiful woman he had known. But she was the only human being for whom he felt personally responsible. Nothing must happen to her. That was as far as he had allowed himself to go. Nothing else had changed. His beliefs were the same. His loyalties were unchanged. He regretted nothing he had done in the name of his political creed and he would do it all again. But Eileen Field was set apart from it. He took the key to her room out of his pocket. There was a mark in his palm. He had never loved anyone in his life since the death of Andrew Barnes. Not his parents, or a close friend, or a woman. Now he did. It was very simple and he didn't argue with it. He put the key back and went inside.

Upstairs, waiting by her bedroom door, Madeleine heard him cross the passage and walk on past his own door. She opened hers and saw him going into the room where Eileen Field was kept.

At six that morning, Resnais went downstairs and into the kitchen. It was fitted with every modern contrivance, looking more like an operating theatre than a place where food was prepared. He passed the stove complex with its eye-level oven and gleaming extractor hood and pressed a switch on the control panel. He then turned the extractor knob anti-clockwise and pulled at the cupboard fitment on the left. It swung outward. Behind it, in a space big enough to walk in, was a room stacked with guns and ammunition. He lingered for a few moments, examining the assorted rifles, revolvers and a selection of the latest small arms, including the auto-loading Armalite AR-IS, a popular weapon in guerilla attacks. He loved guns; they were said to be a phallic symbol. Resnais dismissed the idea as typical bourgeois claptrap. There was nothing wrong with his penis and he still loved to use and handle guns. He chose a Russian M-1930 rifle with a telescopic sight and a box of ammunition. He went back into the kitchen, closed up the cupboard, reset the knob on the control panel, and packed the rifle and bullets into a long case he had brought with him. It came from a sports shop in Nice and normally contained a fishing rod. He went out to the garage. There were three cars: a Renault 5, which was normally used for going short distances, a big Rolls, gleaming white, which was the Algerian millionaire's favourite toy, and a long, low-built, E-type Jaguar. He put the case into the Jaguar's boot, locked it and pocketed the key. He didn't want Peters taking the fast car. Then he went to the terrace, pattered lightly down the fifty rock steps to the sea and went for an early swim. He was eating rolls and drinking fresh coffee when Madeleine came down. He grinned at her and pulled out a chair with one hand, the other waved a buttered roll. He was in excellent spirits, laughing and joking, describing his swim. Madeleine didn't respond. She didn't eat anything. She drank the strong coffee, tight-lipped and sullen. She hadn't slept well and her eyes were tired. Jealousy was a bloody goad, applied by the memory of where the man she had loved had spent the night. There was no mercy, no trace of sentiment left in her now. She looked at Resnais.

'Is everything ready?'

'Everything,' he said gently. 'You do your part and I'll do mine. And smile, chérie. Make it a happy morning for him. He won't see another.'

Peters woke very early. He left Eileen before the dawn broke and it was the only sad note in their lovemaking that she so often woke up to find he had gone. The bedroom was no longer a comfortable prison, a cage in which she paced up and down dreaming of rescue or escape. It was a haven, a private place where she lived a new life with a man she loved. There was no other word to describe what she felt for him. From the first night when he made love to her and the metamorphosis began, her passionate need of him had only increased. Beyond the boundaries of sex, a range of feeling she had never suspected was developing. She had loved Logan but she had never been

166

an integral part of him. The union between her and Peters was so fundamental that it was like being connected to his spinal cord. She understood the meaning of that metaphysical expression in the marriage service about the man and woman being one. She was one with him. When she touched him it was like an extension of herself. And if her commitment to him was complete, then it was mutual. She talked about herself, about her life and her marriage, and it sounded like the recital of someone else's life. Flying from London to Paris to entertain for Logan; dressing in clothes that cost a poor man's yearly wages; dispensing fine food and exquisite wines like some character in a pre-war play; living a life where the values were prefixed by a dollar sign; making relationships with people where there was no common ground beyond expediency. It sounded degrading and telling him made her ashamed. It was all far away and, having told him, she wanted to forget it. He hadn't confided in her about himself. He wasn't the kind of man who looked back in self-analysis. He was himself and she accepted it. And now she never thought about the future. She lived for the day, for their walks in the garden where they sat in the sun and there were no more thoughts of running away from him, of the nights when her door was unlocked and he came in to her. It was like a beautiful dream, filled with tender sensuality.

That morning he brought up her breakfast tray. She insisted that he shared it with her. Afterwards they went to the window; she loved to look out. Peters had his arm around her.

'I have to take her into Nice,' he said. 'I don't like leaving you, but Resnais won't be here. I'll be back as quickly as I can this afternoon. I thought I might take you for a swim. Would you like that?'

Eileen leaned her head against him. Below them the sea was blue and glittering in the sunshine.

'Aren't you afraid I might escape?'

'I can swim pretty fast,' Peters said. He kissed her hair.

He had not thought about another person subjectively for years. Now the quality that added lustre to their relationship was the total generosity with which she gave herself to him. And asked for nothing. He couldn't imagine any woman in a similar position who wouldn't have tried to persuade him to let her go. She didn't ask because she trusted him and because the understanding between them was so deep that neither sought advantage.

She hadn't asked him for the final commitment, but he knew that he would have to make it. On balance, Damascus was confident that her husband meant to carry out the terms for her release. Saiid Homsi believed in him. But neither of them knew that the bargaining card they held had never been a trump. Men like Logan Field didn't throw away Imshan for a woman they no longer wanted.

'I shall miss you,' Eileen said. 'I can try to finish that dreadful sex book you gave me.'

He turned round and kissed her. It took a long time. When he went downstairs Madeleine had brought the Renault out of the garage.

'You drive,' she said. 'I'm sick of that coast road. Let's go along the Moyenne Corniche for a change. We'll see some wonderful views. It's so clear today.'

Logan was having breakfast in his suite in the Okura Hotel when he got Janet's cable. 'Khorvan murdered. No change in the other negotiation. Please telex your progress as am anxious for news. Janet.'

He had slept well, after a long and tedious dinner with a dozen senior Japanese oil men. He felt relaxed in mind and body. The Japanese importers and the Government had agreed to a partnership, the terms of which would provide the extra money needed to finance the building and installation of the new refinery. The heads of agreement were being drawn up and he expected to sign them before leaving for Tehran. He had kept the question mark at bay, ruthlessly excluding it from his calculations. He went ahead as if there were no such man as Saiid Homsi and his wife were at home with their child in England. He closed out everything and brought the negotiations to a successful conclusion. Then he slept, because he knew that in the morning the truth would have to be admitted. He was gambling and he was doing so deliberately because he couldn't bring himself to back away and lose without a fight. There had to be a way out, a way which would save Eileen's life and still leave Imshan within grasp.

When he read Janet's cable he jumped to his feet with excitement. It couldn't have been more fortuitous. Imperial's main enemy and opponent was gone. It was incredible luck. He didn't think in human terms, and the Minister's death was not even a shock. It was a bonus. Without him, it might even now be possible to get the construction of the refinery deferred until Imperial had got the bulk of its investment back. Already he was dealing with Khorvan's successor in his mind. It was likely to be Amir Momtaz, former Ambassador in Washington and known to sympathize with the West. The way was clearing for Imshan. He could never have calculated on the removal of Khorvan. Nothing seemed to stand between him and the apex of his career. The solution to the savage inflationary problem of Western countries was within his personal grasp. He, Logan Field, head of Imperial Oil, was in a position to conclude a deal with the Government of Iran which would result in the break-up of Arab solidarity over oil prices, something that the diplomacy of the West had signally failed to achieve. His company would rank with the oil giants through the development of Imshan. From far below the sounds of Tokyo's frenetic traffic was a muted hum. Sitting in the tenth-floor suite in the luxurious Japanese hotel, Logan felt as if he were standing on the mountain peak looking down at the kingdoms beneath with the promise that all could be his if he would only pay the price.

And the price was Eileen. Deliberately he tried to call her face to mind and nothing came. It was a blank, as if he were subconsciously rejecting her memory. One life, balanced against the solution of a global problem. He had said to James Kelly that if it were no more than his own interests and those of the company, there would have been no conflict, and in that moment of self-examination he persuaded himself that it was true. Janet believed that Eileen would be killed whatever he did. He wasn't prepared to accept that view, but it raised a terrible doubt. It could all be thrown away for nothing. There was a reflection of himself in a mirror across the room. He looked up and saw it, a man sitting hunched in his chair, fighting against two impossible alternatives. To sentence his wife and his child's mother to an assassin's bullet or to destroy his life's work and leave the salvation of the economic and political system of Western Europe in doubt. And then to find that she was not returned alive. 'I don't think you'll ever see her again.' He remembered Janet saying that. He shuddered. Now her face was clear in his mind, the protecting screen dissolved, showing her to him in a dozen guises.

Walking through the soggy Irish fields to show him some horse in which he had no interest, reaching out to him on their honeymoon, leaning over his shoulder as he opened a Christmas present she had given him. He could remember exactly what it was. A little sepia study of hands by an unknown eighteenth-century artist. It hung in his study in London.

The man reflected in the mirror bent over, his head hidden in his hands. He realized he had been thinking of her in the past tense.

Resnais had left the villa early. He checked that the fishing-rod case was in the boot and drove off in the Jaguar. The coast road branched off towards the Corniche about five miles further on and he drove fast. At the junction leading to the mountain road he eased the car back and pulled into a lay-by. He changed his rope-soled sandals for strong shoes with rubber grips and pulled a black sweater over his white sweat shirt. He swung back onto the road and took the route up the mountain side. It was a hot morning and he was oily with sweat. His watch said nine fifty-five. Madeleine would leave with Peters at ten o'clock. He calculated that it would take them just over twenty-five minutes to reach the spot on the road he had indicated to her when they drove back from Nice. They had done the journey in reverse and arrived at the villa exactly half an hour later. He drove on, climbing the twisted road; below him the mountainside fell away, carpeted with pine trees. There was a steep bend, with a blind corner, and he slowed down. Rounding it he drove on for another hundred and fifty yards. The road widened here and there was sufficient room for a car to pull up against the rock verge without impeding traffic.

Resnais stopped the car, pulled out the angler's case and began to run back to the corner. It was ten-fifteen exactly. He climbed off the road, swinging himself up over the rocky overhang; there was a patch of scrub growing up just ahead of the blind corner. He had crouched there the day before and

170

it gave him a perfect view of the road and anything approaching on it before the corner itself had to be rounded. The angle was very steep. No car could hope to take it at speed. On the right-hand side the drop down the mountainside was hundreds of feet into the valley. Resnais unpacked the rifle and clipped on the telescopic sight. He heard the sound of a car and flattened himself in the scrub, sighting along the barrel. He had a clear view of a red Peugeot as it came along the road below him and plenty of time to identify it by the number plate. The Peugeot rounded the corner, slowing as it approached, and then disappeared. Resnais didn't move; he stayed in position, squinting through the tiny range finder on the rifle, waiting for the car driven by Peters to come into view.

Madeleine got into the front seat of the Renault beside Peters; she threw a raffia bag onto the back seat. She remarked on the heat and he said something non-committal; neither of them talked for the first part of the drive. She watched the road ahead through dark glasses and as they swung onto the Corniche she glanced across him and down. The drop was increasing. He drove fast, but without being reckless.

The corner where she knew Resnais was waiting was about two hundred and fifty metres ahead of them.

'I have to get this mended,' she said. She had taken her watch off and was looking at it. 'It stopped last night.'

'There's a place on the sea front,' Peters said. She was putting the watch back on her wrist; her window was down and her arm was lying across the edge of the door.

'Oh, *merde*!'

Peters slowed at the exclamation.

'What's the matter?'

'My watch has fallen off – you'll have to stop.'

He halted the car and Madeleine sprang out. The corner was just ahead of them and he could neither see anything coming round it nor be seen.

'Hurry up,' he said. 'I can't stop here!'

She had been searching along the ground; she straightened up and looked at him.

'Go on,' she said. 'I think there's a lay-by just round the corner. Wait for me there.'

She heard him say something irritated under his breath and

she stood still, watching as the car moved forward, gathering speed. A hundred metres to go. Resnais waiting above the road. She felt nothing but a calm detachment. As the car came into Resnais's view he saw that Madeleine wasn't in it. He sighted on the nearside front wheel and, as Peters came into the straight stretch of road before the corner, he squeezed the trigger. Peters knew the road and the corner; he didn't slow down as much as someone might have done who was unfamiliar with the curve. Without taking his attention off the road he saw up above a movement in the scrub bushes on the overhang. When the tyre burst, there was a second or two when he tried to take avoiding action. He slammed on the brakes and wrenched the wheel to the right, hoping to take the corner. But the impetus of his own speed was too great. The rear wheels slewed round and the Renault nose-dived over the edge.

The sound of rending metal and shattering glass reverberated. There was a sickening distant crash, followed by the dull boom of an explosion as the petrol tank caught fire. A plume of ugly black smoke drifted up over the lip of the road. Madeleine was running towards the place where the car had gone over. Resnais scrambled down and they stood together looking over the edge. There was a fire burning among the pine trees down the mountainside.

'Adieu, Peters,' Resnais said. He slapped her on the back. 'Come on, chérie. Get in the car.'

She turned away too quickly for him to see that her eyes had filled with tears.

The accident was reported to the police within the hour, but by the time the rescue squad climbed down to the site of the fire there were little outbreaks among the trees and a thick pall of black smoke hung in the air. There was nothing left of the car and anyone in it, but a mass of twisted, red hot metal.

Eileen spent the morning lazily. She bathed and passed some time resting on the bed; she dozed for a few minutes, her thoughts full of Peters. She dressed in the cotton dress he had bought her; there were more clothes in the cupboard, an assortment of lipsticks and box of expensive embroidered handkerchiefs which she hadn't the heart to tell him were less use to her than Kleenex. She brushed her hair and made up her lips. She looked tanned from the hours spent in the sunshine and the look of anxious strain had gone. It was a different face that looked back from the mirror, with satisfied eyes and serenity in her smile. She was aware that she looked younger; she felt as excited as a child at the promise to take her swimming when he got back. She went on brushing her hair and when she heard the key in the lock and the door opened she turned eagerly to meet him. Madeleine and Resnais were standing there. Resnais held a gun. Eileen dropped the brush and gave a cry of alarm. The Frenchman smiled.

'You're looking very well, Madame,' he said. 'Our friend has been taking good care of you.'

He walked towards her and she ran to the other side of the bed.

'Go away from me! When he gets back he'll kill you if you touch me again!'

Madeleine moved closer. She was very pale and there was something in her face that frightened Eileen more than the slow grin on the Frenchman's mouth.

'He won't *be* back,' Madeleine said. 'He's dead.'

Eileen stared at each of them. She shook her head.

'I don't believe you! I don't believe you!'

'Put your hands on your head,' Madeleine said, 'otherwise he'll shoot you in the legs. Hurry up!'

'It isn't true,' Eileen was crying. 'You're trying to frighten me . . . He's coming back this afternoon . . .'

'He's dead,' Madeleine shouted at her. She strode round to where Eileen stood, cowering by the bed with her back to the wall. She stepped up and hit her hard across the face with the back of her hand.

'Thanks to you,' she said. 'You corrupted a good man. You ruined him. Now you're going to pay for it. Resnais and I will see to that! Now put your hands on your head, you bitch, before I smash your stupid face.'

She had been trained in unarmed combat; she was fit and very strong. She caught Eileen and spun her round; she gave her a violent push towards the door. Resnais stood by, pointing the gun at her.

'Go on,' he said. 'I wouldn't provoke her, Madame. You took her man away. I don't think she liked that.'

Eileen heard him laugh. She saw the Lebanese girl give him a venomous look. She raised her arms and placed her hands on her head. She walked ahead of them out of the room. She passed Ahmed in the hall as they crossed from the stairs. She gave him a look of appeal but he turned away. They went through into the kitchen and out into a passage, where Resnais opened a door, and down a flight of stairs. She found it difficult to walk down them and she lowered her arms. There was a door at the end. In front of it she stopped. She looked at the Frenchman.

'I don't care if you kill me,' she said. 'If he's dead, I don't care what happens to me.'

'Shut up,' Resnais said.

Madeleine unlocked the door at the foot of the steps.

'Get inside,' she said.

It was pitch dark; blinded by the contrast to the electric lights outside, Eileen could distinguish nothing as she walked into the room. Her hands lowered in expectation of the shot in the back of the head. She felt no fear. Her sole sensation was a grinding pain of grief. But there was no shot. The door slammed and she was left alone. She sank down on the ground and sobbed, not for herself but for the man she loved as she had never loved anything or anyone, not even her child. It was a long time before she got up; she was exhausted from crying. There was a dim light in the room coming from an air vent high up in the wall. She could see the outline of racks filled with bottles and knew she was in the wine cellar. She found the door and ran her hands over the walls looking for a switch, but the lights were turned on from outside. There was a cold, musty smell. She went round the wine racks and made a circle of the room. There was only the one door and the one little vent letting in the feeble light. There were no facilities, no bed, not even a bucket. She sank down on the floor again and knew that this signified their intention to kill her. Her feelings were confused.

Shock had deadened fear; agony for Peters overrode the terror implicit in being at the mercy of the Frenchman and the woman. Now that fear mounted. Eileen began to shiver in the cold and darkness. They hadn't killed her; she gave a moan of fear at the idea that they intended to punish her in some way. 'Thanks to you,' the girl had said before she hit her. They had murdered Peters. They had murdered him because they had discovered that he and she were lovers. And they had brought her down to this cellar – for what purpose? The Frenchman had tortured her and almost raped her; she could imagine what that woman with hate blazing in her eyes would do . . .

Panic swept up on her and she fought to keep control. Peters would want her to stay calm. She fixed his image in her mind and the threat of hysteria receded. She remembered his kisses that morning, the comfort of being held in his arms. It had been a final leave-taking. She had that to strengthen her and give her courage. The end didn't matter. To face it with dignity was important. To keep him in her mind and to go to meet him. The idea gave her peace. She knelt for a time, her face covered by her hands, and prayed for him and for herself. Then she settled down to wait.

'Mr Kelly?'

James went stiff at the sound of the voice over the telephone. He was sitting outside the drawing room, smoking and listening to the gentle night-time chorus in the garden. A French diplomat and his wife had dined quietly with him that evening; most of the time was spent discussing Khorvan's murder. He had retreated into the garden for a last cigarette before going to bed. The British Embassy had obtained an audience with the Shah in three days' time. He picked up the phone and heard Homsi's voice.

'What is it?' James said. 'Is anything wrong?' Alarm made him abrupt. It was nearly midnight.

'That's for you to say,' Homsi answered. 'I've just had a disturbing piece of news, Mr Kelly. I hear that Mr Field has signed an agreement with the Japanese Government.'

'Oh, Christ!' James groaned, covering the mouthpiece. 'Where did you hear this? I'm sure it's not correct.'

'From a private source,' the Syrian said. 'I am afraid this may have very serious consequences.'

'Wait a moment,' Kelly almost shouted at him. 'Listen to me. If it *is* true, I can explain what's happened. When can I see you?'

'Tomorrow,' Homsi said. 'I feel this is very urgent, Mr Kelly. Unless you can give me a satisfactory explanation, I am very much afraid of what may happen.'

'Where and what time?' Kelly said. 'As early as possible.'

'I will wait down the road from your house,' the Syrian said. 'Pick me up in your car at seven-thirty. We can go for a drive and you can go on to your office. I think it is very foolish of Mr Field to go back on his word.'

Before James could deny it, he had rung off. He stood and looked at the phone in his hand; the line was buzzing clear. He put it down and dialled the Hilton hotel. There was a long pause and finally someone on the night switchboard answered. He told them to put him through to Mrs Armstrong. She answered immediately, but he could tell by her voice that she had been asleep. He didn't waste time.

'I've had a call,' she said. 'Apparently Logan has signed with the Japanese. Have you heard anything?'

'Yes,' he heard Janet say. 'He cabled me this morning. The negotiation has been a complete success. They've agreed to finance the refinery. What do you mean, you've had a call? Did he ring you?'

'No,' James said. 'He bloody well didn't. Homsi phoned me. He says this could have serious consequences. They think he's gone back on his word. You realize what this may mean for Eileen?'

'How did they find out?' She sounded wide awake now. 'Nobody knew. It was highly confidential.'

'Listen,' James said. 'Listen to me. If you don't want her death on your conscience, you cable him to get back here. Send it tonight and tell him to take the next flight available. I'm seeing Homsi tomorrow and I can maybe hold him off till Logan gets here.'

'All right.' He heard Janet hesitate and he called her a vile name under his breath. 'I'll send it.'

'He's made his choice, hasn't he?' James said. 'And you knew it. You knew when he signed with the Japs that he was going to rat on the terms. He's a murderer, a cold-blooded murderer. You'd better get him back here.' He rang off.

At seven-fifteen the next morning, Saiid Homsi took a car from his Embassy and it left him at the end of the road leading

176

to Kelly's driveway. It was overcast and hot, with a suggestion of a storm in the air. He walked slowly down the road. His own car had driven off. There was nobody about at that hour. Homsi heard the car coming up behind him and he stopped, waiting for it to draw level. Before it came to a halt, the two rear doors were flung open and three men jumped out. Homsi didn't have time to turn round before they reached him. He was knocked unconscious and heaved into the back of the car in less than a minute. It drove off at speed toward the north of the city. At seven-thirty exactly, James Kelly came out of the driveway and pulled into the road. He waited until eight o'clock for the Syrian to appear and in a mood of desperation gave up and went to Imperial Oil's office on Shah Reza Avenue.

A call put through to the Syrian Embassy gave him no information. Homsi had not come into the building. He left a message asking him to contact him urgently and, when the morning passed and there was no call, he phoned the Syrian Embassy again. This time he was cut off abruptly without being told anything. By the middle of the afternoon, the Embassy itself had begun to make inquiries. The Tehran police were unable to assist them. They took details of the missing trade attaché and Syrian security men visited his rooms. The driver of the car that had taken him to Shemiran that morning was questioned but knew nothing which could explain the mystery.

By eight the following morning, Saiid Homsi had told Colonel Ardalan a number of things which enabled him to fit the vital pieces into his puzzle. The Colonel went home for breakfast; he was very tired because it had been a long day and a long night. He had not permitted the prisoner an hour's respite. There was a SAVAK doctor in attendance, who listened to the Syrian's heart and checked his blood pressure at intervals during the interrogation. The Colonel didn't want him to collapse and die with any question left unanswered. Homsi proved to be wiry and tough. He sustained pain with fortitude and held out until the unbearable threshold was reached and overtaken. Ardalan watched the transformation into a mindless animal and, in the later stages, put a knob of cotton wool into his ears. When he returned to his family and took breakfast, a habit he had picked up during his course at the Military

Academy at Sandhurst, the doctor had advised him that the prisoner would not survive without a respite. He drank coffee and ate hot bread rolls, baked with honey and raisins, and played with his smallest child before it was taken to school. He knew now why Saiid Homsi had contacted Logan Field. He made a report over the scrambled telephone to the Shah's private number at the Saadabad Palace. It was regrettable, but on medical advice he had to defer further questioning until that evening. In the meantime the prisoner was being given protestin injections to raise his blood pressure.

It was the worst day that James Kelly could remember. Contact with Homsi was his only link with the kidnappers. He had presented himself at the Syrian Embassy that evening and asked to see Homsi's superior. He was turned away without an interview and the attitude of the staff was openly hostile. Nobody could tell him anything and nobody would see him. He returned defeated to his house at Shemiran to find Janet Armstrong waiting for him with the telex announcing Logan's arrival from Tokyo the next day. He read it and threw it aside. He didn't ask her to sit down and when he poured himself a whisky, he didn't offer one to her.

'He needn't bother,' he said. 'They've cut off all contact with us. Homsi didn't turn up this morning and the Embassy are denying all knowledge of him.' He looked at Janet. She was cool and smart as always but there were dark rings under her eyes and she seemed subdued. He hoped he was conveying his feelings towards her.

'What does it mean?' she asked.

'It means,' James said slowly, 'that they know Logan was double dealing. Promising one thing and doing another. They don't stand for that kind of thing.' He took a swallow of his whisky. 'My guess is, you don't have a problem any more. I think by now, Eileen is dead.'

He was surprised to see her turn away.

'Don't say that. It wasn't Logan's fault.'

Kelly didn't answer.

'They never meant to let her go,' Janet said. 'Whatever he did, she hadn't a chance.'

'If you don't mind,' Kelly finished his drink, 'I won't come out to the car with you.'

'I suppose you blame me for saying so,' she said.

Kelly shook his head.

'I don't blame you,' he said. 'You had your eye on the main chance. She wasn't your responsibility. Common humanity might have counted with some people, but you don't have any. No, I don't blame you. I'm sure you won't blame yourself.'

She started to say something and then suddenly she burst into tears.

'You bastard!'

She ran out of the room and he heard the door slam. The house was very quiet. It had been better when she was there. He had been able to vent his feelings. The silence was unbearable. He wished he could have gone after her and made her stay. He poured a second whisky and sat down with it. He had to find Homsi. If the Syrian was avoiding him, he still had to find him. To plead, beg, promise – do anything, if there was any chance left.

He put a call through to Colonel Ardalan. It was no good waiting for the Shah and presuming on a relationship which had its origins in political pragmatism. He needed help immediately.

Madeleine had been drinking. Resnais had never seen her drink as much wine as she did that night; they ate a good meal on the terrace and she shouted at Ahmed to bring brandy. She leaned over the table towards Resnais.

'I wonder if that bitch is feeling hungry by now?'

He shrugged.

'If she's thirsty she can open a bottle.' They both laughed. 'You were very good today,' he said.

'So were you.' Madeleine raised the glass to him. 'What did Damascus say?'

'All Arab patriots will mourn.' Resnais imitated the high pitched voice of their radio contact. 'And so they should,' he added. 'He was a hero, killed by a mischance. I said that you were lying down in a dark room.' He looked at her and grinned. She was no longer laughing with him.

'He was corrupted,' she said. 'You didn't know him before. He was like a tiger. But she ruined him.'

'Come on.' Resnais shrugged. 'He's paid for it. Be satisfied.'

Madeleine pushed back her chair. She was drunk but quiet steady.

'I'm going down to pay her a visit,' she said.

Resnais leaned over and caught her wrist.

'No,' he said.

She pulled at him furiously, trying to free herself.

'You said you wouldn't interfere! You promised me!'

'I never said you could beat her to death,' he said. 'You're in a nasty mood, chérie. I'll make a bargain with you. When the time comes, you can shoot her. And I promise you that. But I'm not having any Arab games played with her.'

She looked at him with hatred.

'You want her for yourself! Now you've killed Peters, you want the bitch yourself!'

She cried out as he twisted her wrist and jerked it downwards.

'We both killed him,' he said. He got up and pushed her back in the chair. 'You were the decoy. You set him up. So never say *I* killed him. Never say that again!'

She slumped, rubbing her wrist. She called him a gross name in Arabic and he slapped her face.

'You behave,' Resnais said. 'I'm not Peters. You won't throw tantrums with me. I'm in command here now and you'll do exactly what you're told, otherwise I'll take the hide off you. Understand?'

He hadn't lost his temper; he was cool and calm. He had never liked her and they were only allies through necessity. Peters had never controlled her properly. And Peters was dead. He had no motive in protecting Eileen, except a dislike for women who asserted themselves. The sight of the Lebanese girl drunk had irritated him. Now that he had frightened her, he found her more attractive. He pulled her out of the chair.

'I don't want her,' he said. 'I feel like having you. Get upstairs!'

Ahmed the servant hid himself behind the door of the kitchen as they went. He had been told of the American's death and been surprised at what seemed to be a celebration. He saw the Frenchman and the woman going upstairs and into the man's bedroom. He had been told to leave the prisoner in the cellar without food or water and to ignore her if she called out. He guessed that the other two were responsible for the American's death. Westerners quarrelling among themselves did not concern him; he hated them all. They could starve the woman in the cellar if they liked and it wouldn't have disturbed him. Like his counterpart, Habib Ebrahimi in Tehran, he was a humble servant of the Arab cause. When Peters was in charge, he had obeyed him without question. The radio was never left unattended; Ahmed slept in the room where the transmitter was kept. His Algerian master had used it as an office. He had a bed in the corner, and his instructions were to wake Peters at any hour of the night if a call came through. The Frenchman had given him no instructions. They had both drunk a lot of wine. He had seen them quarrel and not come near to clear the table till they went away. He had respected the American but he was afraid of Resnais. He was Jallad, the executioner. When the transmitter call came through at two in the morning, Ahmed woke and lay awake listening to it. He didn't go upstairs. When it stopped he went to sleep again.

'Why didn't you come to me?' Colonel Ardalan asked. 'I told you I would always help if there was any difficulty. Now, it may be too late.'

James was walking beside him down the passage of the SAVAK headquarters at Niavaran. His call to Ardalan had brought a car round to the house. The Colonel was occupied but he asked Mr Kelly to come to him.

They stopped at a lift, went inside and it descended two floors. The Colonel showed him the way down a yellow-washed corridor with ugly fluorescent lighting overhead. There were several doors on the right and left and he stopped at one of them. He turned to James.

'This isn't very pleasant,' he said, 'but I assure you it has been necessary.'

He opened the door and James went in. The first impression was the smell. It was acrid and bit into his nostrils. Urine, vomit and a stench of human excreta. He covered his mouth with his handkerchief and was almost sick. The room was in darkness except for a single powerful light directed upon something sprawling in a chair, held there by webbing straps.

He didn't recognize Saiid Homsi. There were wires leading

from the chair to a desk. The Colonel sat behind it and offered James a chair.

'We have asked him everything,' he said. 'His answers are taped; sometimes it's difficult to make out what he says. You have a question, Mr Kelly. Ask it.'

The Colonel's hand rested lightly upon a small switch in a portable electric control panel. James couldn't speak at first. He had never fainted in his life but he came close to it in the first few minutes in the room.

'Ask him where they're holding Mrs Field.'

Another voice asked the question; there were several SAVAK officers in the background. There was no answer. James saw Ardalan press the switch. He turned away and choked into his handkerchief.

'We will repeat the question,' the Colonel said, 'but we have to be careful. The doctor says he is near the end. We don't want him to die before he tells us. Why don't you have a cigarette?'

This time there was a mumble; James couldn't distinguish a word.

'Repeat it,' came the order. The switch was pressed once more. James had his back to the scene. But this time there was no sound. He turned and saw a man bending over the figure in the chair.

The Colonel shook his head. He seemed genuinely upset.

'My friend,' he said, 'I am very sorry. You came to me too late. The man is dead.'

Ardalan took him into his office. He gave him a glass of whisky and a cigarette. Even here, in the crisp modern decor, it seemed that the smell of pain came with them. James sat with the glass in his hands; he felt too sick and stunned to speak. 'You came too late.' Nothing would have saved Saiid Homsi. A few hours earlier he could have told them where to find Eileen. Now he was dead and all hope for her had died with him. Ardalan hadn't spared him.

'It must be known by now that we arrested him,' he said. 'Syria has spies even in SAVAK. So they will realize that the whole plot is discovered. I am afraid poor Mrs Field may already be dead.'

'She hadn't a chance anyway,' Kelly said slowly. 'Logan went to Tokyo to make a deal over Imshan with the Japanese

Government. They found out he was going to sign an agreement with them. Homsi told me.'

The Colonel had been monitoring James's telephone ever since the murder of Khorvan; he was aware of all that had passed between him and Homsi including the rendezvous his men had intercepted. But he said nothing.

'Do you really think she's dead?'

'I would think so,' the Colonel said, 'but even so, I have sent for that last tape. We can play it back and see if it makes sense.'

'I don't believe it will,' James said. 'It sounded gibberish to me.'

'He was very incoherent,' Ardalan said. 'Towards the end he was very confused. We will play it over and see. I think you should drink your whisky, Mr Kelly. You look unwell.'

## 10

There was a small pine growing out of the red rock fifty feet down the mountainside where Peters's car went over. The Renault had somersaulted twice before it hit the trunk. The impact threw Peters through the passenger door which had burst open. He was knocked out within seconds of the car diving over the edge. Being unconscious, his body offered less resistance. He was flung into the scrub about ten yards from the tree, while the car went on bouncing and somersaulting down the mountainside. He lay there undiscovered by the police who came to investigate reports of a fire and an accident. When he came to, the sun was blazing fiercely down and the rock was burning to the touch. He had no idea where he was or what had happened. He was bleeding from cuts to the face and his hair was brown and matted with dried blood. Every part of him ached and throbbed and a pain in his side made him jack-knife as he pulled himself up. He knew he was concussed; the ferocity of his headache and a blurring in his vision told him that.

He crouched for some time, fighting the nausea and malaise, trying to regain his equilibrium. Something was driving him, something that wouldn't let him roll over and slide back into darkness. Something sharper than the ribs he sensed were broken and the chaotic pounding in his head. He had to get to his feet. He had been in an accident; there was a memory of a bang, and then a frightful crash of glass and metal...

He dragged himself upright and the sky slid away from him. He began to crawl back up the road on his hands and knees, forced on by the fear which couldn't be identified. A motorist found him staggering along the road. There was a blessed period when he faded out on the way to the hospital in Nice and woke in time to get to the casualty department on his own feet. He gave his real name and genuinely could not remember his address. Although the headache was intolerable, he protested violently, but in vain, when he was given a pain-killing injection, and recovered consciousness to find himself in a side ward with a gendarme sitting by the bed waiting to take a statement from him.

By this time it was dark and he knew now what had driven him back up the mountainside and onto the road. Madeleine had left the car just before the tyre burst; there was no question of coincidence. She had insisted on taking the Corniche road instead of the faster coastline route. She had set him up for Resnais. Seconds before the tyre blew apart, he had seen a movement in the brush above the road. They had tried to kill him.

Eileen. He had to stop himself yelling at the policeman and leaping out of the bed. He had driven off in the morning; he had been unconscious and concussed for most of the day.

'You don't remember your address, Monsieur?'

'No,' Peters said. 'Just my car going over the edge. But my memory is improving. After a night's sleep I will be able to tell you everything.'

'You were very lucky,' the man said, putting his notebook into his breast pocket. 'That car of yours was completely burnt out. Nobody even thought to look for you. I'll send in the nurse.'

He went out and Peters waited. He smiled at the nurse when she came in.

'You're feeling better? Very good. I've got some tablets here. You take these and have a good sleep. That *flic* will be back tomorrow.'

Peters took the tablets; he palmed them, pretending to swallow them with a little water.

'Thanks,' he said. 'I'll sleep now. What time is it?'

'Past eight o'clock,' she said.

She went out, drawing a screen round the end of his bed. Eight o'clock. Ten hours. Ten hours in which they could have done anything to her. He thought of Resnais and flung the bedclothes back. His side was strapped up with adhesive and there was very little pain from the broken ribs. His head was the worst. There was a dressing on it. He crept on bare feet to the locker by the bed and opened it. His clothes hung inside. His shirt was torn and bloodstained, but his shoes and trousers were there. He pushed back the screen. It was a little room, leading directly into a bigger ward. The window was masked by a mosquito screen. He unhooked it and opened the window. The ward was on the first floor and a balcony with a fire escape stairs ran right round each of the five tiers of the hospital building. He pulled his pillows down into the bed, wrapped the cover over them and thumped them into some kind of shape that might deceive a casual glance. Then he climbed out into the darkness and began to make his way down the iron steps into the grounds.

At ten o'clock that night, one of the casualty officers came off duty and couldn't find his car. The police were not very sympathetic when he admitted that he had left his keys in it.

Peters drove slowly. He kept suffering periods of dizziness and in the lights from oncoming cars his vision played tricks. Twice he almost veered across the road. There was a blare of horns from outraged drivers and he swung back to safety. The drive from the centre of Nice took him an hour because he missed a turning and circled for twenty minutes. The pain in his head was getting worse. On the coast road he pulled into the side and rested. Nobody would expect a raid on the villa. They must think he was dead. He remembered that he carried keys to the gates and the front door and frantically searched for them in his trouser pockets. But they and his money had been lodged in the hospital for safe-keeping. He would have to break in. He put the car into gear and drove on. He couldn't take it too near the villa because it would be reported stolen and the police might well call in to houses in its vicinity in case anyone had seen the thief. He parked down a side road and began to walk the three hundred metres to the villa. His watch had been taken and he had no idea of the time. When he approached the house was in darkness. He could hear the sea breaking on the rocks at the back. The gates were closed. He had been taught to pick locks but he had nothing, not even a pin. The only way he could get in was to go down to the beach and swim the distance to the rocks below the villa.

Fortunately the night was clear and bright. By the time he reached the shore, he was staggering like a drunken man. He had climbed a fence and stumbled down three hundred steep stone steps to the sandy beach which was the private preserve of a neighbouring villa built up on the headland. It belonged to a German industrialist who had built a huge swimming pool and never used the sea. Peters fell onto the sand. He fought off the weakness that wanted to give up and fall asleep. The sea hissed and murmured in front of him.

He knew he had to rest before he attempted to swim round the rocks. There was no current there, but a rough sea would have proved too much for him. It was as smooth as black silk, with the moonlight painting a silver path out to the horizon. He leaned back against the rocks and closed his eyes for a moment. He had suffered injury before, but he was very strong and always fit. A bullet wound would have been easier than the waves of dizziness and weakness that were the legacy of concussion.

Peters had always believed in the power of the human will. He had seen men in the jungles of Chile, fighting and surviving in conditions lethal to civilized people. Dedication, fanaticism, these had been the driving forces in his life. Now it was fear that sent the adrenalin pumping, a personal fear so acute that it transcended actual injury to the central nervous system, forcing him to get up when his hurt brain was clamouring for rest.

He tied his shoes round his neck and waded slowly into the water. He had never prayed, even as a child. His family were agnostics who declined religious education for their children. He asked for no external help. He only knew he had to swim the distance and get to Eileen before the dawn came. He made the journey on his back for part of the way; his broken ribs made it impossible to swim effectively over-arm or even breast stroke. His legs were powerful and they drove him round the promontory. The water was warm and buoyant. For the last few metres he stretched out and swam, grunting with pain, and stumbled onto the rocks below the villa, where Madeleine liked to sunbathe. There were fifty steps up to the terrace. They looked as steep as a mountainside as he began to climb. The salt water had soaked through the dressing on his scalp and the wound was stinging. He didn't even notice it; the effort of getting up the steep, narrow stairway was taking all his concentration. When he reached the terrace he collapsed and blacked out. He lay sprawled in full view of the bedroom windows upstairs.

It was light when he recovered consciousness. The blackout had slid into a deep sleep that lasted through the rest of the night. He blinked and moved, confused by his surroundings. His wet clothes had dried on him. There was a rime of salt on his skin. He scrambled up, and froze, listening. There was no sound from inside the villa. The sun was not yet risen and he guessed by the grey light that it must be near five in the morning. His head ached ferociously but he felt stronger. The doors to the terrace were locked, but it only needed his weight to push them open and he was inside.

He stepped into the hall through the big living room and listened. Ahmed slept lightly and would be up within an hour. He came to the stairs and looked up. Eileen wouldn't be there. If she were still alive he knew exactly where they would have put her. He had to find the Algerian first. The door to the radio room opened silently. Peters couldn't see because the blinds were drawn, but after a moment he could hear movement and a grunt as Ahmed turned over on his cot. He edged through the door. Enough light came from outside to show him that the Algerian was huddled up asleep. There was no question of asking him for help. Ahmed had no personal loyalty to him, any more than to Resnais and Madeleine. He belonged to the PLO. Any attempt to rescue Eileen would have him screaming for the others. Peters killed him with a single blow on the throat as he slept. Then he switched on the light and began to search for the keys to the gates which were in Ahmed's keeping. He hadn't found them when he heard the transmitter call sign. He hesitated. His vision blurred again and he swore, catching on to the table to steady himself. His head was churning and pounding like a cement mixer. He had to think clearly. Resnais would have reported his death in the car accident. Damascus would expect Resnais or Madeleine to answer. He put on the earphones and threw the switch to receive. He gave the call sign in French and used Resnais's name. The message came through and was repeated twice. He knew the formula so well he could decode it in his head. 'Our contact arrested in Tehran. The operation is blown. Execute the hostage immediately. Evacuate the villa and disperse.' It was signed by the chief of staff of the Palestine People's Army.

Eileen was sobbing in his arms. She was awake when he

switched on the light and then opened the cellar door. She had slept lying in a huddle on the floor and woken stiff and cold. When she saw him in the doorway, she cried out. He tried to hush her, but she flung herself on him weeping hysterically. He held her in his arms and begged her to be quiet.

'They said you were dead,' she repeated. 'Oh, God, they said you were dead...'

He found it difficult to speak. She was alive and unhurt. It had taken all the effort of which he was capable to find her and suddenly he had nothing left. She found herself supporting him.

'You're badly hurt,' she said. 'Oh my darling...'

There was blood on her hands from the head wound which had opened and soaked through the dressing. She held him and wept. She was shivering with shock and chill. Peters made her look at him. He spoke gently but with firmness. It cost him a great effort.

'Listen to me,' he said. 'You've got to get away. I've killed Ahmed. The others are asleep. There's nobody around. Take the keys in my pocket. They open the gates. There's a car in the driveway – take it. Go on now.'

Eileen looked at him. He was a dreadful grey colour and quite suddenly his legs gave way and he sat on the ground. He put his hand to his head. She knelt beside him.

'I had an accident. I'm concussed to hell. I can't do any more. You take the car and get out of here.'

'No.' She shook her head. She wiped her eyes and face with the back of her hand. 'No,' she said, 'I'm not going anywhere without you.'

He turned on her fiercely.

'For Christ's sake! I've just had the radio order to kill you! Get going!'

He pushed her. Eileen didn't move.

'I'm not leaving you here. If I'm gone those two will kill you. I stay, my darling, or we go together.'

He looked at her and she saw the glaze in his eyes.

'I can't make it,' he said slowly. 'I'm going to black out any minute. I love you. Will you for Christ's sake go now?'

She put her arms around him and drew his head onto her shoulder.

'I love you too. And I'm not leaving you. We'll just have to

189

wait till you've had a rest. It'll be all right. We'll get away together.'

He tried to say something but his eyes closed and he slid into the dark.

Eileen held him. She kissed him gently. The door was open and she had only to reach into his pocket for the keys. She could be free in a few minutes, provided she did as he wanted and left him behind. There wasn't even a moment when she considered it. She held him close to her and soothed him, although he couldn't hear. She felt very little fear. That had been conquered during the long night. If they were going to die, and she felt instinctively that this must be the end, then they would be together.

Upstairs, in the bed she had shared with Resnais, Madeleine awoke. He was still sleeping, his mouth slightly open, one leg stuck out over the edge of the bed. She had hated everything he did; she hated herself for submitting to it, and the situation which bound her to him. There was a moment, as she looked at him, when she thought of killing him and setting herself free. But it wasn't a real possibility and she gave up the idea. He had taken control. He was a vicious and unpredictable man of whom she was justifiably afraid. Until the mission ended, there was no way she could escape him. She went into her own room and took a shower. To her shame, tears mingled with the water, and they were for Peters. Crying for him reminded her of the prisoner in the cellar. She was the one responsible for everything going wrong. It was Eileen Field who was really to blame for Peters's death. She had soft brown hair which Madeleine imagined tearing out in handfuls. Resnais was not likely to wake up for some time. At least she could go down and see how she had enjoyed being left without food and water for nearly twenty-four hours. She dressed and went downstairs. The light was on in the radio room.

'Ahmed?' she called out. She looked round the door and saw him lying in the cot. Blood was running out of his mouth. She had seen men killed like that before. She forgot about Eileen Field. She ran to the foot of the stairs and yelled for Resnais.

Logan was met at the airport by a government car flying the Iranian flag. James Kelly came to meet him. There were no customs formalities. He was hurried through by airline officials and James didn't explain anything until they were in the car.

'The Shah has sent for you,' he said. 'The Minister of the Court telephoned through this morning. Thank God the plane wasn't late.'

'What the hell's happened?' Logan demanded. 'Has anything gone wrong with Imshan?'

James could hardly bring himself to answer.

'The whole thing has blown up in our faces,' he said. 'That's why the Shah wants to see you.'

He gestured towards the driver; there was no partition between them.

'I don't think it's wise to discuss it,' he spoke very quietly. 'A lot of these Palace staff speak English. Anyway we're there.'

Saadabad Palace was a long, two-storey building of dazzling white stone at Tajrish. It was just visible beyond the towering ornamental gates. The car stopped and both men got out. An army officer came forward and James gave their names, which the officer checked against a list. They walked through onto a wide road, flanked on one side by trees, which led directly to the Palace. It was a very hot, clear morning and the sky behind the white building was a dazzling blue. It was a modern conception, built with a strong Greek classical influence, with a steep flight of wide steps to the entrance and flanked by pillars down each side.

'What does he want?' Logan demanded. 'For Christ's sake, what do you mean it's blown up in our faces!'

'Homsi's been arrested,' James said. 'He died under torture. Ardalan knows everything.'

'Jesus,' Logan groaned.

They began the climb up the stairs to the palace entrance. A Palace Chamberlain, dressed in the magnificent blue, gold and white uniform of the Shah's court officials, met them at the door. They crossed a vast white hall, with chandeliers and a few pieces of huge gilded furniture, and were shown into a waiting room. The Chamberlain spoke to James, whom he knew well from previous visits.

'His Imperial Majesty will see you and Mr Field in a few moments.'

The doors closed behind him. It was the largest room Logan

had ever seen and he was not unused to palaces and presidents' official residences. There was an impression of extreme luxury about the furniture, which Kelly's more practised eye identified as French nineteenth-century of the best quality, and there was a huge colourful Qum carpet and alongside it a magnificent Nain, also fresh from the looms. A life-size portrait of the Empress Farah, dressed in ceremonial robes with the priceless Iranian emeralds on her brow, in her ears and round her neck, hung on one of the walls. The impression was one of over-powering wealth newly acquired. The gleam of gilt and mirror and multi-coloured chandeliers was pristine. Age had not had time to mellow anything. It glittered and dazzled like the incredible carpets. It was the showpiece of every self-made millionaire with little taste and a contempt for the antique. Its scale alone subdued criticism.

Logan didn't speak. He was marshalling his forces for the interview. He refused to allow the implications of what James had told him to penetrate beyond the immediate necessity of meeting the Shah. And of all the men in positions of power, Mohammed Riza Pahlavi was likely to be the most formidable. He remembered James's description of him. Cold, supremely intelligent, endowed with a quiet authority. Incapable of being fooled by bluff or intimidated by bluster. Absolute master of his country and his people; holding, by reason of his oil resources, the Western world in supplication at his gate. The Chamberlain came back and held the doors open.

'His Imperial Majesty is ready to see you. Please come with me.'

They recrossed the hall and were shown into a small room, pleasantly decorated in pale green, with a fine reproduction desk between tall windows overlooking the Palace gardens and a comfortable sofa with two armchairs, separated by a long marble-topped coffee table.

The Shah of Iran came forward and shook hands with them. The Shadow of God, Shahanshah, King of Kings, Light of the Aryans. He was of medium height. Logan was the taller by at least four inches but it gave him no advantage. The face was deeply lined and thin, the hair grey and very curly. He wore slightly tinted glasses which made it difficult to see his eyes. His light grey suit and dull red tie were a contrast to the gorgeous uniforms of the court officials. He smiled at James.

'How are you, Mr Kelly?'

'Very well, thank you, sir.'

'Sit down, Mr Field.' It was very informal; the Shah was relaxed and friendly. He reminded Logan of the head of a giant corporation more than a Middle-Eastern autocrat. 'First,' the Shah said, 'let me say that I am sorry we meet in such painful circumstances for you, Mr Field. I am extremely sorry to hear what has happened to your wife. It is a terrible outrage.'

'Thank you, sir,' Logan said.

'I understand that you have been negotiating for financial backing in Tokyo.' The Shah crossed one leg over the other.

Kelly understood that the audience would be conducted between him and Logan from now on. The Shah did not deal with subordinates when the chairman was present. He accepted his relegation without resentment. The Shah had enjoyed talking to him; it might be true to say that he had liked James Kelly to the extent of which he was capable of liking any foreigner, but nobody as experienced as James would have presumed upon the friendship. From now on, it was Logan Field who had to answer all the questions.

'Yes, sir, I did. And I'm happy to say that my negotiations with the Japanese oil importers were followed by further negotiations with the Japanese Government. I saw the Deputy Prime Minister on Thursday. I explained the full potential of the Imshan oil-fields to him and also the terms put forward by Minister Khorvan. He appreciated our dilemma.'

'I'm sure he also appreciated the strategic advantages,' the Shah interposed.

Logan nodded. He was not used to choosing his words with such care and he found it inhibiting.

'You will understand, sir, that I went to Tokyo without consulting my Board in London. It seemed to me that if we were to meet the Minister's requirements, we had to bring in financial support from a new source or a new refinery for Imshan would have been impossible. Our own cash flow could not support the refinery as well as the development of the field.'

'I see that,' the Shah said, 'but since the advantages I mentioned are so enormous to your company personally, and to the Western world in general, I knew this difficulty would be overcome. I assured the Minister on this point. I had no doubt, Mr Field, that an offer such as I made to you of a discount on your share of the oil would ensure that you find a way to agree to my terms and build the refinery which Imshan needs.'

'You were quite right, sir,' Logan said. 'After my discussion with the Japanese Government I was able to conclude a provisional agreement with them and oil importers for the full financing in return for a guaranteed oil supply for the ten years after full production is achieved. That will build the refinery.'

'Good,' the Shah said. 'That is the news I hoped to hear from you. When the Minister was assassinated, there was some doubt about your sincerity in the matter. Understandable in view of the discoveries Colonel Ardalan made from the terrorist and from the Syrian Homsi. I am completely satisfied with your report, Mr Field.'

'Thank you, sir,' Logan said.

He had thought the Shah relaxed; he saw now that it had been an attitude adopted for the interview. The man was coiled like a spring. He spoke faultless English, having learned it in his teens; Western languages do not come easily to the Iranian ear. Educated at Le Rosey in Switzerland and widely travelled in his youth, there was a deceptive period in his life when he had seemed another Eastern playboy, until the British deposed his father in 1941 and placed him on the throne in expectation of a puppet who could be managed from Whitehall. Thirty-four years later, Logan Field faced the product of that uneasy assumption of a throne. He had given him his refinery, produced by his own efforts the crucial agreement which permitted both Iran and Imperial Oil to get what they wanted. Mohammed Riza Pahlavi had loved his second wife, the Empress Soraya. For an Eastern king, with an unsecured succession, he had shown considerable sentiment towards his childless consort, even after he divorced her. Logan had never given anything in a business negotiation without trying, and usually succeeding, in getting something back. The idea came very suddenly to him, as he looked at the head of the Iranian state, a man like himself and a man who had just been accorded everything he had demanded.

'Sir,' he said slowly, 'you were kind enough to express your sympathy over my wife.'

He could feel James going stiff on the sofa beside him. The Shah nodded.

'You know that the price of her release is our withdrawal from Imshan?'

'I believe that is what the Syrian admitted under questioning,' the Shah said.

'I realize,' Logan went on, 'that I made a serious initial mistake. When Homsi first approached me I should have come direct to you with the problem.'

'It would have been wiser,' was the answer.

James watched him, desperately trying to see what lay behind the tinted glasses. He could distinguish nothing.

'Although,' the Shah continued in his quiet voice, 'I don't see how I could have helped you, Mr Field. Your wife was not kidnapped in Iran. On the other hand, my Minister Khorvan might still have been alive.'

'I know that,' Logan said. He sounded genuinely humble. 'I regret it very much. But I was told that unless I kept the blackmail secret my wife would be killed. I didn't think I had a choice.'

'I appreciate that. It was a difficult decision.'

'Sir,' Logan leaned forward towards the figure in the armchair, 'it is possible to save my wife's life even now, if you will help me.'

The Shah took a cigarette box, opened it, took one out and offered it to Field and James. It was a gesture that robbed Logan's last words of their dramatic effect.

'I would be glad to, if it *were* possible,' he said calmly.

'It is possible,' Logan said. 'I will lodge my agreement with the Tokyo government with Minister Khorvan's successor. There can be no doubt about our sincerity in concluding this agreement with the National Oil Company here. We need Imshan desperately. You know this even better than I do, sir, because I'm just a businessman, not a politician. But if you will allow me to make a public statement withdrawing from Imshan, then my wife will be released.'

'I don't understand your proposal, Mr Field.'

'Let me appear to give in to their terms. Then when my wife is safe, we resume the final negotiations and the deal goes through. It could be a question of a few days, no more.'

'As I understand it,' the Shah said, 'you wish to publicly withdraw from Imshan and then resume when your domestic situation has been resolved?'

He shook his head and removed his concealing glasses for a moment. The eyes were very dark and cold.

'I'm sorry, Mr Field. It's an impossible proposal. I cannot consider allowing any Western company to break off negotiations with us and then come back. It is not consistent with my policy to re-admit anyone to Imshan if they have once withdrawn. I sympathize with your dilemma but I must advise you to divorce all personal considerations from your dealings with Iranian oil.'

He got up, quite casually, and held out his hand to Logan.

'I am very glad about your deal with the Japanese,' he said. Then he turned to James. 'It was nice to see you, Mr Kelly.'

The audience was over. They went out and the Chamberlain was at the door to see them though the hall. They walked down the steps side by side and didn't speak. Outside the gates Logan saw the blue Rolls Royce. There was a shadow in the back and it was Janet.

'I tried,' he said suddenly to James. 'There was just a chance he might have agreed to it.'

'No chance at all,' James said. 'Why the hell should he bail you out? It's your choice. We're going round to Ardalan's office now. I told them to bring my own car. I'll follow behind you.'

Janet put her arms round Logan and kissed him.

'Darling, thank God you're back! How did it go?'

'Fine,' Logan said. He withdrew to his own side of the car. 'He's got what he wanted.'

He didn't want to talk about it. His choice. Kelly had kept on saying that from the beginning. Choose between the oil-field and Eileen.

'Darling,' Janet said gently, 'I've got some bad news for you. Ardalan thinks Eileen may be dead.'

'What?' He swung round on her. 'What do you mean?'

'Homsi died under interrogation,' Janet said. 'Ardalan thinks they may have killed Eileen by now. If it is true, they did it because they knew Homsi would give everything away. So it's not your fault. You mustn't blame yourself.'

She took his hand and pressed it. He pulled it away from her and stared out of the window.

'We're going to their office to listen to a tape. I'm afraid it's just a waste of time. Don't be upset. Please. It's not your fault if the worst has happened.'

He didn't want to listen to Janet. He didn't want to hear that calm reasonable tone, telling him that his wife was very likely dead and reminding him that his only link with the kidnappers had gone. He felt sick with shock. He remembered that chill injunction from the Shah. He had to divorce himself from any personal considerations. So long as he held the power over the negotiations he could achieve that balance; he could do the thing at which he was an admitted master. Juggle a dozen possibilities in the air without letting one drop, bluff and promise and somehow come out with the advantage on his side. But not now. The Syrian was dead, the secret was out. And if Janet was right and Ardalan's judgement not at fault, then Eileen was already lying dead in some cellar. He leaned his head against the window glass. It couldn't be over. It couldn't have happened so quickly before he had time to make a final decision.

'Darling,' Janet said and, reaching over, touched him.

'For Christ's sake,' Logan said without turning round, 'leave me alone.'

At one point on the journey James's car had overtaken them. When they went into the SAVAK headquarters and up to the Colonel's office, he was already there. The Colonel had given him a drink. He offered one to Logan and Janet which both of them refused.

'Well,' Logan said. 'I've heard the news. You arrest the man who knows where my wife is being kept hidden and you bloody well kill him without finding out!'

The Colonel waited a moment. He could appreciate the Englishman's distress. He was the type of man who would have to blame disaster upon someone else.

'Mr Logan,' he said patiently, 'I'm afraid you cannot hold me responsible. You did not tell me the truth. You had every opportunity and instead you treated with terrorists who were acting against the interests of Iran and you persisted in lying to me. So did Mr Kelly, who I am sure was acting on your instructions. If you had dealt honestly with me, Mahmoud

Khorvan would have been alive today. And so might your wife. So don't try and lay the blame for this ugly mess onto me.'

'You're talking as if it was certain Mrs Field was dead,' Janet said. 'Can't you see it's distressing Mr Field? There's no proof...'

'Don't be a bloody fool,' Logan said angrily. 'He knows perfectly well that the minute his thugs arrested Homsi, the Syrians knew the whole plan was finished. I don't know what the hell you asked me to come here for. I can't do anything to save my wife, even if there was a hope of her still being alive!'

'The Colonel asked you to listen to a tape,' James Kelly said. 'We asked Homsi where Eileen was hidden, just before he died. He said something but it doesn't make sense. Colonel Ardalan is doing his best to help us.'

'I will play it to you,' Ardalan said. 'See if you can understand what it means. To me it is merely gibberish.'

He switched on a portable tape recorder and re-ran to a certain point. James's voice came over clearly. 'Ask him where Mrs Field is being held.' Another voice repeated the question. A dreadful gurgling yell followed a few seconds later. Janet gasped. The same voice asked again. The words were a jumble when they came through; the voice was slurred and thick. There was a garbled plea for mercy, with English and Arabic intermingled, and then quite clearly the name, 'Mrs Field', followed by a single Arabic word, '*kwayyis*'. Then a groan that ended in a sigh.

'That was the last thing he said.' Ardalan switched the machine off. 'Mrs Field, *kwayyis*.'

'What does it mean?' Logan said.

The Colonel shrugged. 'Pleasant, nice, sweet. It makes no sense.'

'He was very confused,' James said. 'I'm afraid it's useless. It was some association of ideas between a woman and being sweet and nice.'

Logan looked at the Colonel.

'What did you use on him?'

'Electrodes. Unfortunately prolonged shocks over a period do disorient the mind. But he told us all about the plot to prevent Imshan being developed by a Western company; there was strong Soviet influence at work as well as Palestinian. A very serious threat to the independence of my country has been averted, Mr Field. His Imperial Majesty has been fully informed.'

'I know,' Logan said. 'He told me.'

'Colonel,' Janet said suddenly, 'could you put that word "*kwayyis*" into a sentence for me?'

'*Al hawa kwayyis ktir*. It is nice weather.' He looked at her and shrugged. 'The word doesn't mean anything, Mrs Armstrong. It was just the wanderings of someone nearly dead.'

'Of course it doesn't mean anything,' Logan said bitterly. 'You'd torn the bastard to pieces! If you'd gone a bit more slowly with him...'

'Please!' Ardalan held up a hand. 'Don't try and tell me how to do my job. We got everything of importance out of him.'

'Important to you...' Logan turned on him angrily.

'Wait a minute,' Janet said. 'For God's sake, I'm trying to think...Sweet, nice...nice weather...Colonel...you say he was very confused...'

'More dead than alive,' James broke in. 'He didn't know what he was saying.'

'Perhaps he didn't know how to say it,' Janet said slowly. 'Perhaps he couldn't think of the English word so he used the nearest Arabic equivalent. Supposing it wasn't an adjective. *Nice* – Nice in the South of France!'

The Colonel raised his eyebrows.

'That is possible,' he said. Then he shook his head. 'But not very likely.'

'Why not?' James demanded. 'Janet could be right. He was trying to answer your question. Where are they holding Mrs Field? *Nice*. For Christ's sake, it's worth a try!'

'It's too far-fetched,' Logan said angrily. 'You're going into the realms of bloody fantasy. Nice, in the South of France – nobody would take her there!'

'On the other hand,' Ardalan interrupted him, 'it is not as fantastic as all that. There is a large Arab work force in that part of France. I think we should ask Interpol to investigate. They will know if there are any suspects in the area.'

'She's dead,' Logan burst out at them, 'I know it.' He glared at Janet. 'I wish you'd mind your own bloody business!'

'I think the lady has been very helpful,' the Colonel protested. 'I will send a telex through immediately and see what the Interpol reaction is. If they consider it a possibility, Mr Field, I will arrange for you to be flown out. Whatever has happened, you will want to be there.'

Logan didn't answer him.

'We'll wait at your house,' he said to James. He walked down ahead of them, leaving Janet to follow with James beside her. Outside the building he turned to them. 'You can both wait at Shemiran,' he said. 'I'm going to the office. I've got work to do.' He got inside the Rolls and it drove off.

James hesitated for a moment. Janet looked very pale and it was probably his imagination but he thought there were tears in her eyes. He touched her on the arm.

'Come on,' he said. 'We'll go home. To hell with Logan. I think you've got the answer.'

'What happened with the Shah?' Janet asked him. As they got into James's car she kept her head averted. Now he was certain about the tears. He slipped the automatic gear into place and they moved off.

'I'll tell you when we get back,' he said. 'But I'm happy to say Logan met his match.'

Eileen heard Madeleine shouting for the Frenchman. Peters lay like lead in her arms. She was overcome with sudden panic and she began to shake him.

'Wake up! For God's sake, wake up, wake up...'

He groaned and she began to struggle to lift him into a sitting position. She was not nearly strong enough. The cellar door was open. Even if she shut it, they would be certain to look inside. The Lebanese girl had found the servant's body. They would know Peters was alive. There was no resignation left in her now, no sense of calm or fatalism. She pulled and shook at Peters, frantic with fear.

'Darling! Wake up! Come on...please, please...'

He opened his eyes, trying to focus. Eileen began to heave at him, holding him under the arms.

'They're coming,' she gasped. 'We've got to hide. Get up. Oh, try, for God's sake.'

'All right,' he mumbled, fighting the lethargy that didn't want to hear or know, but only to slide back into sleep. 'All right...' He could hear Resnais's voice. It came from the radio room. At any moment they would come to the cellar.

With Eileen's help he dragged himself to his feet. Hide, she had said. There was nowhere. He couldn't think clearly. All he knew was that she was still with him and in danger.

'Behind the door,' Eileen whispered. 'Hurry, get into the corner by the wine bin, hold onto it, but don't make a noise! I'll pull the door back.'

She heard footsteps running across the tiled floor of the kitchen above them. She pushed Peters into the corner, dragged the cellar door open and slid behind it to hide with him. The bottles in the wooden wine rack rattled. She held herself rigid, praying wildly that he wouldn't move or lose consciousness. They were coming down the stairs.

'*Merde!*' Resnais's shout exploded a few feet away from them. 'She's gone!'

They were standing at the open doorway. Eileen could see their shadows on the floor. Instinctively she closed her eyes and gripped Peters with all her strength. Outside, Madeleine turned to the Frenchman.

'He wasn't killed,' she accused. 'You fool – you should have made sure!'

'They haven't gone far,' Resnais said. 'Ahmed's not even cold. And they can't have taken the car – you would have heard them! If they're on the road, we'll catch them. Come on!'

Peters was fully awake. The sound of Resnais's voice had driven away the urge to give in and drift off again. He was supporting himself fully and Eileen felt his hand on her, telling her to stay absolutely still and quiet even when they heard Madeleine and Resnais going back up the stairs to the kitchen.

'I'm all right now,' he whispered.

They came out from behind the door.

'Jesus,' Peters said. 'They'll find the gate's still locked and they'll think we're still in the grounds. When they don't find us there, they'll come back and search the house!'

'What are we going to do?' Eileen said.

'Fight it out,' Peters said. 'There's no other way, can you shoot?'

'No,' she said. 'No, I've never touched a gun in my life.'

'We'll get weapons,' he said. 'If my head would stop lifting off...We've got to get to the kitchen, and quick. You'll have to help me.'

Going up the stairs to the kitchen he stumbled and fell on his knees. The pain in his head was so excruciating that he groaned out loud. Eileen helped him up, sobbing with the effort. He got to the kitchen and stopped, holding onto the door.

'Go to the cooker,' he gasped. 'Push button number 4 on the control panel. Hurry.'

She did as he said and the cupboard fitment swung back from the wall. Peters went inside the little armoury.

'Take this,' he mumbled to her.

He couldn't carry the weight of the Browning 308 and the box of ammunition; she took both. He pushed a grenade into his trouser pocket. They came back into the kitchen.

'Push button 4 twice,' he said.

The cupboard swung back into place. He leaned against the wall, exhausted.

'Why the hell didn't you go?'

'Because I'm not leaving you,' Eileen answered. 'So don't try and make me.'

'Bull-headed Irish,' Peters said. 'Christ – we'll never make it walking. So I'll have to lay for them. I want you to do exactly as I say. No argument. We need to get to the garage. There's a way down through the outside door here. It's a covered way and there's only one exit. Let's go while they're out in the grounds.'

It seemed to take them a long time; twice he had to stop and wait, attacked by dizziness. She watched him in agony, praying that he wouldn't black out. But will-power kept him on his feet. He staggered like a drunken man as they reached the exit to the garage. They went in by a side door. Inside was the white Rolls Royce laid up on chocks. The electrically operated garage doors were open. Resnais hadn't bothered to garage the Jaguar; it stood in the drive. Peters leaned against the Rolls. He took the grenade out of his pocket and gave Eileen a ring with two keys on it.

'The big one opens the main gate,' he said. 'I want you to run and unlock it when I tell you. Okay?'

'While you stay here? What happens if you black out?' she said.

'I won't,' Peters said. 'I'm feeling better. I'm going to take cover here. They've got to pass the garage to get back in the house. That's when I pick them off. You go to the doors and look out. Be very careful. Signal if you can see or hear anything.'

Eileen kept in the shadow to the side of the garage entrance. She listened and at first heard nothing. Then there was a voice, calling something indistinct. It was the girl. The Frenchman answered.

'They've split up,' she said to Peters. 'I can hear them shouting to each other.'

Peters swore. He had loaded the Browning and the grenade was on the ground beside him.

'Which direction?'

'To the right,' Eileen said. 'Not very close.'

'Okay,' Peters said. 'If they're round there the driveway is screened by the oleander bushes. Run and get those gates open. And stay put till I come out. Go on!'

He watched her go. There wasn't a hope in hell that he would join her. But the way was clear for her escape.

Eileen darted out of the entrance and ran as fast as she could down the drive to the main gates. She was gasping for breath; she could hardly fit the key into the lock. She turned it and the gates swung open easily. She leaned against the supporting pillars; she was weakened physically from lack of exercise and her legs trembled. Outside was the road; she had only to walk through the gates and she was free. That was what Peters intended when he sent her to open them. He was going to stay behind and fight Resnais and Madeleine off while she escaped. Telling her to wait there had been a ruse to make her leave him. He knew when the firing started that she would be unable to get back. She would have to save herself. She hesitated, but only long enough to scan the way back to the garage. She saw nobody and heard nothing. He had called her bull-headed Irish. She remembered that as she began to run towards the garage. As she reached it, Madeleine rounded the corner.

She and Resnais had split up to search. She was carrying her gun at the ready, but her attention was not fully engaged. She had decided that Peters and the woman were hiding in the house. She and Resnais had searched every bush in the garden. Resnais thought they might have climbed down the rocks and attempted to swim, but Madeleine disagreed with him. It was a long swim against the tide and she derided the idea that anyone as soft as Eileen Field could have attempted it.

She was completely unprepared to see Eileen running for her life only a few yards away from her. So taken by surprise that she shouted out after her and loosed a couple of shots without taking proper aim. Eileen vanished into the garage and Madeleine raced towards it. She didn't get the chance to shoot again. A burst from Peters's Browning caught her full on; three bullets hit her in the chest; the impact threw her violently backwards; her pistol went spinning into the oleander bushes. Madeleine gave a single scream and then lay still. She felt a massive pain and the metallic taste of blood. She knew that it was Peters who had shot her and as she died she spoke his name.

Resnais, who was twenty yards behind her, came from the other side of the house as the shooting began and saw her lying in the driveway. He didn't open fire. He froze while Madeleine died. Peters was in the garage. There was no way to the front or back doors unless he crossed in view of the open garage doors. Unless he climbed to the first floor. Once inside the house he could use the only method of attack which would turn Peters's strongpoint into a lethal trap. Inside the kitchen was the armoury. He needed grenades.

The Interpol branch in Nice had recently been strengthened due to an influx of Algerian criminals into the area. There had been an outbreak of robberies and an attempted hold-up of a German millionaire industrialist within the last nine months. The rich and influential raised an outcry and the gendarmerie was also brought up above its normal strength. It was essential that the fashionable resorts along the strip of coast should remain peaceful for the rich inhabitants and for the tourists which were its livelihood. Ardalan's telex caused a furore in the police headquarters. The suggestion that a Palestinian terrorist organization was at work in the region convulsed the prefect with alarm. The police were urged to act with all possible urgency to weed out and deport possible trouble makers. If the kidnapped woman was being held in the environs of Nice, then the French police would find her. There were large numbers of

Algerians and Arabs working locally, in restaurants and cafés, as hotel staff, and in the building and construction work undertaken on the coast. A list of them was already in the possession of the police, who kept records of all aliens with Arabic connections, and the name of the Algerian millionaire was among them. While a squad of police set out on a dawn raid on the districts where the poorer suspects lived, a single squad car was despatched, more as a gesture than for serious investigation, later that morning. In the meantime a telexed reply informed the head of SAVAK that while no incidents of a suspicious nature had been reported, there was a strong nucleus of Arabs in the district and it was not impossible for a European to be kept prisoner among them. On receipt of this news Logan Field was notified in his office. He had been forced into hiring a private jet and he had no excuse ready when Janet and James insisted upon coming with him.

It was a bumpy uncomfortable flight. James sat apart from Logan and Janet. He had felt sorry for Janet Armstrong and this surprised him. It had seemed impossible that she had feelings which could be hurt, but Logan proved him wrong again. She was miserable, and it was her flash of brilliant intuition which had broken the jumbled message of the dying Saiid Homsi. James had no doubt that she was right. Unlike Logan, he felt confident that Eileen would be rescued. She was being held somewhere in the French resort. A surprise raid by police didn't recommend itself to him, but Ardalan assured him that Interpol would handle the situation carefully. In the meantime, on the Shah's instructions, the Syrian government had been asked officially to help in contacting the terrorists holding Mrs Field and negotiating her release. No mention had been made by either government of Saiid Homsi. He had been buried along with SAVAK's other victims in a lime pit outside Tehran.

Logan had hardly spoken since the plane took off. Janet didn't try to talk to him. He hadn't seen her the night before and his attitude was cold and hostile. She had amazed herself by crying till she fell asleep.

He didn't thank her for finding out where Eileen might be hidden. He didn't want to know. Not because he was callous; Janet knew him too well to attribute it to that. Not because he didn't care; but because he cared more than he had ever admitted to himself.

He fastened his belt as the plane turned for the descent to Nice airport. They would find nothing. Everything in him, every intuitive sense told him that Eileen would never be found alive. The night before, in the privacy of his room in James's house, Logan had broken down and wept. He hadn't wanted to come to Nice, but he had no excuse for staying in Tehran. It was Colonel Ardalan, cool and polite as usual, who offered to transport him by military jet if he was unable to charter a flight out at such short notice. They were all pressuring him to go and face the prospect of finding his wife dead in some empty house. Nobody would ever know the agony and horror which overcame him at the thought of it. He could hardly bear to feel Janet sitting beside him. If the nightmare became reality, he would hold her responsible, however unfairly.

They landed smoothly and an airport official met them off the plane and escorted them through customs. A *capitaine* of gendarmes and a young officer came forward and saluted them. Logan broke out in a sweat even before the *capitaine* spoke.

'M. Field? I have a car outside. I'm afraid we have found your wife. Please come with me.'

'Why did you come back?' Peters turned on her furiously. His head was pounding and sweat was running, stinging into his eyes. Madeleine was dead; he could see her sprawled on her back on the drive. But the Frenchman was the real opponent. A professional killer, a trained expert. Peters felt so weak and nauseated that he could hardly see what he was doing. Yet here was Eileen kneeling beside him instead of having taken advantage of the opportunity he had given her and got safely away. He had a crazy effeminate desire to break into tears because nothing was solved. He loved her enough to have knocked her down for coming back.

'I told you, I'm not going without you,' Eileen said fiercely. 'I've opened the gates. Come on, let me get you into the car and we'll run for it!' She was pulling at his arm. He shook her off.

'Resnais is out there,' he said. 'We'd be shot to pieces the moment we came through the doorway. For Christ's sake, Eileen – you go in the car! I'll give you covering fire!'

She shook her head.

'We're going together,' she said. 'I'm not leaving you behind, so you can just forget it. Think of a way for us both to get out.'

'There isn't one,' Peters said wearily. 'I'm as weak as hell. If I black out and Resnais rushes us, we're finished.'

Eileen looked at him.

'Show me how to fire that gun,' she whispered. 'Tell me what to do and I'll do it!'

'You wouldn't be quick enough,' Peters said. 'He'd blast you before you got to pull the trigger. He's a pro – I'd never get him like I did Madeleine.' He closed his eyes for a moment and panicked as the slide into unconsciousness began. His head felt heavy, his limbs numb. He fought against it with all his last reserves. 'I'm going to pass out,' he mumbled to her; he saw the terror on her face, but he couldn't even hold onto the Browning; it slipped out of his hand onto the ground.

'Grenade,' he said. 'If he comes in firing, stay down. Pull out the pin and count...count three...then throw it. On the floor...take it, darling...'

He slumped to the side, collapsed against the body of the white Rolls Royce. Eileen bent over him. He was breathing hard, his face grey and filmed with sweat. There was no sound in the garage but the harsh laboured breathing of someone who was deeply unconscious. Eileen moved the Browning to one side; the grenade lay on the ground. It was oval-shaped, corrugated; it looked evil, with the little pin on a ring sticking out of the side. You pulled out the pin, counted three and threw... The blast was what killed in a confined space. She remembered war films, with the inevitable pill box or fox hole exploding under a grenade attack. She picked it up and held it. It was cold and heavy. Her hands were shaking. If the Frenchman crept up on them, she had to remember the sequence and throw it at him. If she dropped it or miscounted...

She looked at Peters lying against the sumptuous car and she was glad that she hadn't done what he wanted and run through the open gates. She was all the protection he had; the idea made her calm. She settled down to wait for the slightest sound that would warn of Resnais's approach.

Resnais swung himself up to the low balcony on the first floor. He had climbed by means of a drain pipe and a storeroom window, shuttered from the inside but with a substantial sill. He shouldered the window and it opened easily inwards. He didn't waste time. He hurried down the stairs and as he passed the study where Ahmed's body was lying he heard the transmitter. He waited for a moment and then decided that he had better take the message. Peters wouldn't know he wasn't lying in wait for them in the gardens. He wasn't likely to make a run for it at that moment, so soon after killing Madeleine. He picked up the earphones and took down the message. It was brief. 'Confirm previous message. Operation cancelled due to Homsi's arrest. Request confirmation of hostage execution. Repeat. Confirmation necessary and call sign for dispersal.'

Homsi arrested. Resnais let them send the message a second time, while he registered the shock of the information and the fact that Damascus was repeating a message already received. Received by Peters... Eileen Field was to be executed and the team was to disperse. It was all for nothing. Madeleine's death, his attempt on Peters, the highly organized exercise in top-level terrorism. He didn't answer the message. He left it clattering through a third time. Let Damascus think the villa was empty. The radio should have been destroyed if instructions had been properly carried out. But the hero he had personally reported killed in a car accident had come back from the dead and was holed up in the garage with the hostage. Resnais didn't know what final explanation would be offered but he wouldn't be the one to make it. Not until he had time to get a story sorted out in Paris. He couldn't do that unless Peters and Eileen Field were both dead.

He ran on to the kitchen, opened up the armoury and stuffed two grenades into each of his trouser pockets. Then moving at a light run and making no noise, he sped down the covered passageway which Peters had taken to the garage. As he approached the door, he crept like a stalking cat. He took one grenade out of his pocket, held it in his right hand, and with his left he very gently depressed the handle of the door.

As it opened, he was standing at the back of the garage. He took a single step forward, well hidden by the angle of the door. He knew that Peters and Eileen Field were still there; he had an animal's sense for the presence of an enemy. Two grenades should do it, one after the other. He took the second out of his pocket and very slowly and carefully opened the door wide enough to lean forward and throw.

The patrol cars made their first raids on the houses occupied by Algerians and Arabs soon after dawn that morning. Searches revealed nothing suspicious. Several suspected sympathizers with the Palestinians were taken to Nice police headquarters and questioned.

A special squad, carrying a senior officer in the local gendarmerie and an Interpol liaison officer, accompanied by three armed gendarmes arrived at the villa belonging to the millionaire Arab just after eight in the morning. The Algerian was a well known member of the smart set in the resort. He was on excellent terms with the *maire* and the police; he owned a large yacht which was at that time on a cruise round the Greek islands; and apart from rumours of his political affiliations he had done nothing to justify a raid on his house in his absence. Such nicety hadn't been evident in the case of the poor Algerian workers who had been dragged out of their beds and beaten up in the police station. It was unwise to upset the wealthy and the police were reluctant to take any chance of doing so. At eight fifteen the *capitaine* of gendarmes, who later met Logan at the airport, was the first to jump out of the car as it came to a halt in front of the villa. His men sprang out after him. They drew their revolvers.

Tact was not needed. The scene in the garage on the left of the entrance was enough to tell them that they had come to the right place. The stink of death and explosions hung over the air. The *capitaine* was standing in a thin trickle of blood that was making patterns on the gravel. He went to the garage, looked inside and shouted to the Interpol official. He in turn shouted back.

The search was over. Within a few minutes, after a radio call from the car to headquarters, the villa was cordoned off and a team of police experts were going through the rooms and the grounds. The *capitaine* undertook the unpleasant duty of meeting Logan Field and bringing him to the scene. He was a hard man, inured to violence, but the inside of the garage had upset him.

He wondered what effect it would have upon the chairman of Imperial Oil.

## II

It seemed to Eileen that she had been crouching beside Peters
for hours. The sun was up and there was a cheerful bird that
twittered in the trees. It was a horrible contrast to the body of
Madeleine which lay in full view, her arms at her sides. She
looked as if she had been laid out after death. Blood had
gathered in a pool on the ground. There was little shadow
immediately in front of the garage; the oleander bushes and
the pines were further back; there it was dense and impossible
to see if anyone were hidden. Eileen placed her hand on
Peter's forehead. It was cold and clammy. His colour was a
frightening grey. Somewhere out in the garden Resnais must
be waiting, preparing to rush them. Madeleine had been
killed by a fluke, thrown off guard by the sight of Eileen
running in the open. Now Resnais was alone but, as Peters
said, he was the more deadly of the two. She listened, her
nerves taut beyond endurance. The bird no longer sang and
the silence in the garden was horrible, unreal. Suddenly
something snapped; the sound was like a pistol shot to her
over-stretched imagination. She grabbed the grenade and half
rose, ready to pull the pin and throw it in the direction from
which the noise had come. But there was no movement, no
shape behind the shadows.

What she had heard was the shutter being forced open on
the first floor window. She held the grenade ready but had no
idea where to throw it. Resnais must know there was something
wrong inside the garage. They would have tried to escape in
the car otherwise. If he rushed them from the front, the
tremendous firepower from the Browning would cut her
down before she could throw anything. But he wouldn't be
expecting to face her; he might think one of them was hurt

but he couldn't be certain it was Peters. And Peters had the same weapon. It would be crazy for Resnais to attack direct. And then she remembered the door back into the house, the door through which she and Peters had got into the garage. That was where the Frenchman would come. She gave a cry of terror and tried to shake Peters, but it was useless. He was slumped across the Rolls. She almost panicked then; for a moment she felt paralysed with terror, as if her body were frozen into immobility while at any moment that door might burst open. She ran to it, scrabbling desperately for a bolt, a key. There was no way of locking it from inside the garage. Naturally it would be fastened from inside the house. She crouched by it, listening, and heard nothing. No footsteps, no creak of boards, nothing. But she knew that this was the way he would come.

She made her way back to the white Rolls. Peters hadn't moved. Eileen bent over him; tears fell on his face. Then she picked up the grenade. She sat on her heels and watched the door.

When it began to open she thought at first it was an optical illusion. It seemed there was a crack between it and the wall. For a second she closed her eyes tightly and as they opened the crack was wider. She gave a gasp of terror and raised herself from behind the shelter of the Rolls Royce. There was no possible doubt. The door was opening, very slowly and without making a sound. She pulled out the pin on the grenade and counted. 'One, two, three.' Then she threw it with all her strength at the gap which was widening. She had a glimpse of something like a hand coming round the edge of it, just before she threw herself on top of Peters. The force of the explosion blasted her into unconsciousness, as the grenade in Resnais's hand blew up a second after the one she had thrown. The wood of the door shattered into splinters as lethal as bullets, a rain of steel fragments bombarded the inside of the garage. Human remains spattered the walls and ceiling. Acrid fumes filled the area and hung over the wreck of the Rolls Royce, which had been in a direct line to the explosion. Its body was holed and pockmarked with splinters, its rear doors buckled. Eileen and Peters lay under a coverlet of broken glass from the windows; her arm was flung across him as if she were trying to shield him. It was Peters who recovered first. He came back to consciousness, confused and shocked. He could hear nothing and his ears throbbed painfully from the force of the blast. He raised himself slowly and the broken glass slithered off him. He began brushing it frantically away from Eileen's body. He cut himself and at first he thought the blood was only his own. He lifted her, staggering and dizzy under the slight weight, and dragged her outside. The stench and fumes were choking in the garage; there was a loathsome charnel-house smell.

'Eileen! Eileen! For Christ's sake. . .'

He thought he was shouting but all sound was muffled. Her dress was soaked with blood. A long jagged splinter of wood had holed her in the side like a spear. She was just breathing.

Peters lifted her over his shoulder. He swayed on his feet and then began to walk down to the gate. It didn't occur to him to go back into the house. He had to get help for her and all he could remember was the car in the driveway. It hurt too much to think beyond the total necessity of saving her life. He knew as soon as he saw the nature of the injury that unless she was attended to quickly she would die. He had to reach that car and drive to the hospital. His ears were buzzing and blocked. His blinding headache was in rhythm with every jarring step along the road. When he saw the blue sports car he broke into a stumbling run. He lifted her into the passenger seat and bent over her, feeling the pulse in her slack wrist. Her eyes opened and she gave a groan of pain. She was losing a lot of blood. His shirt and hands were crimson with it.

'You'll be all right,' he mumbled. 'I'm taking you to hospital. You'll be all right. Oh Christ, don't fade out . . . hold on . . .'

She was unconscious again, but for a moment she had known him. He got in beside her and started the car. His concentration was too erratic to risk driving fast. All he could hope was to stay conscious and reach the hospital. It took him half an hour, much less than the previous night's journey when he was hopelessly confused, and then he pulled into the entrance to the hospital. He went to the enquiry desk and saw the girl behind it open her mouth in horror at the sight of him.

'There's been an accident,' Peters said. 'There's a woman outside in a blue sports car. Her name is Mrs Field. Get someone quickly. No . . . I'm all right . . . that's her blood.'

In the confusion while two orderlies came running with a stretcher and a crowd of spectators surrounded the car, Eileen was lifted out and taken inside. The receptionist thought she was dead and turned to look for the man who had reported the accident. But he had disappeared.

They had covered the body with a rubber sheet. The policeman pulled it back and the *capitaine* stepped aside for Logan. Logan looked down at the face of Madeleine Labouchère. He turned to the *capitaine*.

'That's not my wife,' he said. He walked a few paces back to James Kelly, who was waiting, sick and stricken, with Janet beside him.

'It's not Eileen,' Logan said. He brushed one hand across his forehead. James saw it trembling. 'It's another woman, shot in the stomach.'

The *capitaine* had joined them.

'M. Field,' he said, 'we are certain that your wife has been held here. There is a dead Algerian in the house and a radio transmitter. Grenades were used in a battle in the garage. There are human remains. I think you had better go with your friends and wait in our headquarters.'

He hesitated. Logan's rejection of the woman's corpse had embarrassed him. From the way it was lying, it looked as if it had been arranged after death. The cruelty of death by having half the stomach blown out had been dignified into an execution. This theory was disposed of when Madeleine's Walther P.38 automatic was found in the oleander bushes. It did not occur to the *capitaine* or to Logan, or James, that Eileen was not among the victims whose mangled remains were in the human débris in the garage. Janet had not gone near it. She stayed apart, looking so pale that Logan heard James ask her if she were feeling faint. He didn't bother to turn round. She shouldn't have come on the trip and she certainly shouldn't have come out to the villa. If she called attention to herself by fainting, it would be the final error in a mounting total. He walked away to the car, leaving James to bring her along, and they drove to police headquarters in silence. They were shown into the *capitaine*'s office and a policeman brought them a tray with brandy and Perrier and ice. Janet poured them each a drink. She handed one to Logan.

'I think she's alive,' she said quietly.

Logan looked at her.

'That's the most bloody stupid, insensitive thing. . .'

'M. Field!'

He swung away from her to the police lieutenant who had accompanied him from the villa. He was in the doorway and he shouted in excitement.

'M. Field! The Pasteur Hospital has just phoned a report that a woman with that name was brought to the hospital twenty minutes ago! We go to the hospital immediately!'

Logan was pushing past him through the door, followed by James. Janet didn't move. James turned and called to her.

'Come on. Aren't you coming?'

She shook her head.

'No. He'll be all right now. I'm going back to England. If Logan wants me, he knows where to call.'

She shrugged a little and managed to smile.

'You go along, James. And good luck. Don't let Logan push you out.'

'I won't,' James promised. 'I'm going to be right there.'

The surgeon who operated on Eileen found a badly damaged rib cage and a hole in the abdominal wall, with extensive internal haemorrhaging. He removed the part of the wood splinter which had penetrated too far for Peters to see. It measured seven and a quarter inches. He came down after the operation and told Logan Field that he could see his wife for a few minutes later that evening. In his opinion she would recover but there was always the risk of post-operative shock.

The hospital was under siege from the press and television. Logan was offered a room and an appeal was put out over the television networks for the man who had brought Mrs Field to the hospital to come forward.

The gruesome scene at the villa was making world headlines. Logan saw the French papers. He and James were together in the little waiting room off the private ward where Eileen lay. He had taken James's presence for granted. He was his employee and liaison with the authorities. He spoke perfect French and he acted as a buffer between Logan and demands for an interview. He had gone outside the building and spoken briefly to the press on Logan's behalf. Until Mrs Field had recovered enough to tell them what had happened, Logan Field could not issue a statement. He admitted that Eileen had been the victim of a kidnapping by an international terrorist group but he refused to go into details at this stage. James was adroit with the press where Logan wouldn't have trusted himself to remain calm. He was the diplomat, expert at smoothing over difficulties.

A nurse brought them coffee and asked if they wanted to eat something. Both refused.

'You haven't asked where Janet is,' James said.

Logan frowned.

'I'd forgotten about her. She can get herself into a hotel.'

'She's gone back to England,' James said. 'I think you've been pretty rough on her, Logan. You ought to ring her up and let her know what's happened.'

'I don't know myself, yet,' Logan said. 'I'll wait till tomorrow. I think you'd better fly back to Tehran after I've seen Eileen. Work out a statement for me and it had better be very guarded. We don't want to start a political row and embarrass the Shah. I'll join you as soon as I know Eileen's out of danger.'

James took out a cigarette and lit it. He looked at Logan.

'I'm not going back to Tehran,' he said. 'I'm resigning. I'm staying here.'

'Don't be a bloody fool,' Logan said. 'You're throwing everything away. Imshan goes ahead now and you can reach the top in Imperial. All right, if you don't want to go to Tehran, stay on here for a few days. Think it over.'

'I have thought it over,' James said. 'Whether you kick Janet out or not, Eileen will never go back to you. You think you've won, Logan. You risked her life for your bloody oil-field and you come out with Imshan in the bag and think you can walk back to her as if nothing has happened. To hell with Janet by the way. But it isn't going to work out like that. You're not going to have your cake and eat it this time.'

There was a nurse sitting by Eileen's bed. The single light was shaded and when Logan first came in he didn't see that her eyes were open. He came to the bed and bent over her. The nurse got up.

'Only a few minutes, Mr Field. She is still feeling the anaesthetic. I will wait outside.'

Eileen saw Logan through a fog of analgesic. His face seemed to loom independent of his body. For a moment she thought she was dreaming in the half-world of returning consciousness. Then he spoke and the fog cleared a little.

'Darling,' she heard him say. 'You're going to be all right.'

Her lips were dry and she felt thirsty. The nurse had allowed her a sip of water at a time when she first came round. She opened her eyes fully and focused on Logan. He bent down closer to her.

'Where is he?'

'Who? Who are you talking about?'

Logan thought for a moment that she was wandering, but the expression in her eyes was clear. She raised her head from the pillow.

'Where is he? What happened to him?'

'I don't know what you mean,' Logan said.

'He brought me here,' Eileen mumbled, 'in the car . . . I remember seeing him, just for a second.'

'Somebody got you to the hospital,' Logan said, 'but he disappeared afterwards. They're trying to find him now.'

There was a very slight smile on her lips. It made Logan uncomfortable. He had never seen her look secretive before.

'He got away then. Thank God.' She turned her head and closed her eyes. 'I'm going back to sleep,' she said.

He stood watching her. He heard the nurse come back into the room and touch him on the arm.

'You can see her in the morning,' she whispered. 'She'll be better then.'

'Thank you,' Logan said.

He walked out of the room and asked to telephone the gendarmerie headquarters. He spoke to the *capitaine*.

'I've just seen my wife. You'd better get the man who brought her in. From what she said, I believe he was one of the kidnappers.'

Road blocks were set up, the strictest security was in operation at the airport and no sailings were permitted from the harbour. An extensive search was carried out through the town of Nice itself. An identikit picture of Peters was flashed on the television screens and put on the front page of the newspapers. There were stories in the world press that Eileen Field was winning her fight for life and pictures of Logan going in and out of the hospital.

Fifty miles outside Nice harbour, a motor yacht was on course for the Italian coast. The tiny yacht marina at Bocca di Magra had a berth reserved for it. Normally the boat remained at anchor there, going out for a day's excursion to Porto Venere or the Cinque Terra with tourists. Since Eileen Field arrived at the villa, the yacht had been waiting in Nice, its two man crew spending their time drinking in the bars and fishing.

It was a big, powerfully engined craft, capable of thirty knots, with a tiny cabin that slept three. Peters was lying on the bunk. The taxi driver who picked him up outside the hospital had thought that he was drunk. He seemed unsteady and when they arrived at the quay, the driver had to help him out. He brought him to the boat and hung around, beginning to fret about his fare, while one of the crew came and helped the American aboard. He was paid off, with a generous tip, and thought no more about it. He was used to Americans being drunk early in the morning on the coast.

The yacht's captain was an Italian; his home was on the Magra, the river that runs into the sea hard by Lerici on one of the most beautiful curves of the Italian coast. He lived by hiring his boat out during the summer season and he was an active member of the Marxist group who had settled in the little river port. He had been sent to Nice to take the commando group to safety if the operation failed. He knew nothing about their mission in France and he didn't ask questions when only Peters appeared. He brought him downstairs to the cabin, cast off and started out of the harbour. He would take a full day to reach the Magra as he had to go well out to sea to avoid searching aircraft. Once they were safe in the Magra, his own people would care for the terrorist. And it was obvious that he would need care, because he was confused and became unconscious while they steamed at a full thirty knots out into the Mediterranean. The second crew member, a young and dedicated activist, sat by his side and watched him. He didn't know how best to help his injured comrade.

He could have coped very well with a physical wound. Brain damage frightened him. Twice during the day Peters woke up and asked for something to drink. The boy left him and reported to his captain that there was some improvement. They heard the news of the hunt for Peters on the short-wave radio. Neither commented. They had a very long start and in any case the papers they had given to the port authorities were forged and gave the yacht's place of origin and registration as Marseilles. They wouldn't be traced. The American had got safely away.

It was early afternoon. In the hot, cramped little cabin Peters lay propped up on the bunk, awake. The pain in his head was continuous and excruciating; the thud and rumble of the engines made his conscious periods unbearable. The heat and the smell of fuel was overpowering. He lay soaked in sweat, the lower half of his body covered by a sheet. A carafe of water was on the narrow ledge beside the bunk and he drank continuously. They had given him aspirins to ease the pain but the effect was negligible. It was a part of him, the pounding of a hammer, wielded with such force that it felt as if his head would split like an apple under the pressure. The movement of the boat was steady; the powerful engines were running at full throttle, her bows were out of the water and they were racing through a calm sea towards the haven of Italy. He didn't think about his own safety. He seemed to have no control over his thoughts. His last memory was of seeing Eileen brought into the hospital on a stretcher. He couldn't remember taking the taxi and getting to the arranged escape point in the harbour. He kept seeing Eileen's face, smiling at him. It was the only pleasant part of being awake and he couldn't hold onto it for long. He saw other faces, floating like balloons in a void. His mother, with her disappointed expression, and her voice in his head accusing him. 'You talk about loving humanity – you're not capable of loving even one person...' It made him very angry. He called her a liar and her face drifted away, as if someone had loosed the string on the balloon. His father – a teacher from High School; he didn't call them but they came, without sequence or relevance to each other. Madeleine. Lying dead in the villa garden. He closed his eyes against her. He felt nothing. His mother said he had no feelings . . . Incapable of love . . . He tried to bring Eileen back, fighting the whispers and the faces which were merging into a sad confusion.

The little door to the cabin folded back and the young Italian came in. He had heard Peters call out and hurried down.

'Are you all right?' he asked in French. 'Do you want anything?'

Peters tried to lift himself. The Italian was very dark, with a drooping moustache and serious eyes. Peters wanted to say something but suddenly the pain in his head became a crescendo; the embolism lodged in the frontal lobe of his brain finally burst; a massive haemorrhage spread in seconds and he fell back on the bunk. His eyes closed and he called out one word. The young man bent over him and then ran up on deck to call the captain. A few minutes later they stood beside the bunk. The yacht idled on the water, its engines shut off. The older of the two Italians shook his head.

'If you don't rest with a severe concussion, this can happen,' he said.

'Did he say anything?'

The boy looked distressed.

'It sounded like a woman's name.'

'He died for the cause,' the older man said. He raised his clenched fist in salute over Peters. 'We can't take him into port. We'll bury him here.'

In the early afternoon of that day, Eileen woke from a deep sleep. The room was full of flowers; a large vase of roses sent by James were the first thing she saw. She felt no pain, only a feeling of profound disquiet as if something were terribly wrong. The blinds were half drawn, the room was cool and shady, scented with the flowers. The nurse sat knitting in a chair near the bed. She heard a sound and saw Eileen with tears pouring down her face. She hurried to her.

'What is it? Are you in pain, dear? I'll get you something. . .'

She couldn't explain the indefinable, the sense of grief which had no explanation. She took the analgesics and held onto the nurse's hand. Under their influence she fell asleep again. She didn't know and never would that it was the precise moment when she woke that Peters died a hundred miles away.

In the autumn Logan gave a press conference in the VIP lounge at London airport. He had flown in from Tehran and a crowd of press photographers, television cameras and a special BBC reporter were waiting for him. He sat in the lounge with a glass of whisky and soda and read out a short statement. It was the last thing James Kelly did for him before he resigned. He drafted the statement. It was brief and anticipated most of the questions. Imperial Oil had signed an agreement with the National Iranian Oil Company to develop the massive field at Imshan. He had no comment to make on the reactions of the United Arab Republic to the suggestion that the price formula would lead to lower oil prices.

'Did you see the Shah, Mr Field?'

Logan glanced towards the questioner.

'I saw His Imperial Majesty yesterday,' he said. 'I had a long audience with him.'

'Would you describe him as a friend to the West, sir?'

Logan shook his head.

'I would describe him as dedicated to the interests of his own people,' he said.

James had told him to say something like that. He waited, enjoying himself. Publicity of this kind didn't frighten him; he looked fresh and good humoured, a man returning from a triumphant conclusion with the right amount of modesty and authority. One of the reporters was writing that down. Logan was concentrating on the television interviewer. He was a widely travelled man with experience in Middle Eastern affairs. Logan explained the implications of Imshan and touched on the attempt to blackmail him into abandoning it. He repeated his answer to the questions which had been asked both publicly and in private so many times.

'It was an impossible choice. I couldn't sacrifice my wife, but I couldn't put personal feelings before my responsibility to the economic survival of our Western society. Thank God the problem was solved for me.'

It was an answer that pleased everyone. The interview with television was concluded and Logan stood up. He wanted to get to the City in time for a meeting with his directors. It was a woman reporter who edged up to him. He paused politely.

'Your wife is living in Ireland, Mr Field. Is it true that you have separated?'

He changed colour; his face flushed red and he half turned away from her.

'I have no comment to make on my private affairs.'

The reporter raised her voice as he began to push his way to the door.

'Will you be seeing your wife, Mr Field?'

He didn't answer. He thrust his way through the exit door and hurried away to be taken through to where his company car was waiting. The conference had ended upon a painfully sour note.

The library at Meath House was a shabby room. Generations of dogs had scuffed and worn the leather sofa; there were stains on the chairs where Fitzgeralds had lounged in muddied hunting clothes; and the big mahogany bracket clock was incapable of keeping accurate time. The room was walled with books, many of them unread and untouched for years. It was supposed that there were valuable first editions among them but it didn't occur to anyone in the family to think of selling them when money was short. It was a room that Eileen associated with big fires and smoke and the smell of leather and whisky; a place where her father loved to stand warming his back and talking with a glass in his hand.

She had arranged flowers in two massive Waterford vases, just as her mother used to do, and she had come there after playing with Lucy in the garden. The child was very changed. She had lost her subdued passivity. She laughed and shouted and her grandfather and Bridget spoiled her. There were animals instead of fluffy toys. A spaniel puppy which slept in her nursery, the same room which Eileen had used until she married Logan, and an ancient pony which she was learning to sit on in a basket saddle. She was a free and happy child, over-indulged perhaps but growing visibly. It made Eileen contented to watch her; their love for each other was very close. When she was still convalescing and unable to do more than sit in the garden if it was warm and the rain held off, she had found complete absorption in her child. By the time Logan came over to see her, she was well enough not to be disturbed. She greeted him calmly and with courtesy as if he were a stranger calling on a visit. He had not suggested anything about Lucy's future because he had hoped to persuade her to talk about their own. Eileen had told him quite without rancour that there was nothing to discuss. It was two months since he had arrived at Meath and gone away the next morning, sped on by her father who hadn't attempted to be friendly. She had read about him in the newspapers and felt no personal interest. Her detachment from him and her past life was so complete she felt neither curiosity, resentment nor regret. It was all part of the life lived by another person. A person with her face and her name, but who had never really existed as she existed now. She spent a lot of time now that she was strong walking round the countryside; there was an air about her of expectancy which no one at Meath understood. It was Bridget, greeting James Kelly that autumn afternoon, who put it into words.

'How is Mrs Field?'

He had written, asking to come and see her. To his surprise she telephoned inviting him to stay. They hadn't talked on the telephone. He had seen her twice in the hospital and found that she didn't want to talk about anything. There was a closed secrecy about her which disturbed him.

'She's fine now,' Bridget said, 'but she's not herself, Mr Kelly. What she's been through left its mark on her. Everyone at Meath sees the change in her.'

James paused. They were outside the library door.

'What kind of change?'

'She lives inside of herself,' the Irish girl said. 'It's as if she was waiting for something. Go in, sir. I'll bring the tea in a minute.'

He thought she looked very beautiful; she was thin, but there was brightness in her eyes and genuine pleasure in her smile as she came to meet him. He held both her hands for a moment and she didn't draw away.

'Dear James,' Eileen said, 'I'm so happy to see you. Come and sit down.'

They sat on the sofa side by side. She asked him questions about himself and he described his resignation from Imperial

Oil. He had taken a job as a consultant to a firm of merchant bankers. His description of it made her laugh.

'You don't really fit into big business, do you? Why didn't you go back into the Foreign Office?'

'No future in it,' he said. 'I've decided to become a nine-to-five bore like everyone else. When are you coming back to England?'

'I don't know.' She turned away from him, pouring tea which he didn't want. 'I'm quite happy here. Lucy loves it.'

'What about Logan?'

'He's busy with his oil-field, I suppose. You know as much about him as I do.'

James looked at her.

'You're never going back to him?'

She smiled and shook her head.

'No. That's all over and done with. I hope he marries Janet Armstrong. I told him I thought he'd treated her very badly.'

'Funnily enough, I don't think she'd have him. She resigned too.'

'He won't mind,' Eileen said. 'Logan isn't the kind of man to be lonely without people. He's never really needed anyone. I read about Imshan in the papers. They called him the tycoon who saved the West. It sounded like a title for a cowboy movie.'

He put his hand out and touched hers.

'You're looking very well,' he said. 'Bridget said you'd changed. I was worried about it. But she's right. You're a different woman.'

'I feel different,' Eileen said. 'An awful lot happened to me in those three weeks. That's what Logan couldn't understand. He thought we could start all over again, living the same kind of life. Me playing hostess in that dreary house in Eaton Square. Lucy growing up in that artificial atmosphere. Him living for his business and me living for him.'

'And now you're living for yourself,' James said quietly. 'For the first time.'

'Not altogether.' The secret look was there again, lurking round her mouth. 'I've found myself as a human being; that's part of it. And I've freed Lucy. She's having a wonderful life here. Father adores her and everyone spoils her to death.'

'I suppose,' James said, 'you wouldn't tell me what really happened at the end?'

She said to him what she had said to the police and to Interpol.

'I can't really remember. We were in the garage. There was an argument between the men and the woman. There was an explosion. I woke up in the hospital.'

'You said they were Arabs,' James said. 'The man who brought you to the hospital was an American.'

'So I was told. Have some more tea.'

'I wish you'd trust me,' James said gently. 'I wish you'd tell me the truth. They won't find him now. He's got clear away.'

She didn't answer. She stopped putting the tea cups in a pile on the tray and turned round to him. She sat very still and let him take her hand again.

'I love you very much,' James said. 'I came here to make sure you and Logan were finished and to remind you about what I said in Tehran. Tell me about him, darling. It may help us both.'

'I can't,' Eileen said. 'I know you fought to get me freed while Logan was hanging on to the oil-fields and trusting to luck that they wouldn't murder me. While he was excusing himself he was telling me how much I owed to you. And I'll say this much, because I do trust you. There was a man but I can't talk about it. All I can do now is sit here and wait.'

James went on holding her hand. The room was quiet, peaceful. Outside the pale Irish sunlight dappled the garden and made patterns on the faded carpet.

'He may never come,' James said. 'You realize that?'

There were tears in her eyes.

'I know, but I have to hope. I have to give him time.'

'All right.' He gave her his handkerchief and slipped his arm around her. 'You wait for as long as you want to and, if you don't mind, I'll wait with you. If he doesn't come back, maybe you'll settle for second best.'

He leaned over and kissed her lightly on the cheek.

'Let's go and find your father. And I want to see Lucy.'